DINING WITH DEVILS

Set in 11 pt. Plantin.
Printed on permanent paper.

LIBRARY OF CONGRESS CATALOGING-IN-PUBLICATION DATA

Aalborg, Gordon.
  Dining with devils : a Tasmanian thriller / by Gordon Aalborg.
  — 1st ed.
    p. cm.
  ISBN-13: 978-1-59414-749-4 (alk. paper)
  ISBN-10: 1-59414-749-3 (alk. paper)
  1. Tasmania—Fiction. 2. Police—Tasmania—Fiction. 3. Serial murderers—Fiction. I. Title.
  PR9619.3.A22D56 2009
  823'.914—dc22   2008053580

First Edition. First Printing: April 2009.
Published in 2009 in conjunction with Tekno Books and Ed Gorman.

Printed in the United States of America
1 2 3 4 5 6 7 13 12 11 10 09

This book is dedicated to Deni, for her unswerving faith and support.

And to the Jack Russell terriers of the world, all of whom have a bit of "Bluey" in there somewhere, just waiting to escape and create havoc.

And, not least, to Foothills Mocha Magic and John Whitten, who loved her as I did. They are both gone now, hopefully to a better place, and together again, as they should be. R.I.P.

ACKNOWLEDGMENTS

I got a lot of caving information and help from people in Tassie, so thanks must go to:

Stephen J. Phipps, who was a PhD student and scientific programmer at the University of Tasmania in Hobart when I began the book, and is now (doctorate completed) an earth systems modeler in Sidney, and Michael Lichon of the Mole Creek Caving Club, who found a place in the book on the premise that no good deed goes unpunished.

A plentitude of literary license was taken, partly to disguise known and protected caves in the Mole Creek region and partly just for the fun of it, so any errors relating to caving are mine! These guys were extremely helpful.

Of course, my old mate Grant Vowles came good again on police procedural matters, being a policeman himself (if a vastly different one than the fictional Charlie Banes in this novel and in *The Specialist*). Once again, the errors, if any, are mine.

Ian Beaumont of Queensland, retired gun dealer and all-around good fellow, deserves his place in this book.

My computer gurus at DTI Computers—Tom Esplen and Neal Sheppard—have saved my bacon more than once, and hopefully will do so again. You guys are amazing.

My thanks to all of you. Many, many thanks!

And a special thank you to my splendid editor, Diane Piron-Gelman, who deserves it!

CHAPTER ONE

At first, everyone thought the retrieving trial judge had been killed by a blind man shooting blanks at a dead pigeon. With typical Tasmanian logic and the blinkered focus of hardened gundog trial fanatics, they ignored the fact that the judge had been standing behind the blind man when the gun went off and the blanks in the blind man's shotgun were loaded only with primers, and therefore harmless.

Instead, they focused on the obvious, which was that blind John had the shotgun in his hands and all the motive in the world for shooting the judge, who, the evening before, had callously told John, in front of everyone, that he should give up entering his guide dog Magic in retrieving trials because, "You can't possibly win." Insensitive and unkind words to a highly competitive individual like John, so in the eyes of most observers, the judge deserved shooting!

And then the judge had compounded the offense by growling back when John's guide dog/retrieving trial entrant sensed John's anger and curled her upper lip in the beginnings of a snarl. Foothills Mocha Magic was not known to snarl without good and sufficient reason. The chocolate Labrador bitch took her work as a guide dog seriously, and reading John's moods, not to mention protecting him, was part of her chosen role in life. A short-lived incident, but a memorable one that gained the judge no credit even in death.

When he died, nobody was actually watching the judge

anyway. All attentions were focused across an arm of the South Esk River, on the place where the mechanical catapult was set up to fling dead pigeons for the trial dogs to retrieve. The trial site was on Ormley, a grazing property nestled in the Fingal Valley east of Avoca between the looming bulk of Ben Lomond and the lower Fingal Tier to the south.

It was a typical late autumn morning in which everyone had awakened to a river valley swirling in a fog that roosted in the tall blue gums and stringy-barks along the river and shrouded the gorse bushes and lower scrub. It took quite some time to burn off, but by mid-morning the day was as splendid as anyone could ask for. Except maybe the judge.

Thus, this astonishing chain of events:

The judge raised his clipboard in a signal.

The bird thrower was released, flinging the pigeon into the air for Magic to see and John to shoot at even though he couldn't see.

John, who'd been a shooter before losing his sight in an accident, heard the thrower and fired at the appropriate moment the bird should have been at the zenith of its flight.

And both the hapless pigeon and the trial judge ended up face-down and dead on the boggy ground, a hundred yards and a river between them, but equal in death.

Foothills Mocha Magic, splendid dog that she was, kept her attention focused on the pigeon—if the idiot judge wished to do his job lying face down in the dirt, that was none of her concern. John, of course, didn't see the judge fall, so he waited the requisite mental ten-count, then ordered his dog to fetch, whereupon she took off like a rocket, launched herself into the river, swam across, ran straight to the bird, picked it up, and was swimming the river on her way back almost before the judge stopped twitching. She threw him a scurrilous glance, then presented John with her trophy in a perfect, ten-point delivery, and walked back to heel, neither knowing nor caring that her best run ever wasn't going to count.

Hardly anyone even saw the delivery; most of the gallery had, by this time, realized that their trial judge had just fallen down dead.

About seventy-five people and half that many dogs watched it all, but nobody saw anything that Sergeant Charlie Banes, head of the St. Helens police station, out of uniform and trying to enjoy a rare Saturday off, didn't also see from his position in the gallery of onlookers. A gun was fired and a man whom many people actively disliked fell down dead. That simple. It made no sense, at first, to anyone. Nobody'd heard any shot but John's shotgun going off, and it wasn't until they went to look that the bullet hole in the judge's back became suddenly, brutally obvious. So did the pool of his own blood, welling out under him from where the bullet's exit wound had blown apart his chest.

Charlie's first reaction, like that of the other onlookers, was disbelief. His second, as he licked idly at a fang-bloodied knuckle, was that somehow this was more of Bluey's revenge for having been collared and leashed. Bluey was the rough-coated Jack Russell terrier that Charlie was dog-sitting for the day, a singularly independent reprobate beast famed for his irreverent temper and noxious habits, and Charlie's personal nemesis. Technically, Bluey shouldn't have been on the trial site in the first place, not being a registered gundog, but Charlie's status as an officer of the law had been duly noted and the presence of the scruffy little terrier grudgingly accepted.

Charlie's third reaction—and this was the one that would not go away; it scurried around in his mind like a demented, caged hamster for months afterward—was to wonder how he could ever explain to the higher-ups in the Tasmanian police department how he, a senior policeman, could stand and watch as a blind man stood before a crowd of people with a loaded shotgun in his hands, fired the gun, and somebody died.

That terrifying thought was forcibly shoved to the background as he thrust Bluey's lead into the hands of Teague Kendall, who was standing next to him.

"Stay here, and hang onto this bugger, lest he eat somebody," Charlie snapped, then rushed toward the fallen judge, waving his police ID and letting professionalism take control.

"Police! Everybody stay where they are!" he shouted, and was gratified to see the stentorian tones have their effect on the crowd of now totally confused onlookers. Within moments, he had the crowd under a semblance of order, and had thankfully managed to keep everyone at least several feet from the dead judge.

Kendall did exactly as he'd been told. He remained in place, torn between watching his police officer friend take control of the situation and hoping the recalcitrant Jack Russell terrier wouldn't decide to vent his evil disposition on Kendall himself. Beside Kendall, Rex Henderson also remained in place, scanning the scene with quick, observant glances and, Kendall thought, already rewriting the scene in his mind.

Both men were writers. Kendall's best-selling true-crime thriller *The Specialist,* recounting the exploits of a crazy serial killer who'd operated in Tasmania and near Kendall's home on Vancouver Island in Canada—nearly claiming Kendall and his lady friend Kirsten Knelsen as victims—was topping the charts in North America, while Rex's latest crime novel had done so well his publisher had sponsored an Australia/New Zealand book tour for the Houston, Texas, writer. Their being together in a muddy paddock in the Tasmanian backblocks, observing the aftermath of what seemed to be a sniper attack on a retrieving trial judge, was the result of having met quite by chance at

LAX on their way to Australia on two different flights.

Rex Henderson was a quiet, unassuming, middle-aged man whose gentle demeanor belied the sometimes harsh violence of his crime novels. Originally from Minnesota, he'd found it necessary to put on a Texas drawl during his Australian visit just to please his audiences. Now he appeared lost in thought, calmly observing the chaos around them as Charlie sheep-dogged the crowd into order. Rex was also rubbing nervously at his left ear lobe, or so Kendall assumed until he noticed the trickle of blood down Rex's fingers, and realized there was more involved than just nerves.

"What've you done to yourself?" he asked, leaning over to peer closely at the injury.

His companion lowered the hand, then stared wide-eyed at his bloodied fingers before turning to look at Kendall. Only then, apparently, did Rex actually feel anything like pain.

"Ouch!" he said. "They sure have vicious bees in this country. Or was it a hornet, do you think?"

Kendall moved in for a closer look, first dragging a handkerchief from his back pocket so he could wipe away the still-oozing blood. Rex flinched at the touch of the hanky, but flinched more visibly when Kendall had finished his assessment.

"A lead hornet," Kendall declared with genuine surprise. "Bloody oath, mate . . . I think the bullet that got the judge must have nicked your ear on the way by."

"A bullet?" Rex stared at Kendall with a calmness the younger, taller man couldn't help but envy. "Surely not. It was an insect of some kind. I heard it."

"So did I, now that you mention it," Kendall replied. "And it was no insect." He thought for a brief moment, then handed over Bluey's lead to Rex. "Here, hold this mongrel while I let Charlie know about this. And don't move. Where you were standing might turn out to be important when it's time to see where the shot came from."

"Should we be standing here at all if somebody's actually shooting at us?" Rex answered his own question before Kendall could think of a reply. "I guess it hardly matters, now. There's been enough time to have wiped out half the people here, if that was the plan."

Both men glanced nervously around them and behind, across boggy riverside paddocks to the nearest real cover, a slight ridge adorned with bracken fern, blackberry scrub, and a few tall stringy-barks—Tasmanian oaks. Assuming Kendall was right about the direction involved, this was the logical place for the shot to have originated.

"Helluva shot," Kendall said. "Must be near-as-damn-it a thousand meters." He ran his glance in a line between the judge's corpse and the distant ridge, then returned to his announced course of action. "You stay here while I tell Charlie," he said, "and don't, for God's sake, let that mongrel dog get loose. We've got enough chaos already."

Teague paused for an instant, peering intently at his companion, then added, "Jeez, but you're lucky. If I was you, I'd go buy a lottery ticket today." Then he shook his head in a gesture of disgust. "And I'm an idiot," he said, and reached out to retrieve the Jack Russell's leash. "You're the one needing attention. Get yourself to the catering tent—they're sure to have a first-aid kit. There's all the time in the world to tell Charlie about how you almost got yourself shot."

authority was legend.

At Fingal, he turned north into the maze of back roads and forestry tracks that meandered through paddock and scrub and rugged timber country along creeks and over ridges, angling always north and east before he finally turned back northwest to reach his destination, the Pub in the Paddock at Pyengana. It was a route Ian could have driven dead drunk or half asleep, and often had. He knew every back road and track in the northeast of Tasmania, courtesy of a lifetime spent thieving and poaching. The northeastern quarter of this small island south of Australia proper was Ian's spiritual home, one he'd left only once in his sixty-plus years of rough, hardscrabble existence.

He'd joined the Australian army during the Vietnam years (it was, in the magistrate's words: "Join the army or it's off to gaol, boy!") and found his shooting and bush skills highly enough valued—usually—to compensate for his incorrigible insubordination. He already knew about killing. There was hardly an animal or bird species in Tasmania that Ian Boyd hadn't shot at one time or another. He'd shot possums for their skins while still just a boy, and wallabies and Forester kangaroos for dog tucker, fallow deer for the table and the sheer thrill of poaching them, bandicoots and wombats and even, once, a platypus, just to see how they'd cook up. And he'd killed feral cats and the ubiquitous Tassie Devils and, occasionally, other people's dogs and livestock just for the hell of it.

The army taught him to kill humans. As a sniper. From ambush. Ian took to it well, seeing no real difference in what sort of animal fell to his accurate shooting. The only real difference, he'd decided early on, was that people were a lot more noisy about their dying if the fatal shot wasn't quite perfect.

The army experience in 'Nam also taught him about hashish and cocaine and heroin and a barrage of other abusive substances his body and mind came to crave. His history and heritage provided the means to finance his addictions once the army had used him up and spit him out, sending him back to Tasmania with diagnosed but untreated posttraumatic stress disorder and a taste for anything that would placate the demons in his mind. From the day of his discharge to this, the day of his first unsanctioned murder, he'd seldom drawn a breath untouched by drugs or alcohol.

Ian was the last ("Thank God!" said those few who knew him well) in a long, long line of thieves and poachers and ne'er-do-wells that traced back to those ancestors who'd come off a convict hulk in chains when Tasmania was still Van Diemen's Land, been flung into the living hell that was the Port Arthur penal colony, then eventually released into bonded servitude or groveling poverty and a return to the noxious habits that had seen them transported from Britain in the first place. Now, past sixty and far more interested in abusive substances than sex, he was probably incapable of furthering his branch of the Boyd line, and unlikely to try.

He paused on a quiet, isolated stretch of road and stowed the Finnish rifle with its built-in sound suppressor carefully beneath the truck seat, and tucked away the spent casing for eventual reloading. Then it was on, to the Pub in the Paddock, nearly fifty kilometers as the crow flies away from the murder scene, and nearly as much again by convoluted, twisting, often barely passable bush tracks.

Ian had no idea if the woman who'd ordered the shooting would be at Pyengana, waiting for him, waiting for a full debriefing. Nor did it matter. She would find him, if not at the Pub in the Paddock, then at some other of Ian's regular watering holes, perhaps in St. Helens, on the coast. She'd found Ian there before, after all. She had strode gracefully into a St. Helens pub with unique familiarity, for a stranger, but greeted Ian with the warmth and intimacy of an old mate.

Or so Ian remembered, vaguely, as he sipped on his first of many draught beers at Pyengana. He'd been both drunk and high at the time, and had only flitting recollections of how she had bought them both beers, then sat across from him at a corner table and begun to speak in that strangely familiar velvet voice, a voice both deep and mellow, smooth and seductive as Bailey's Irish Cream. It was the voice that had triggered Ian's reactions, offsetting the unease he first felt at not recognizing the woman immediately, out of uniform as she was, then his confusion when he did recognize her.

The one thing he did recall was that somehow the woman knew him, seemed able to read his mind, to know what Ian was going to say before the words had passed his yellowing, tobacco-stained teeth, knew his very thoughts, and knew also the inner demons that provoked those thoughts, that fueled his reactions.

Certainly she'd known all about his almost paranoid hatred of anything and everything American. Had even asked, Ian vaguely remembered, if he still went about kicking the doors of the Ford F100 pickup trucks that were becoming increasingly common in Tasmania. Or had she asked? He had to think about that, but decided it didn't matter. She might or might not have asked the question, but she'd known the answer, just as she'd known that he had once shot out his own television set at the sight of Australian Prime Minister John Howard snuggling up to American President George W. Bush as the two conspired to send young men out to die in Iraq, as young men from both countries had died in Vietnam, and for as little reason.

It seemed to Ian that the woman had known everything about him, not that she'd come at any specific issue directly. Instead, she'd punctuated their discussion with gentle swirls of the nurse's-style upside-down pocket watch she dangled from its fob, letting the timepiece spin in a pendulum-like, hypnotic pattern.

At Pyengana, as he sat nursing a beer and watching the tourists en route home from St. Columba Falls, a few kilometers to the south, Ian found himself wondering just how much the damned woman did know. Did she know, for instance, that now, as the alcohol brought him down from a fierce cocaine high, he was certain sure that he'd actually shot the wrong man?

At Pyengana, he learned for the first time that in addition to missing his shot, he'd actually killed someone. It was all over the television news and everyone was talking about it. Everyone but Ian; he was already seriously into the grog, but not so drunk he couldn't break with tradition and keep his mouth shut for a change. He would have to talk about it eventually, but that would come later.

It was the jack-jumper's fault, anyway, but try to explain that to the woman who'd offered such good money for a simple shooting. Selecting his target had been easy enough; even amongst the crowd at the gundog trial, and even at the extreme range, it had been easy to distinguish the features of the man whose photo graced the dust jacket of the book he'd been shown. An American book, an American author. And, according to Ian's new employer, a Republican . . . a distinction that meant nothing to Ian except that it meant the man was a George W. Bush supporter, and therefore deserved shooting, whether for five dollars or five hundred, which was what Ian had been promised along with copious quantities of what he craved even more than the money—enough drugs to keep him going for months.

Easy identification, an easy shot even at that extreme range. So why had he allowed himself to be distracted so much that he'd missed seeing the ant nest? He didn't know the answer, only that he was on the edge of being, in the vernacular, pissed as forty cats, and would have to take to the back roads in order to get home without risking a breathalyzer check. He'd already gone without his driver's license twice in recent years, and wasn't quite so drunk that he wanted to risk losing it forever. Besides, there was the Vaime SSR under the seat—an illegal, unregistered firearm even before Little Johnny Howard had forced through the most draconian anti-firearms legislation in Australian history and made criminals of the country's honest farmers, shooters, and bushmen just to placate the growing numbers of city people who knew nothing about guns but were insistent on removing them from society.

Bad thoughts for a freedom-loving renegade already drunk. The next thing Ian knew, he was raging about the Iraq war to a couple of tourists he assumed were Americans. They were actually Canadian and would have agreed with his views if he'd been sober enough to make any sense at all. But Ian was in one of his "eyes closed, arms waving" episodes, and wasn't making sense even to himself. Nor to the publican, who eventually got sick of the disturbance and sent Ian packing. The Canadians, who'd seen far worse behavior in watering holes throughout their own frigid north, thought it something of an overreaction, then put the incident into their mental scrapbooks and ordered another beer.

Ian, for his part, managed to drive his battered vehicle a few kilometers back into the scrub, where he found a convenient and secluded side track where he could unroll his swag and try to sleep away the memory of his mistake. He'd had a long day, traveling first to Launceston to find his target, then having to follow the man south and east to the dog trial site. Easy enough work but damned long hours, Ian thought. The sleep part now was easy; he was out cold almost before he reached the horizontal.

Waking up was less easy. Ian struggled out of a nightmare filled with demons that tormented him with the smell of fresh roasted coffee, and he eventually opened his bleary eyes to find that it hadn't all been a dream. The coffee was real, as was the slender figure of the velvet-voiced woman brewing it, a woman who stared at Ian through reflective sunglasses despite the earliness of the hour, then smiled. It was not a nice smile. The last time Ian had seen a smile like that, it was on the grizzled face of old Viv Purcell's dog Bluey, just before the evil little Jack Russell attempted to bite off Ian's balls.

There was also the small matter of the Vaime SSR, lying across the woman's lap with the muzzle casually aimed in Ian's direction, but he managed to ignore that as he struggled upright and lurched his way to the fire and the lure of the fresh coffee.

He'd poured the coffee and even raised the tin cup in a casual sort of toast when he noticed the woman was holding his rifle in hands that wore latex surgical gloves. And the rifle was cocked.

Then Ian really began to worry.

CHAPTER FOUR

The man who dropped the knife didn't always enjoy being dead, but he enjoyed being shot at even less.

When the grazier's shotgun exploded the morning, startling the sheep and dispersing a mob of magpies from the scrub around him, the man with the knife in his hand was already terrified. It had taken him fifteen minutes just to reach the cave opening from the point where it had become visible to him. Fifteen minutes to cover fifteen yards, and each minute a lifetime . . . even for a man already dead.

Until the point where he'd actually seen the entrance to the cave, he'd moved with the grace of a dancer, flitting across the open paddock as if shifted by the dawn breezes. He'd ghosted along behind Kirsten's party like the faithful scout in some Western movie—seeing but unseen, at one with the very universe around him, indomitable, all-knowing, *amazing* . . .

But sight of the opening had struck him like a slap across the face, a sucker punch exploding outward from his own mind. He'd stumbled, nearly fallen as weird colors swirled through his vision and terror thundered in his ears. He'd been forced to approach on his hands and knees, which was perhaps just as well; his trembling legs couldn't have supported him. Sweat poured into his eyes and his hands were slick with it, despite the coolness of the autumn morning.

The cave opening gaped before him like the entrance to hell, and in his perverted mind it was exactly that. Half the world

31

believe you think like them, too. The first reaction you had to this gaping wound in my ear was that I was lucky it didn't kill me, and therefore I ought to go and purchase a lottery ticket."

"So what's wrong with that?"

"Nothing, except that no less than six—count 'em!—*six* other people said the same thing in almost the exact same words while the veterinarian was tending my injury. A vet!" Rex sighed, deliberately being over-dramatic. "Still, better than no doctor at all, I suppose."

"Heaps better, I'd reckon. They're trained to fix up patients that can't tell them what's wrong." Kendall leaned in to inspect the injured ear. "At least it's quit bleeding. Just wait until you get back to The States; you'll be able to tell everybody you were attacked by bloodthirsty Aboriginals."

"Who'd believe that?"

"Most Americans I've met. Although, yeah, maybe you're right. Americans only believe what they see on television."

"If this had happened at home, at least everybody wouldn't be sitting around complaining about how it wrecked the dog trial." There was a sharpness to Rex's voice that caught Kendall's attention. "And they certainly wouldn't be arguing with the authorities about whether they should be allowed to move a hundred yards downstream and continue the damned trial with a new judge! And I've had three offers to buy my hat, if you can imagine it. And . . . and . . ."

Rex's mouth kept moving, but no words emerged. Kendall suddenly realized his companion was genuinely upset by the day's events. Rex wrote fairly chilling and dark mysteries, to the delight of his many fans, but Kendall thought him to be a gentle and caring soul at heart, despite that vivid imagination.

"Steady on, little mate," he cried, reaching to grab Rex if the man should suddenly decide to faint. The move surprised the rough-coated Jack Russell terrier leashed to Kendall's left hand,

and he responded by erupting into excited barks and rushing around in a demented circle that resulted in Kendall, not Rex, tumbling to the ground.

"You rotten mongrel of a dog!" Kendall snarled at the dog, then clambered upright, making sure to maintain a hold on the leash. Bluey's response to the insult was an evil glare; the dog liked Rex (most dogs did) but was unsure about Kendall, who wasn't really a "dog person."

"Give him to me before you trip again and injure the poor creature," Rex said, obviously recovered from his spate of shock. Bluey scampered happily through the transfer of guardianship, pausing only long enough to sprinkle Kendall's boots as he departed. Rex laughed. Kendall didn't see anything funny about it.

"You're overdoing this famous bit, you rotten mongrel," Kendall said. "You'll get your comeuppance, mark my very word, and there'll be no sympathy from me when it happens. Nor from anybody else, either, I'll wager."

"Not from me, and that's sure and certain." The voice of Charlie Banes rumbled from behind them, and Kendall, Rex, and Bluey all turned to meet the approaching policeman. Even in civilian clothes, Charlie tended to carry himself with alertness and precision, and despite the lack of uniform, he exuded authority.

"You're an evil animal, little mate," he said to the Jack Russell, who glared ferociously, one yellow eye fixed on the grazed knuckle he'd already inflicted on his tormentor. "Still," Charlie continued, turning his attention to Kendall, "this evil little bugger's responsible for solving your Specialist case, and probably saving your life, too, at least in a roundabout way." Charlie then turned to Rex.

" 'The Specialist'," Charlie said in sneering tones. "Not hard to tell our Teague's been a journalist, eh? Typical. Can't have a story without putting some fancy-dancy name to it, and taking everything all out of context, and indulging in a little journalistic feeding frenzy, eh?" His voice lost no authority, but revealed his views on the journalistic profession, not that Charlie Banes would have dignified it with such a description.

Rex didn't reply. He'd already heard, chapter and verse, how the diminutive dog and his geriatric master, a stereotypical Tasmanian bushie, had led Charlie to discovering the Tasmanian exploits of the psychologist serial killer/cannibal Dr. Ralph Stafford, whom Teague had christened the Specialist.

"He didn't save my life, and even if he did—that's no excuse for pissing on my boots," Kendall retorted as he traded scowls with the totally unrepentant dog.

"It's why sensible people wear gumboots to dog trials," Charlie replied, turning his attention again to Rex. Charlie leaned down to inspect the injured ear, obviously having been told about it before he'd joined them. "Bullet burn, for certain," he said. "Now come show me precisely where you were standing. We've got bugger-all else to work with on this thing so far, so anything constructive would be helpful."

The three men spent some time estimating sight-lines and possible places the shot might have come from, but Charlie refused to allow any closer inspections of the ridge in question. "I'm being sent the entire mob of recruits from the police academy in Hobart," he said. "They'll do a proper line search— part of their training, if nothing else. And I expect there won't be much else, either. The local coppers are busy interviewing everybody, though, for what it's worth." Again that thoughtful pause before he continued. "Nobody saw anything, nobody did anything, nobody knows anything. Well, not surprising. The judge certainly wasn't shot by any of these people."

"I'm not so sure," Rex interjected. "At least half of the ones in the tent when I was being looked at by the vet were bound and convinced he deserved shooting. It was about the only thing most of them did agree on."

"Well he did deserve it, going by what I understand the silly bugger said to that blind man last night," Teague said. "Insensitive peckerwick, if nothing else, although I guess that doesn't really make him deserve to be shot."

Charlie seemed unimpressed by the line of reasoning. "They're just nervous, and I don't blame them," he said. "And of course he was over from Australia, which is one strike against him, and from Canberra-our-nation's-capital (running the words into one) is a pretty sound second strike. Add the incident with the blind bloke and Bob's your uncle—he was a bad bastard and deserved shooting."

Rex Henderson, ever alert to semantic nuances, started to reach up and touch his wounded ear, then thought better of it. "Why do you refer to Australia as if it was a foreign country?" he asked. "Isn't this part of Australia?"

"This is Tasmania!" Teague and Charlie replied almost in unison, then looked at each other, and laughed outright at the perplexed expression on their companion's face. It was left to Kendall to explain that in the eyes of most fair-dinkum (genuine) Tasmanians, Australia *is* sort of a foreign country, or at least a second-rate cousin to Tasmania, which everyone knew to be far more significant than the mainland. "We're the tail that wags the dog, or at least that's how native Tasmanians think of it," he explained.

Charlie's cue: "Speaking of dogs, is there any chance you could—?" He got no further.

"Not on your bloody life," Teague interrupted. "We're staying in a posh hotel, for starters, Charlie; not someplace he can piss on what furniture he doesn't try to eat. Besides, that mongrel hates and loathes and detests me, and the feeling's mutual. I'd be lucky to get him back to Launceston without being eaten by the bugger. And Rex can't take him either, because he's in the same hotel, and because . . . well . . . just because."

"Don't make such a production of it. I was only about to ask if you'd mind holding onto him a bit longer. The problem is that I'm going to be stuck here until the CIB and forensics teams arrive, at the very least, and I can hardly do me job and look after this evil creature"—with a sideways glance at the grinning dog—"at the same time, can I?"

"So lock him in your car. At least that would protect everybody else from him. I don't think *he* needs much protecting."

"He'd destroy the car's interior in five minutes flat, and I'm likely to be here for hours." Charlie again glared at the animal he'd become lumbered with when Bluey had been dumped in Charlie's care by his geriatric owner, Viv Purcell, en route to the hospital for a checkup. Viv had handed Charlie the dog and made his escape before the policeman could think of any useful excuse.

"So borrow a crate and lock him in that," Kendall said. "I'm not having him with me, and not in my rental car, either."

It was Rex who salvaged the situation. "Unless there's some law against it, I'd sort of like to stay and watch whatever's going to happen," he said, firming his grip on the leash. "You," he said, turning to Teague Kendall, "can go back to Launceston if you like. I'm sure I can scrounge a ride with somebody once the dust settles. One thing about these Tasmanians, they're very obliging to strangers."

"Don't be daft. If you want to stay, I'll stay too," replied Kendall. "In fact, I'd best stay, or these *obliging* Tasmanians might talk you out of that fancy Stetson and con you into trading those Lucchese boots for Blunnies."

"It is *not* a Stetson. It is a Charlie One Horse 'Desperado,' if you can imagine such a thing." Rex lifted the offending hat from his head and regarded it soberly. "The publishers insisted I wear this," he said. "Part of my *image*." He snorted, clearly not impressed by the concept. "And these Lucchese boots, I'll have you know, cost me $549. I've had them for about seven years and I'd sooner trade my car! These boots are like bedroom slippers."

Teague Kendall had no real comeback. His own battered Akubra bush hat, once a top-of-the-line example of Australian hat manufacture, was nearing the end of its useful life, and his battered Blundstone boots weren't much better. Both had been back and forth between Australia and Canada more than once.

"Going to be a long, boring day," said Charlie. "Be another couple of hours before the trainees get here, and then there'll be a bun fight over jurisdiction and whether it's safe to let the cadets even *do* a proper line search. Safe!" He spat out the word. "There's a hundred people standing around here, and nobody else has been shot yet, but they'll be arguing about safety, you mark my word. Whoever's in charge will be mortally afraid of being criticized for endangering his troops, and just ignore the fact that's what they were sent here for—to do a line search!"

"Jesus! Maybe you should go home, Charlie. This is getting to you, I think," said Kendall.

"Of course it's getting to me. I'm off my turf, out of bloody uniform, and lumbered with this evil bloody animal, but I'm still the senior officer on the ground and, whatever else, I'm the one who'll cop the shit when it flies from the fan. As it will!" Charlie's voice belied his obvious enjoyment of the situation.

"And speaking of things hitting the fan," he continued, "oughtn't you be getting yourself back to Lonnie, like Rex suggested? You surely ought to be there when your girl gets back from wherever she is. Leaving her to find you missing and no idea where you are or why is hardly honeymoon behavior, I'd say."

"This isn't a honeymoon, and well you know it!" Kendall's flush was half anger, half embarrassment. He knew his friend was—in the vernacular—having a lend of him. A laugh at Kendall's expense. But it didn't ease his real concerns on the subject of Kirsten Knelsen, their trip together, and their fragile, highly questionable relationship. He wasn't about to disclose those concerns to Charlie Banes or anyone else, but he didn't enjoy being led into a risky corner about them, either.

"Not if the woman's got any sense at all; no sane woman would marry you," was the reply. "So, where did you say she was? Down a cave somewhere, as I recall."

"Mole Creek, with a mob of equally crazy caving enthusiasts." Teague wasn't afraid to show his feelings on that subject. After his experiences with Kirsten in the cave she'd discovered on Vancouver Island, and the terror of being trapped in icy water that came to his knees but froze his very soul, in total darkness for hours that seemed like a lifetime, positive he was going to die there, Teague had sworn never to venture underground again. Indeed—and he did not admit this fact—he doubted he could summon up the nerve to do so! It was among the many difficulties he faced in developing a relationship with Kirsten, whom he thought he loved dearly but was totally uncertain he could ever live with. Their journey to visit Tasmania had been planned, in fact, to see how they got on together under more or less normal circumstances, few of which had yet come to pass.

First there'd been her delight at being contacted by members of the Mole Creek caving group almost before she had her bag unpacked at their Launceston hotel, and now . . . this! Kirsten had been, in Teague's opinion, a bit too enthusiastic about being invited on the caving expedition at Mole Creek, a little too pleased that Bruce Wilkinson, a retired insurance type from

Hobart and a Golden Retriever fancier, had invited Kendall and Rex to join him for the weekend's gundog trial. Or was this all just his fragile ego talking? Rex was no help.

"You barely get off the plane and you trot off to this dog trial with me, instead of . . . well . . . instead of something," he said with a cautious grin. "Doesn't sound like any sort of honeymoon to me, either."

Which allowed Charlie to rejoin the fray, much to Kendall's discomfort.

"It isn't a honeymoon?" Charlie said, raising his bushy eyebrows in an exaggerated gesture of mock indignation. "You mean you're staying together in the same hotel room and you're not married? Good thing this is the twenty-first century, my lad. In the old days, I'd have been duty bound to have you up for cohabiting! Although, to be fair, the term was usually reserved for relations between, uhm, partners of, uhm, mixed races if you take my point. Still, I am shocked, Kendall—truly shocked."

Which—truly—he was not! Charlie's own relationship situation was equally fragile, perhaps even more disturbing. So much so that he actually felt guilty—if not *too* guilty—about twitting Kendall in the first place.

Charlie thought that he, himself, might actually be getting serious about someone, and the concept frankly terrified him. Police of both sexes, he knew only too well, faced fearsome odds when it came to relationships and marriage and family life. Yes, there were exceptions. He knew of a Burnie policeman who was married to (horror of horrors!) a journalist, but seemed to be making it work very well indeed. And, to be fair, Charlie's friendship with Kendall had begun when the novelist had been a journalist, and had only grown stronger over time.

But it isn't marriage. Thank God!

For himself, having managed to survive one marital meltdown only because he was young enough, dumb enough, and tough

41

enough, the entire issue now loomed like a gigantic wave. He was old enough now to know his limitations, and in the relationship field, they were legion.

Half your bloody luck, mate. He offered the silent tribute to his Burnie colleague with the journalist wife, then glanced down at the reprobate terrier he'd been lumbered with. *And half yours too, little mate. If today's any example, I'll end up with you as a chaperone come Monday night. Wouldn't that be just fucking wonderful? They'd better let your boss out of hospital before then, or you'll be facing up to a lead injection.*

As if!

Bluey, nonplussed by Charlie's silent thoughts, regarded him haughtily through unreadable amber eyes, and curled his upper lip in something that could have been a sneer, or a smirk, or even a smile.

Or all of the above.

Chapter Six

The four cavers hovered in silence for what seemed like an hour. They just stood there, staring first at the knife, then at each other, then back at the knife again. But they hardly needed to voice their obvious concerns aloud. Was the knife there because somebody had tried to cut the abseil rope and somehow managed to drop the knife in the process? Or, hideously more terrifying, in a way, somebody had cut the rope just enough to weaken it, just enough that a climber might get partway or most of the way up, only to find the rope giving way beneath the strain? It seemed illogical, somehow, and yet also terrifyingly possible. Surely nobody would *deliberately* . . . ?

No. It made no sense at all. If somebody wanted to trap the cavers below ground, they would have needed only to throw the rope down. It was simply rigged through a hanger hidden beside the entrance.

The possibility of such a problem had even been raised, apparently in jest, but the Tassie cavers had been certain, they said, that the property owner didn't even know of this cave's existence. Or did he? If they'd been spotted during their stealthy approach so many hours ago . . .

"The bloke that owns the property *has* been known to take to trespassers with a shotgun," Michael commented, barely above a whisper.

"They said in court that he was using quail shot, and he fired way above everybody's head, too," Sue replied. But Kirsten noticed a shudder of fear as the words emerged. Again, they looked at the knife, looked at each other. Waiting, but for what?

Kirsten stood there in the eerie group silence, suddenly aware that everyone was looking at her, and also suddenly aware that they were seeking something. Leadership? She shivered inwardly at the mere thought.

Hey, guys. I'm just a tourist here. This is your country, your cave. Don't expect me to have any answers. It isn't fair.

But she said nothing. Nor did they, until Kirsten finally, decisively, stepped over to and grabbed the dangling rope, pulling on it first tentatively, then with all her strength, leaning back hard and bracing her feet.

The rope held, showed no sign of any inherent or newly created weakness. (*But how could it? What the hell signs should we be looking for?*) Kirsten dropped her side-pack and reached high, then hitched herself up along the rope, not using the abseiling gear, merely shinnying up the rope until she was several feet above their heads.

"Well, don't just stand there," she said, voice already harsh with the exertion. "Somebody else grab on and come up behind me. We should be able to get *all* our weight on it before anybody's dangerously high."

Which they did, and the rope did not break. Then they settled down for another round of staring at the rope while everyone caught their breath and waited, watching each other to see who would now be first to tackle the *real* climb.

"I'm the heaviest. Might as well be me," Michael said, then scurried to attach the climbing gear as if he feared losing his courage if he didn't get started right away.

But before he began his climb, he took a clean handkerchief from his pack and gingerly picked up the knife. He made no attempt to close the blade, just wrapped the open knife in the handkerchief.

"Anybody got a spare piddle jar?" he asked, and when one was produced, he dropped in the knife and stuck the bottle into his pack.

"There might be fingerprints on it," he said somewhat lamely. "Or . . . something, anyway."

"You've been watching too many American cop shows," quipped one of his companions. But the look they all cast upward at the rope suspended from above held no humor at all.

CHAPTER SEVEN

It was full dark when the Mole Creek mob dropped Kirsten off in front of her Launceston hotel after their day underground, just as it had been when they'd collected her that morning.

She was exhausted. The ardors of her day, coupled with residual jet lag from her flight from Canada, were combining to produce a skull-shattering headache. But she was jazzed, too, almost giddy with excitement at the underground wonders she'd been privileged to enjoy.

Also, despite having been told not to be, she was feeling just a touch guilty. Her newfound friends faced not only a long drive home—the cave was, after all, only a few minutes' drive from Mole Creek in the first place—but they had the task of cleaning up her borrowed caving gear along with their own.

And the shocking price they had to pay for gasoline, high even by Canadian standards, merely added to her guilt.

And the Americans scream blue murder when they're not paying half what we do. Spoiled, that's what they are! They should all come here, maybe. No. Transport to Tasmania—that's how they settled the place in the first place, although thankfully not with Americans. The irreverent thoughts produced a hiccup of giddy laughter.

But the expense issue, at least, she could partially atone for the next day, she thought as she made her weary way through the lobby and into the elevator. She'd insisted they return for lunch the next day . . . tomorrow. Her treat!

Kirsten stared blearily at her image in the elevator's mirrored

46

wall, less than impressed by what she saw. A medium-height, slender enough figure, but one hardly enhanced by muddy hiking boots and jeans stained by grass and mud as well. Her bush shirt was half out at the waist and her long, strawberry-blonde hair was disheveled to the point of being outright unkempt. Then she smiled, and that, at least, was genuine Kirsten . . . tired, exhausted or not. And why not? She'd had a helluva day. A wonderful day. A day to remember always and forever.

Kendall wasn't in the suite when she entered, and she couldn't help feeling slightly guilty about being glad for that. All she wanted now was a shower, then a drink and something to eat. If she could stay awake that long. Then the oblivion of sleep, beautiful sleep. She moved through to "her" room, glanced at the bed and felt drawn toward it, here, now, her entire being suddenly magnetized by the illusion of slumber and peace.

I'm in the wrong business; I should be designing TV commercials.

Kirsten dropped her fanny pack just inside the door and was headed for the bathroom, fingers already fumbling with her shirt buttons, when she paused at a soft knock at the outer door.

"Who is it?" She almost recoiled at the impatience in her own voice. *Get a grip, girl.*

The response was muffled, or too soft for her to catch all the words. She walked back, opened the door and found herself facing a total stranger, a tall, lean man, taller than Kendall and slimmer, his eyes hidden behind reflective sunglasses. Standing quiet, not threatening, not aggressive. She had an instant to notice dark hair under a broad-brimmed hat, regular, normal, casual clothing, expensive casual footwear. Then he spoke.

"How do you like Pauline's blue hair?" His voice had the texture of rich chocolate fudge. It was deep, resonant, hypnotic.

The nonsense of the question didn't register. Neither did the voice, nor the words themselves. Not consciously. But subconsciously . . . Kirsten straightened, her body functional if strangely rigid but her mind . . . gone! She didn't notice the man's quick, savage smile of pleasure, was unaware of the hypnotic suggestions that followed.

He waited, still with that predator's smile, while she gathered up her fanny pack, checked to make sure it held her passport, her wallet, her ID. Then he took her arm and guided her out into the corridor, moving slowly, patiently, as if leading a blind person.

CHAPTER EIGHT

The breathalyzer stop near Scottsdale caught Ralph Stafford by surprise, but only because it wasn't where he'd expected it to be. He'd nearly taken to the back roads to get around Scottsdale, knowing it was Saturday night, knowing a police breathalyzer unit was possible in that region of the Tasman Highway. Then he'd decided not to waste the time.

And in any event he hadn't considered this particular stretch of highway, which was little more than a wide spot in the steep, twisty section known as "The Sideling." It was an unlikely spot for a breathalyzer stop, but one that offered no escape routes. The locals could have told him that.

Stafford came around a curve, saw the police lights, tasted panic like acid in this throat, then swallowed it in a convulsive gulp. If they stopped him, he could brazen through it. He hadn't been drinking, hadn't been speeding, his license and reggo were in order.

As for his sleeping passenger . . . Kirsten Knelsen was no worry at all because she would stay asleep. He'd made sure of that. Her face was obscured by the inflatable neck pillow at her nape, and the travel blanket he'd draped her with obscured the bonds that confined her wrists and ran down beside the seat to further confine her ankles.

Stafford was hugely, enormously pleased with how the post-hypnotic suggestion he'd implanted more than a year ago had survived, even perhaps strengthened in Kirsten's subconscious.

She had succumbed perfectly to the seemingly innocent question about Pauline Corrigan, his former office assistant in Canada and Kirsten's best friend in the whole world.

It had, with hindsight, perhaps been risky to even try it, but now . . . ? A sign; it could be nothing else. Fate!

No, he thought, he'd get through this. There was no way known her disappearance could have been flagged yet, no way this could be more than a routine breathalyzer stop.

Fate wouldn't do this to me. Fate loves me.

And Fate did favor him. The police, with two other vehicles already lined up, waved Stafford through without a second glance.

Thankyouthankyouthankyou.

Stafford, no longer a doctor, no longer, technically, Ralph Stafford for that matter, didn't believe in God (except on those increasingly frequent occasions when he thought he, himself, might *be* God) but he had a curious sense that some things were governed by fate.

In his mind, it had surely been fate that had allowed him to escape from the Canadian cave in which Kirsten Knelsen had left him trapped. Once free, albeit with the help of the cougar that had physically dragged him from the cave mouth and nearly killed him in the process, it had been his own brilliance for pre-planning that had let him tend to his own wounds, flee to Mexico, endure months of painful reconstructive surgery, and then make his way to Australia despite the post-9/11 increases in airline security.

During his early years in practice, Stafford had worked in a variety of prisons and mental institutions, where he'd been as fascinated by what he could learn about identity theft and criminal methodology as he was with the inmates themselves. He had put that knowledge to good use over the years, and had sufficient identities, documents, and funds cached in various places around the world to let him roam almost at will.

Now back in Tasmania, he'd used one identity to buy a 4 × 4 with nearly a year's reggo in place, rented modest accommodations with yet another identity. He had access to vast amounts of funds stolen from patients over the years. His biggest worry had been keeping busy.

Until now.

Stafford was brilliant, and knew it. As a young man, on a lark, he'd taken the Mensa application test and passed. Later independent tests proved he wasn't just in the top two percent of IQ scores, but the top quarter of the top one percent. Maybe higher than that, since IQ tests were of questionable accuracy in the first place. But he thought it exemplified his oft-stated opinion that ninety-five percent of Mensans couldn't pour piss out of a boot without written instructions and the other five percent wrote the instructions—in Japlish.

This arrogance in the young doctor was eventually tempered, if only slightly, by the realities of his profession, but by that time his own mind was going awry anyway, synapses dissolving, reality shape-shifting with little or no warning.

So he'd come to rely on fate as he understood it, and rely on it in ways nobody else would or could understand.

Fate, he was certain, had caused him to glance at the newspaper on the day it made much of Teague Kendall's visit to Tasmania, providing him with Kendall's book-signing schedule for the entire state. And with that knowledge, the dessert, the delicious bonus that Kirsten Knelsen would be accompanying Kendall to Australia. To Tasmania. To him.

Stafford had hardly been able to believe his luck. Kendall, in his eyes, was more or less irrelevant. A nuisance factor at best. But Kirsten! Stafford salivated like Pavlov's dog just at the thought. He'd been so close that first time to being able to compare the taste of Kirsten with that of her sister Emma, but the older sister had eluded him in the end. A second chance, having her come to him as if served up on a platter, well . . . could it be anything *but* fate? As for the incident near the cave mouth? A mere glitch. Of no importance. Certainly not now!

All these elements hummed around in Stafford's mind like contented bees as he steered carefully through the night, running east from Launceston on the Tasman Highway almost to St. Helens itself, aiming to turn south on the bush tracks below Goshen and Gould's Country into the jungle of scrub above Loila Tier. His destination was an isolated shack he'd been shown by Ian Boyd, who, coincidentally, had also guided Stafford to the abandoned mining setup he'd previously used as his hideaway butchery during his incarnation as the Specialist.

At that time, it had been a tossup which of the two locations to use, and he'd chosen the one on Blue Tier for its ease of access. He'd not wanted to risk damage to the borrowed SUV that had come with his work at the St. Helens mental health facility. But that wasn't an issue now. The 4 × 4 he was driving was already scratched and nondescript, and there was nobody to care but himself.

Beside him, Kirsten slumbered peaceably, courtesy of the sedative he'd administered even before he'd got them out of Launceston. She was properly buckled into her seatbelt, not that he expected anyone to notice or care, now that he'd passed the breathalyzer unit. The highway was virtually empty.

Then he came around a tight curve, almost at the turnoff to Pyengana, and found the road bright with police flashers and a uniformed officer waving him down with a bright red baton.

Stafford kept both hands in sight, one of them very much so. He held it to his nose in the universal sign for silence as he used the index finger of his other hand to point to where Kirsten stayed slumped in the passenger seat.

"She's had a really tough day," he said in a voice rich as chocolate fudge, barely even a whisper but adequately audible to the policeman at the window Stafford had just rolled down.

Stafford's voice, in addition to its rich, melodic quality, was a tool of his (former) trade, a professional instrument he had honed and perfected over the years. He expected the policeman to respond to it, wasn't surprised in the least when the man whispered back.

"Just a routine stop, Sir. May I ask if you've had any alcohol this evening?"

"Not a drop," Stafford replied with a pleasant smile. "Not a drop in weeks, actually." He knew the qualifier would grant him no leniency, was totally unsurprised when the officer produced the breathalyzer and asked politely for a breath sample.

DNA . . . DNA . . . DNA. No!—not to worry. He'll discard the sample into a bag with a hundred of them and that'll be the end of that problem.

He took a deep breath, blew into the mouthpiece exactly as he knew the policeman wanted, watched the green figures come up 00, nodded politely as the policeman, still whispering, thanked Stafford for cooperating and waved him onward into the night.

After that, things got easier, except for an annoying number of wrong turns and false starts as he meandered through a maze of tracks that became harder and harder to negotiate as he threaded his way into the scrub jungle above Loila Tier. He was exhausted by the time his vehicle lurched to a halt in front of the shack.

The shack was little more than a hovel, its iron roof pitted and pocked with rust where it hadn't rusted through entirely. The windowless slab walls were constructed from sleeper flitches—the half-round leftovers from logs milled for railway ties—and the floor was native soil and half-rotted planks. It squatted in head-high bracken fern, blended into the background like some illustration for a particularly ghastly kiddies' nursery rhyme. The whole structure sagged drunkenly, but it was sounder than it looked and, Stafford reasoned, would serve his purpose. It would have to . . . he wasn't long on choices.

I could use a drink, just about now. A cold glass of nice, full-bodied Piper's Brook would go down well. If I had any, which I don't.

He was even thirstier by the time he got the vehicle unloaded, almost filling the shack with a folding table, camp cots, the cooking gear, the various boxes of food he'd hurriedly collected, the tools—most of them gathered earlier from a cache that hadn't been found in the investigation of his earlier crimes. Then came the task of finding a suitable means to confine Kirsten while she recovered from her sedation. He didn't want drugs in her system when the time came; adrenaline would be problem enough.

Eventually, he settled on installing a six-inch eyebolt, drilling a hole for it into a solid section of wall, then arranging a suitable length of chain so that he could allow her some freedom of movement with no hope of her getting loose. She would be able to recline on the camp cot provided, reach the latrine bucket if needed, but little else.

Kirsten, still satisfactorily sedated despite the roughness of the journey, was a heavier load than he'd expected, and by the time he had her properly installed in the windowless, lopsided shanty, Stafford was breathing heavily and very much feeling the effects of having let himself get out of shape.

Two glasses. Maybe even three. Surely the event calls for a celebration?

He slumped into a folding camp chair and let his breathing come back to normal, all the while watching his captive in her drugged slumber on the camp cot he'd set up for her.

Kirsten would stay sedated until well into the morning,

Stafford reckoned, then lapsed into a convoluted mental calculation of how long it would then take for the drugs to work their way out of her system.

Forty-eight hours, minimum. Seventy-two would be better. Plenty of time for us to get to know each other again. I can probably use hypnotic means to keep her calm, which is good. No sense in flooding the tissues with adrenalin, not when tenderness and flavor are at stake.

He dozed awhile himself, but was wakened by maniacal kookaburra laughter with the onset of dawn. Stafford yawned, stretched, let his gaze roam around the squalid interior of the hut. His first task on rousing was to check his tools, just for the reassurance that he'd brought them all, that they'd traveled without mishap. Stafford was, indeed, a specialist, and whatever else he thought about Kendall's true-crime thriller, he quite liked the title.

He'd managed to salvage some of the precision, top-quality butcher knives and surgical tools he'd cached before leaving Tasmania the last time. He'd had no inkling at the time, of course, that he might be caught out in Canada, that discovery of his main headquarters here in Tasmania would mean the loss of his best, most favorite tools.

But Stafford had always been a careful, organized individual, even before his mind began to disintegrate, before his psychoses began to take control and change him from a healer to a butcher. So he'd kept a few tools cached here and there—just in case.

His skills, of course, went where he did. He could dismember a human carcass with a boning knife alone and do it as quickly and more neatly than a butcher could do the same with a lamb or a quarter of beef. He could turn the carcass into recognizable cuts of meat. And cook them to perfection. And eat them.

None of which he'd done since escaping from Kirsten's cave

and wending his circuitous route through healing, facial reconstruction, and identity theft back to Tasmania, where it had all begun. But now he had his tools. And the time. And he had Kirsten.

Stafford spent a moment rearranging his few remaining favorites, keeping half an eye on Kirsten as he did so. Then, suddenly, he remembered what he'd forgotten.

The wine! Idiot! How could you forget the wine? You were quick enough to think about it last night.

Whereupon he began to dither, which annoyed him even more but which, for some reason, he couldn't stop. Would they even *have* a decent wine in St. Helens, or would he be faced with the long drive back to Launceston? His mind flooded with annoying, sometimes embarrassing scenes with ignorant clerks in the local bottle shops when he'd worked in St. Helens. Before. Clerks who thought, as did most of their customers, obviously, that wine only came in cardboard boxes and should be evaluated by lowest-of-price and drunk by the four-liter cask. Peasants.

Kirsten showed no signs of stirring, even when Stafford lifted her wrist to check her pulse . . . which was slow, steady, as normal as he would have expected. She'd be out until midday, at least. But . . . ? Another dose of sedative—just to be sure? He would have to be gone several hours, perhaps into the afternoon . . .

But then I'd have to wait that much longer for it to clear her system.

Which might not be a bad thing. We have so much to talk about, after all.

Except . . . the poor girl will be terrified beyond belief if she wakes up and finds herself all alone, chained up like an animal, not knowing where she is, or why.

But I wouldn't be here to enjoy it.

But if I was here, she wouldn't be alone.

And yet . . .

I wonder which would be more terrifying.

Stafford began to chuckle, and was still chortling as he thumped and bumped his way along the rough track that led to the slightly better track that led to a half-decent bush track that would lead him to a decent road and, eventually, St. Helens.

Where there would be wine. Good wine. Piper's Brook, for preference. Stafford liked nothing better than Piper's Brook with his meals.

CHAPTER NINE

Rose Chapman dearly wanted to shoot Ian Boyd. She was that angry with him, with how things had gone so horribly wrong. But she was equally angry with herself for depending on such an unreliable fool in the first place.

It seemed like such a good idea at the time.

She had recited that mantra over and over and over as she'd tracked him from the Pub in the Paddock at Pyengana to the seclusion of his hidey-hole in the scrub, as she'd waited through the night, dozing fitfully on the back seat of her own vehicle while trying to decide what to do. And when. And how.

Watching his apparent lack of fear as he slouched over, drinking the coffee as if providing it for him was her proper role, Rose's temper, never the calmest on her best day ever, overflowed.

"You bloody fool!" The words emerged in a hiss of exasperation coupled with frustration so extreme it crippled her tongue. "Do you know what you've done?"

Rose knew. They both did. It had been all over the electronic media within an hour of Ian's bullet smashing the life from the gundog judge.

"Wasn't my fault," he replied, trying to look defiant about it and failing in the face of his own rifle staring at him, the menace of that growing more and more threatening.

"You weren't meant to kill anyone!" The words hissed and her eyes blazed. Rose had wonderful eyes, huge eyes that complimented her raven hair and milky complexion. Eyes that could change from the palest, softest, dove-breast gray to the hard black of cast iron, depending on her mood. And, usually, she knew precisely how to use those eyes to greatest effect. She could appear vamp or virgin, soul mate or sex goddess with the merest flick of one dark eyebrow, the slightest widening or narrowing of her eyes. Combined with her natural good looks and truly splendid figure, her eyes were lethal weapons where most men were concerned.

Now, she was too angry to bother with such tricks, and instinctively knew they'd have no effect on Ian Boyd anyway. Ian was far past being influenced by feminine wiles—seduction to him came in the form of white powder in a plastic sachet, or illicit pills in a plastic bottle. Thankfully, she had those, too, at her disposal.

"All I wanted was for you to scare him, maybe hurt him a little," she hissed at Ian, her voice kept low despite the fact there was nobody within miles of them. "Threaten him, frighten the hell out of him . . . that's all."

"That's what I was trying to do," Boyd mumbled, never meeting her eyes, his own gaze focused on the wavering rifle barrel but his mind already straying into speculation about what drugs she'd maybe brought him, and in what quantities. If she was going to shoot him, she'd have done it by now, he reckoned. Certainly no sense trying to explain that he hadn't shot to kill, that if it hadn't been for the bull ant, the flinching . . .

With all the night to think about it, Rose had made a similar decision. Ian Boyd was a clumsy, inept tool, but better than none at all. Maybe. And perhaps still a useful one. Maybe. Nobody would ever connect him to the slaying of the gundog judge, not without Ian himself doing or saying something stupid, and once he'd served his purpose she could make sure he never said anything at all. Ever.

Rose had spent much of the night reviewing all she knew about Ian, which was more than he could have imagined. During her stint as a psych nurse at the Birch Clinic in St. Helens, where Ian Boyd was in and out with boring regularity, Rose had come to know a good deal about his lifestyle. He was a big man, rough as guts and mean as a snake. A brawler, easily provoked. Quick to anger, equally quick to forget the reasons for his anger. When he was high, Ian raved. When coming down, he raved. During his rare periods of stability, he would talk if anyone showed the slightest interest in listening. But he hardly ever made sense.

He'd appeared to understand when she'd originally set him against his target, and she'd expected him to provoke an incident, maybe even a fight. She'd tossed off the shooting suggestion, a throwaway line, never thinking he'd take it seriously.

No matter. Too late now to worry about things already done. For now, she needed merely to keep Ian away from public places, under control, and useable if and when she might need him again.

"You've still got that shack up behind Loila Tier?" She hadn't intended it as a question, exactly, but Ian took it as such, and was quick to nod agreement.

In point of fact, he'd have agreed to almost anything that would make Rose stop pointing his own rifle at him, but she couldn't know that.

"Good," she continued. "Let's go. It's a better place to talk about things than here."

She was on her feet, the rifle still in her hands but less threatening, now, before Ian could even think. Then he had to think, at least a little, following her directions as he doused and kicked apart the fire, collected the coffee pot and implements. Then he rolled his swag and got everything loaded into whichever of the two vehicles Rose Chapman directed.

He was not happy that she kept his cherished rifle when she climbed into her own SUV and fired off her final orders for the journey.

"I'll follow you. Drive properly . . . no speeding. Remember I'll be right behind you, and remember I've got this!" She punctuated her final remark not with the rifle, but with little waves of a baggie whose contents gleamed snow white in the morning sunshine.

Rose knew about manipulation. She was an expert at it, whether the method be emotional blackmail or substance deprivation. She hadn't expected Ian Boyd to be overly frightened by the rifle, but she *knew* what his reaction would be to the mere sight of the drugs he so desperately craved.

For his part, Ian practically salivated at the sight of the drugs. Their image filled his imagination as they made their way in tandem, first out to the Tasman Highway, east past Goshen, then south into the maze of tracks and trails and bush roads that eventually brought them to the decrepit old shack Ian thought of as his own.

He was so focused on the rewards awaiting him that he paid no attention to the condition of the track during the final few miles to the shack. Merely drunk, or at least undistracted by having Rose hot on his tail, he might have noticed the broken branches and disturbed underbrush as he forced his battered vehicle through, but today . . . ? No chance.

Rose had no inkling of the situation. She merely followed in Ian's wake, doing her best to keep her SUV from being destroyed by the exertions she forced upon it. The SUV was a high-end model with all the bells 'n' whistles, but she'd never used it in conditions like these, and it took all her energy just to keep the damned thing on this wallaby-pad that passed for a vehicular track.

The last few hundred yards were as much creek as track, and

the shack itself was nearly drowning in the bracken fern that surrounded it. It was close to invisible in the dank shadow of towering gum trees until one got within spitting distance.

Ian got to the shack door before Rose, not least because it took her a moment to regain her equilibrium and another to reach back for Ian's rifle as she clambered down from her SUV. But they were together when he opened the door, and shared equally the surprise at what greeted them when the rough-hewn plank door squeaked open.

CHAPTER TEN

There are degrees of worry. Sort of like the semantics of "lies, damned lies, and statistics," as voiced by Benjamin Disraeli. Or was it Mark Twain?

Teague Kendall was busy putting names of his own to the degrees of worry when the telephone in his hotel suite rang just before noon on Sunday and the leader of the Mole Creek caving group asked for Kirsten.

"She's not with you?" Kendall asked automatically. Then the ultimate definition he'd been seeking and trying to avoid at the same time came to him unbidden, leaping into his consciousness like some predatory animal.

Terror.

He'd felt it before, also with Kirsten involved. Not quite like this, but frightening nonetheless when he'd realized, back in what sometimes seemed the distant past, in what sometimes leapt out of his nightmares as if only yesterday, that Kirsten had gone caving alone with Ralph Stafford.

Doctor Ralph Stafford.

Serial killer.

Cannibal.

Terrifying, but not quite like this. This was worse, even with no real reason that it should be. There was no Stafford anymore, and whatever was going on, there would be a logical, reasonable explanation.

Maybe.

Hopefully.

Please, God!

"Stay there. I'll be right down." Then he paused, tried to force the panic from his mind and make his voice calm. "On second thought, you come up, if you wouldn't mind."

He gave his suite number, hung up the telephone, then did his best to force his tired, confused brain into functioning with some degree of efficiency. Not an easy task.

Kendall had been awake most of the night, worrying. Without any real reason, he'd almost-but-not-quite convinced himself that worrying might be normal, but it was unnecessary. He knew enough about caving to recognize that sometimes things happened and delays and changes of plans were called for. Somebody could sprain an ankle, a rope could come out of its mooring, any number of things could force an overnight delay in a cave.

He'd given Rex Henderson a veritable shopping list of such excuses earlier that morning, when he'd phoned his fellow writer to ask if Kirsten, by some miracle, was with Rex. Which of course made no sense at all and both men knew it, but at least, Kendall reasoned, it was doing *something*. He'd also checked with the front desk, asked around in the hotel's coffee shop and everywhere else he could think of, but there'd been a shift change from the night before—nobody'd seen Kirsten. There had been no undelivered messages. The telephone in the suite sat silent and stared at him without blinking: no phone messages waiting, either.

Nonetheless, he'd been able to keep his worst fears at bay—until now.

When Michael and his caver mates arrived at the suite, Kendall had to force himself to show calm, to ask his questions in a quiet, ordered fashion, giving them time to answer, even to expand on their answers.

It was a trial, especially when the subject of the knife came up. Kendall's stomach lurched, then boiled in foul-tasting bile, when Michael showed him the knife—still in its piddle container.

Then Kendall phoned the police.

Then he followed Kirsten's intentions and bought them all lunch. From room service, because he wasn't about to let them out of his sight until the police arrived.

CHAPTER ELEVEN

Charlie Banes was sprawled uncomfortably under the geriatric Land Rover he'd bought for a song but which was costing him an arm and a leg to renovate into something even remotely useful. He wasn't accomplishing much, but the tinkering seemed to help him think, and he had much to think about.

He was about as good a mechanic as he was a plumber, but he had a vague working knowledge of what he was about, and was actually enjoying himself when old Viv Purcell's disreputable damned dog rushed in under the vehicle and playfully butted Charlie in the balls.

"Christ on a bloody crutch!" he cried, then repeated the oath less noisily after rearing up to thump his head on the driveshaft so hard it nearly knocked him out.

"G'arn . . . get out of that, you mongrel bloody dog, or I'll kick yez into the middle of next week," shouted old Viv, who meant not a word of it, as both Charlie and the recalcitrant Jack Russell terrier well knew.

"Dammit, Viv. That evil dog of yours will be the death of me one day," Charlie said as he rolled out from under the vehicle, one greasy hand pawing at where his head was already smeared with grease from its impact with the undercarriage.

"Bluey didn't mean nothin'. He likes you is all."

"He doesn't like me. That bloody mongrel doesn't like anybody. I'm half surprised he didn't *bite* me in the balls. Or piss on me. It wouldn't be the first time."

"He only pisses on people he likes." The old man graced Charlie with a nearly toothless grin, while Bluey sat at the diminutive ancient's feet, grimacing at the policeman through too many teeth, his yellow eyes alight with an unholy glee.

Charlie kept his eye on the dog as he rolled over and got to his feet, using the Land Rover's bumper to give him leverage . . . and something to hang onto if he was forced to defend himself against Bluey's affections.

"Any road," the old man continued, "that's not what we're here for."

"Good," said Charlie. "Just don't tell me I've got to dog-sit the brute again, that's all I ask."

"You did fine . . . a ripper job." There was a slight note of condescension in old Viv's tone.

Charlie tried to ignore that. He kept his eyes on Bluey, trying in fact to hold the dog in place with his own gaze, like a sheepdog dealing with a recalcitrant ewe. Fat chance! Bluey returned the stare, not in the least intimidated and indicating that with a slightly curled, sneering upper lip.

"But I'm worried you might have missed some of the more important aspects of our case there yesterday," Viv continued, his voice now holding the tones of a superior officer addressing an underling.

Charlie winced, but tried not to show it. Nor did he speak his unbidden thoughts.

OUR case? Bloody oath, Viv . . . give it a rest!

Ever since the old man and his damned dog had been (admittedly) influential in the solving of Teague Kendall's Specialist case more than a year earlier, the old man had been a right royal pain in the arse. Hardly a week went by without him dropping by the St. Helens police offices to deposit gratuitous, generally useless advice about some case or another.

It was annoying beyond all logic, would have been funny if it wasn't so annoying, and—worst of all—showed no sign of abating. Viv had become the Jessica Fletcher of St. Helens, but with none of Angela Lansbury's grace and charm.

The problem for Charlie was that he genuinely liked the old reprobate, even if he couldn't put the "why" into words and actually didn't dare to try. Old Viv was a genuine *rum'n*—bush Australian for an incorrigible, unrepentant rogue. Which, in Viv's case, was putting things mildly. The old man was incorrigible, had been (and probably still was!) a poacher, had absolutely no regard or respect for authority of any type, and could be depended upon in most circumstances to do the wrong thing for even the most right reasons. And he drank. A lot. And he had that damned dog . . .

But Viv was an honest scoundrel, a man liked and even respected by far more people than the few who didn't like him, and those few didn't really know him. Charlie knew him. Respected him. Couldn't help but like him. The old bushman was the living essence of rural Tasmania, a sort of fossil that lived and breathed and walked around in a world that was slowly but surely outgrowing him. Not necessarily for the better.

To Charlie, that was a pity. His own view of the world as it was and should be still had plenty of room for Viv and his unique set of values. But . . . he could be *such* a pain in the arse sometimes.

"Okay, Viv," Charlie said, wiping ineffectually at his greasy hands with a rag that was already dirtier than the fingers it touched. "Has that damned mongrel been talking to you again? Does he have a workable theory about yesterday's shooting, or is this one something you've come up with all on your lonesome?"

"He was there, wasn't he?"

"And don't I bloody know it? If there was justice in the world, it would've been him got shot, if you want my opinion." The dog's eyes flared yellow and he sneered his indifference to the slight, but Charlie ignored that and carried on bravely. "Come on, out with it. It must be pretty top stuff for you to come all this way to tell me about it."

The old man met Charlie's eyes with a defiant stare, glanced down at his geriatric dog, then back up at Charlie, who braced himself for a possible assault by the creature.

"They shot the wrong bloke." The words were spat out like warm beer.

"They? There was more than one shooter? Christ, Viv . . . did the damned dog tell you that, or what?"

Viv merely glared. "It's all over the wireless and the telly, not that I'd expect you to notice. Nobody can come up with a single reason why anybody'd want to shoot that dog judge. The bullet didn't hit who it was aimed at is what I'm telling yez."

"So who was it aimed at? There were only about a hundred people there on the trial site—take your choice." Charlie's patience was flagging, not least because he'd already come to the same conclusion as Viv . . . even before he'd handed over the crime scene and made the long drive home in the dark. With that damned dog.

"How should I know? I wasn't there."

"So what are we talking about, then? Bloody hell . . . I spent all the day there at Ormley, half the night getting home and delivering your mongrel dog, and now you want me to solve riddles?"

"You're a copper." Spoken as if that was what policemen were there for—to solve riddles for curious old bushies with nothing better to do than make them up.

"And a bloody tired copper, in the bargain," Charlie replied. "So can you just cut to the chase, so I can get back to my tinkering with this wreck of a vehicle?"

"Huumph. That thing's a piece of shit and I would have told

you that before you bought it, if you'd asked. If you knew what I know about where it's been and what it's done, you wouldn't have bought it at all."

Charlie hesitated. He knew the geriatric Land Rover wasn't on anybody's "hot" list, and it wasn't worth enough to have a lien against it. But he didn't know the vehicle's unarguably lengthy history . . . and suddenly feared that Viv might. It wouldn't be any huge surprise from a character who was filled with surprises.

"Look, Viv," Charlie began, keeping his rising temper under control. "The bloke that got shot was a judge in an area where everybody's walking round with their egos on the end of a leash. He mightily pissed off that blind bloke, from what I heard, and that suggests he's probably done the same for God only knows how many other people back down the line. Just because no obvious suspect has turned up doesn't mean there isn't one."

" 'Twasn't him they was shooting at." Not one iota of give in the old man's voice.

Jesus! I might as well talk to the bloody wind.

"Well then, who was it?" Charlie growled, trying to intimidate Viv with his strongest policeman's stare and having even less success than when he'd tried it on the dog.

"It could have been that writer bloke—Kendall." The old man didn't sound convinced, so Charlie held his peace. Teague Kendall was no more logical a target than the Canberra retrieving trial judge, in his view, but maybe no less logical either.

The silence grew, but Charlie couldn't tell if Viv had gone to sleep mentally, was waiting for a response, or merely building suspense. *Kendall? Might as well say it could have been that other writer, Henderson. Or me, for that matter.*

Viv's next words echoed Charlie's last thought, and he couldn't halt the shiver that crept up his spine.

"Don't *do* that!" he muttered, as much to himself as to the diminutive old man in front of him. Being shot at was, in theory, part of any policeman's potential fate, but it had never been high on Charlie's risk list. He'd never, in the line of duty, been shot at, had never fired his gun, seldom so much as drawn his gun, and fully expected to end his career the same way.

"Well yez might think about it, any road," the old man muttered in reply, clearly unimpressed by Charlie's response. He half turned away, then swiveled back to ask, "And I suppose yez didn't remember about my book?"

So this is what it's about. I should have bloody well guessed. Charlie sighed.

"No, I didn't forget. Things just got a little bit busy out there is all. Not that it matters. Kendall will be stopping by sometime during the week, he said, and I'm certain he'll sign a copy of that damned book for you while he's here. Although," he added, suspecting as he did so that he was wasting his breath on the unsubtle hint, "you're usually supposed to *buy* a copy of a book before you ask the author to personally autograph it."

"Bugger that for a joke," was the half-expected reply. "He should be giving me a share of the royalties. There wouldn't even *be* a book if it weren't for me. And Bluey, of course."

The dog, half asleep against the old man's Blundstone boots, perked up at the sound of his name and looked from Charlie to Viv and back again, his fangs bared as if in anticipation of an attack command. The evil in his yellow eyes was so fierce that Charlie had to force himself not to flinch.

"Yeah, sure. Maybe I shouldn't tell you that Kendall expressed a specific desire to meet you, although I can't for the life of me imagine why," Charlie added. "He's already met that damned dog, and the mongrel bastard must have decided he likes Kendall, too, because he pissed on *his* boots. So there you go, Viv—lessons from your dog on how to deal with the rich and famous. Piss on 'em! How'd ya go with *that?*"

Charlie couldn't hold back a staccato snort of laughter that drew a snarl from Bluey and a filthy glance from the beast's master. Charlie laughed even more gaily when old Viv could only glare in reply, clearly—for once—lost for words.

Two minutes later, old Viv's bush ute departed in a cloud of oil fumes and a cacophony of rattles and bangs and shudders that made Charlie look at his own "project" with renewed skepticism.

"I wonder what the old bugger does know about you," he muttered as he slid back under the vehicle, but it was only moments before his mind turned back to the discussion with Viv about who had been the intended victim in the sniper attack.

Like the old man, Charlie didn't believe for a moment it had been the dog trial judge—the concept made no sense at all. At least to him. It was the man's first-ever visit to Tasmania, so it was unlikely he'd mortally offended anyone else locally, and those at the trial had said anybody high enough in the local trialing fraternity to have been that significantly offended during a mainland visit were there, on the ground, when the sniper struck.

But if not the judge, then who? Charlie didn't believe for a minute it had been himself. The old bugger had merely been stirring him with that suggestion. But who? Illogical it could have been Rex Henderson, despite the American's bullet-burned ear. But Kendall? That made no sense either that Charlie could see. Still, they'd been the three people closest to the line of fire, or what was assumed to have been the line of fire.

For all anyone really knew, the damned bullet could have come from a mile away, a total freak accident—except that Charlie was sure that wasn't the case. The massive hole in the dead man's chest from the entry wound was enough to tell him that. The fatal bullet was a long-range shot from a high-powered rifle, but not an accident from a mile away.

"Not my problem. Thank God," he muttered as he reached for a misplaced spanner and concentrated on his tinkering. He was able to stave off the offending thoughts for a short time, but old Viv's visit had ruined his Sunday afternoon and Charlie eventually had to admit it.

He stopped work and went inside to make a cuppa, and noticed the blinking light on his answering machine. That was enough to make him check the cell phone that lolled on the kitchen counter instead of being on his belt where it should have been, day off or not. And found it, too, bristling with the promise of voice-mail messages floating out there in cyberspace.

He knew before he heard a single one that it could only be bad news, and for once it was no surprise at all to be right.

CHAPTER TWELVE

Kirsten swam up into consciousness, a slow, confusing ascent made worse by the dryness in her mouth and a hammering headache. It felt as if someone was banging on her skull with something that managed to hurt and boom, echo and tinkle . . . all at the same time.

She opened her eyes to find light, but not much of it. The space surrounding her was huddled in shadow, obscure. And it smelled. Despite the dryness in her mouth, her nose was conscious of a damp, musty odor, one of age and decay and neglect.

She rolled over on her side, realizing as she did so that she couldn't move her hands properly. Peered down through barely focusing eyes to see what her sense of touch had already told her—her hands were bound in front of her with some sort of plastic, the cable ties used by electricians, she thought.

One major difference between a horse and a mule—apart from the obvious—is their reaction to fearful things. A horse will fly into panic over nothing more threatening than a blowing leaf, a swooping bird. A mule's reaction is the opposite of panic; a mule will almost always prop, or balk, and stay immovable until it has figured out what the problem is. Mules generally get into far less trouble than horses.

This bit of trivia scampered about in Kirsten's mind as she stared at her bonds, then slowly, patiently, let her gaze roam around the interior of the dank-smelling hovel. Noting, assessing, questioning. Learning nothing that made any sense at all, except that she seemed to be alone.

Good. I hope. Don't panic. Be a mule. No need to panic. Yet!

Managed then to swing her legs over the side of the cot on which she lay. She struggled to her feet, aware that there was a light chain wrapped twice around her waist. Snugly. And fastened behind her, somehow. She couldn't figure out the fastening, but she could turn and see where the other end of the chain was run through a large eyebolt in the wall. And padlocked.

Standing, now, choking back the bile of panic, she once again scanned the entire room, noting the boxes of food, the camp stove, the folding table already set up, the second camp bed still folded away. Noted how everything was neatly arranged, a sharp contrast to the overall aura of the hovel itself. Recognized her own fanny pack, neatly laid out on the folding table.

Realized, suddenly, that despite the darkness in the window-less shack, there was light peeping through pinholes in the roof, through cracks in the slab walls.

Daylight? Must be. But . . .

She ran her mind back, tried to replay the tape that mentally catalogued where she'd been, what she'd done. Got as far as returning to the suite she and Kendall shared in the hotel. The knock on the door. The vague, blurred memory of the tall, lean man who'd stood there when she'd answered it.

Then nothing.

But it was night, then. Last night? When?

Now, panic began to nibble at her equilibrium. Not a lot of it. Yet! But enough to increase the dryness in her mouth, enough to turn the headache into a sense of somebody trying to open up her skull with a jackhammer.

And she had to pee.

Her eyes found the bucket at the end of the cot. She was, barely, able to drag it closer. Getting her jeans undone, managing to actually *use* the makeshift toilet was somewhat harder. Getting her jeans back in place was hardest of all. But she managed.

And then—blessings upon blessings—she noticed the two-liter bottle of water there on the foot of the camp cot, and with it a small container of headache tablets.

Fat chance I'll be taking any of that! God only knows what's in there.

But the aspirins were in an unopened cardboard box, and when she fumbled the childproof lid off the plastic bottle inside, she found it, too, sealed. New. Unopened. Kirsten had random thoughts about how somebody might tamper with aspirin tablets, then the jackhammers at her temples took control.

She dug her way through the seal with a thumbnail, gave the tablets a cursory inspection, then swallowed four of them with a gratifying swig of water from the bottle, which was also new and unopened, for what that might be worth. It didn't matter. If she couldn't cure the headache, she couldn't think. If she couldn't think . . .

At first, the only thing eased was her raging thirst. A second quaff of the water, which tasted fine, helped that. Then the jackhammers in her head slowed, faded. Her mind took at least a semblance of control and she resealed the bottle and set it safely away on the cot. Who knew, who could even imagine how long she might be here before more water was provided? Who knew anything?

Now the panic was beginning to take larger bites.

She tested the chain, at first tentatively, then by yanking on it with all her strength. It might as well have come off a logging truck for all her efforts accomplished.

Then she tested the limits of her reach. First standing, then kneeling, then on her hands and knees and reaching out with her feet to see what she could somehow drag close enough for it to be of use to her.

Nothing. She could reach not one damned thing that might help her.

She slumped on the camp cot, lowered her head and closed her eyes for an instant.

Think, dammit!

Again, she surveyed her surroundings, hoping to make some sense of it all. Failed. There *was* no sense to this, or at least none she could think of.

Kidnapped? But why? I'm not worth anything to anybody. This is Australia, not some obscure, third-world country where the peasants automatically assume anyone who looks American must be rich, must be worth holding for ransom.

She took some gratification from not having been beaten up, not having been sexually assaulted. Not having been killed. Judging from the stock of foodstuffs and the neatly arranged gear in the shack, there was some intention to keep her there for a time. But none of it made any sense.

And where were her captors? Or captor.

They'll be back, she thought, looking once again at the preparations. *So how long do I have, I wonder? And what can I do?*

Her mouth was dry again, her furry tongue practically demanding another drink. And the raging headache was not defeated, merely retired temporarily to regroup and prepare a new assault. That much she was sure of, if nothing else.

Think, Kirsten.

She looked around once more, then felt the panic gnawing, feeding, growing. Thinking wouldn't be enough. She had to actually do something, and better sooner than later.

So do it, dammit!

Her attention focused on the eyebolt in the wall. She knew about eyebolts, knew about all manner of bolts and pitons and clasps and clamps. It was part and parcel of being a caver. She couldn't break the chain, couldn't chew through the plastic cable ties at her wrists in less than a month, if that. But the bolt . . . ?

Kirsten looked down at the camp cot, speculated, wondered.

"Maybe." She spoke the word aloud, half expecting her voice to echo in the dankness of the shack's interior. It was, vaguely, cavelike, all shrouded in shadows and uneven wall shapes. She was far less afraid of *where* she was than of why.

First, Kirsten carefully set the water bottle and aspirin off to one side. Still within reach, if barely so, but safe from her next set of actions. Then she tipped over the camp cot, and nearly cried out in delight to find that she'd guessed right—it was the type with strong, springy, W-shaped supports that fitted into sockets along the side rails.

That fitted in, therefore could be *un*fitted. Easily, by somebody with both hands free and balanced leverage. Not quite too easy for Kirsten, but not all that hard, either. A good grip, a kick here and there, and she had one support free, then another.

What was left of the camp cot she moved aside so she could kneel and insert the steel support into the eyebolt. The rest, she thought, should be easy. Even with her hands bound, she could exert leverage.

She thrust the steel rod into the eye of the bolt, positioned herself, braced, and heaved on it, tentatively at first, then with all the strength she could muster. It wasn't as easy as it should have been . . . the W shape and the smoothness of the steel made getting and keeping a grip difficult. The support twisted in her grip, was almost impossible to control.

She had to try three times before she found the right angle, the right position. But she did. Whereupon the improvised lever bent and the eyebolt remained in place. Open, staring, taunting her.

"Son of a *bitch!*"

She grabbed up another section of cot support. Tried again. Failed again. Cursed again.

She stopped, panting as much from the sense of growing panic as from the exertion. Looked over the situation again, thought some more.

Fool!

She flung down the support rods and grabbed up the main structure of the camp cot. Side rails . . . in sections . . . all short, *straight* pieces of steel designed to be threaded through the canvas of the bed and locked together so the W-shaped bits could be inserted last.

Not designed to be pulled apart by someone with her hands bound together, with no way to get the sort of grip that would allow them to be twisted apart, but pieces she'd be able to get a decent grip on, once she got them separated. Kirsten wasted valuable time, cursing the growing panic she could now taste, until she figured it out, until she sat down on the filthy floor, locked her feet on one of the unions as best she could, took the best grip she could on the end section, and tried to pull and twist at the same time.

She was exhausted by the time she got the first piece loose. Her hands were cramped with the strain by the time she got the second one. The third was, paradoxically, no problem at all.

Kirsten needed to rest, didn't dare take the time. She thrust two of the straight steel pieces into the eye of the bolt, momentarily thought of trying to fit in a third, then thrust away that thought. No room. No time.

She flexed her cramped fingers, positioned herself, took a careful grip . . .

And watched, hoping against hope, praying silently, as the eye of the bolt moved, then moved some more.

Yes. Yes, yes, yes!

79

No, no, no! Once the eye of the bolt was parallel to the floor, her leverage was gone. Worse, she couldn't get her levers into the eye from below to take a fresh position. There simply wasn't room.

Damn it!

She tried every angle she could manage, but working almost flat against the eye, she couldn't manage the torque to twist it up so she could get a new grip, another half-turn. The floor was old, the wood spongy . . . and she was exhausted.

She took a sip of the water, only a small sip. At least, she thought, her headache was gone, driven away by the exertion. The panic remained, gnawing at her, growling, demanding her attention.

No!

She sat back, pulling her knees up and clasping her arms around them. There had to be a way, if only she could figure out what it was. She looked at where the other side of the cot frame was still inside the canvas . . . a six-foot length of jointed steel. Could she use that, she wondered? Could it help her reach something that might help her?

Then she heard the sound of arriving vehicles.

Too late.

Even before the door was flung open, Kirsten was on her feet, one of her steel bar levers in her bound hands. She crouched, listening as vehicle engines stopped and the faint sound of footsteps grew less faint as they approached the shack.

CHAPTER THIRTEEN

The panic in Kendall's voice flowed through the telephone lines like quicksilver. Charlie didn't need the raft of earlier messages to recognize how agitated his friend was, how angry, how frustrated, how terrified.

"Thank you, God! Charlie—would you please speak to this officer? Would you please tell him, explain to him—I'm sorry, what was your name again? . . . oh, shit! Just talk to him, Charlie. Please!"

The next voice on the line was all Charlie needed to know what half the problem was. Had to be. He knew that voice and the policeman who owned it, could visualize the scene just by hearing the voice.

"This is Constable John Small. Who am I speaking to, please?"

It's "To whom am I speaking?" . . . asshole! Not that I'd expect you to know that.

"This is Sergeant Charles Banes at St. Helens," Charlie replied. Heavy on the *Sergeant.* "What seems to be the problem, there, Constable?" Even heavier on the *Constable.* Not that it would matter, or at least not much. Charlie knew that, but it couldn't hurt to establish rank right from the start.

There is a fine, fine line between what makes a cop and what makes a crook. Maybe no more than a flip of a coin at some point in time. Maybe even at birth. The best in both worlds are often cut from the same cloth, poured from the same mold, shaped—some authorities suggest—by the same mental quirks.

81

Most cops know it, few admit it (at least in public) and
Constable John Small epitomized it. He was one of the worst
cops Charlie had ever encountered—and, perversely, one of the
very best. But in Charlie's mind, Small should have been a
crook and, Charlie often thought, very likely was. He had a
fleeting moment of wonder at what stupidity Small had managed to get him posted to the city, of all places, then focused his
mind back to the issue at hand.

Charlie knew instinctively that Small wouldn't like Kendall,
would like nothing better than the ability to rattle Kendall's
chain. He'd obviously been doing exactly that, and pleasure was
reflected in the tone of his voice, which Charlie had always
thought had been borrowed from a whiny, spoiled infant.

The voice was too light for the man who spoke in it: Small
was of medium height, with a stocky, athletic build slowly going
to seed. And it might have been only the phone, but Charlie
found himself thinking that Small's whiny, perpetually sneering
voice had actually gotten higher as his hairline receded. Charlie
had a mental picture of the words issuing through a rust-colored
moustache that matched the thinning hair.

"We have a situation here, Sir," the constable said, letting
each word grudgingly escape. "There *seems* to be a knife
involved, and it *may* be involved in the possible disappearance
of a female person."

"It damned well *is* involved, and it's not a *possible* disappearance—she's been abducted, dammit!" Kendall's voice was
distant thunder, his agitation clearly getting worse. Charlie
wanted to shout back, to tell his friend to settle down, shut up,
and let *him* get on with handling this.

*You're only making it worse, little mate. You're playing right into
Small's hands, doing exactly what he wants you to do. And I'd best
not do the same.*

So he clung to the slight advantage of rank as he slowly drew from the Launceston constable sufficient details so that Charlie could actually make sense of it all. Such sense as there was!

It was like pulling teeth. Charlie had no authority advantage in Launceston and Small damned well knew it. They both knew it. Whatever was going on with Kendall and Kirsten was none of Charlie's business, officially, either—and they both knew that, too. But he could ask, and he did, bracing his ears against that goddamn whiny, supercilious voice, half wishing he dared to scream at the constable, to pull rank with a vengeance. Which he couldn't, didn't dare to even try.

And they both knew that, too.

Charlie and John Small had a history. Both were of an age, both had come up through the country cop system in Tasmania. But Small was a cowboy, always bending the rules, always traveling just a whisker off the straight path. Which partially explained why he still held only constable ranking, while Charlie was now a sergeant, and more than likely explained what he was now doing on duty in the city. Charlie didn't know, hadn't heard. Charlie did his best at all times to avoid office politics, even in his own office.

You must be hating it. Poor bugger. Wonder what you did this time. I really should keep track of things better.

Most people, at least occasionally, get into a rut. Alcoholics, it's sometimes said, compound the situation by furnishing their ruts and hanging up pictures. Charlie wasn't an alcoholic, but he had that element to his makeup. He'd found his niche in St. Helens, dug his rut there on the east coast of Tasmania, furnished it, hung pictures on the walls, curtains on the windows, carpets on the floors. And would be totally content to retire there. He was a country copper to the teeth, had never wanted to be anything else.

John Small, Charlie thought, was much the same. They'd been stationed in the same places, occasionally, had never gotten along well, never would. But Charlie had a grudging respect for the other policeman; he was a damned good cop when he bothered to work at it. Except . . .

Small was as phony as a political promise and smarmy as a snake-oil salesman. But he was tough, utterly fearless, doggedly persistent when it suited him, and a man Charlie would far rather have on his side than against him.

But he wasn't going to like Kendall, and the dislike would be reciprocal. That was made even more obvious when Small cautiously raised the issue Charlie had been waiting for. The constable didn't even get all the words out before Charlie heard Kendall's voice in the background, hoarse with outrage.

"Goddamn it, why can't you just say it? Charlie? This silly bastard thinks it's all a fucking publicity stunt!"

No surprise, that. Worse, Charlie couldn't blame him; he'd have wondered the same in Small's situation, although he might have been more circumspect about voicing it. But then he knew Kendall, whose volatility was legend, once provoked.

Fuckaduck . . . fuckaduck . . . fuckaduck! You bloody idiot, Kendall!

Which was not what he said to Constable John Small. Instead, he forced calm and appeasement into his voice. Where Small might eventually fit in all of this, Charlie didn't know, but he did know this was no way to gain any help from him at all.

"Sorry, John," he said in his most engaging voice. "Would you please put that fool on the blower for a tick, before he does himself an injury?" Charlie was far less appeasing when the telephone had changed hands.

"Dammit, Teague," he swore. "Will you stop carrying on like a pork chop and let *me* try and deal with this? The policeman you've got there is known to me. He's a friend, Kendall. He's on our side." Charlie surreptitiously crossed himself, glanced skyward for forgiveness, then continued. "So will you just go in the corner, shut up for a change, and give us a chance to sort things out?"

"But . . ."

"But bloody nothing! Do it—damn it!"

There was no doubt his voice had carried throughout the room at the other end. Constable John Small's voice held a tone of smarmy satisfaction when he took up the phone again. But it took only a few moments of quiet conversation before Charlie could see that he'd done the right thing by taking Small's side.

By the time Charlie finally hung up, it was established that the knife would be taken into the Launceston offices for fingerprinting, the prints sent to the data bank in Hobart for processing, and that John Small and his patrol partner would immediately begin reviewing the hotel security footage to see what that might tell them.

And Charlie had told Kendall that his friend would be better served if he could somehow hold his temper and cooperate with John Small!

Fat chance of that.

CHAPTER FOURTEEN

"Bloody oath!"

Ian Boyd stopped dead in his tracks, his tall frame blocking the entry to the shack momentarily until Rose shoved her way in with him, placing them side-by-side as their eyes adjusted to the dimness inside, as their minds adjusted to what they faced.

A slender woman with long, unkempt, strawberry-blonde hair was crouched, facing them, her eyes narrowed, her entire body poised for action, a length of steel rod in her bound hands. She wore jeans, hiking boots, a worn, faded bush shirt, and, they quickly noted, a chain that encircled her narrow waist, then ran to an eyebolt in the wall behind her.

She looked angry, terrified, vulnerable, and dangerous, all at the same time. Like the sort of mad person folklore said every old rural family in Tasmania kept chained up under some tree in a back paddock someplace. A nonsense, of course. Usually.

Rose knew all about mad women from the back paddocks. Knew also that this wasn't one of them. Knew, once her eyes had adjusted to the gloom inside the hovel and she was able to get a clear look, exactly who this woman was. Rose had seen her picture all too often on international television and in Kendall's damned book.

But here? Now? She knew who . . . but not why. It made no sense at all, but it was certainly interesting. Fascinating, in fact.

"Get yourself outside and keep a lookout while I sort this out," she demanded, her voice a whip crack aimed at making

86

Ian obey before he said another word. She was so certain of her domination that she didn't even bother to look at him. She kept her eyes fixed on the disheveled figure at the end of the chain, willing the captive also to stay silent.

Ian muttered an indistinct obscenity, then shambled outside, slamming the heavy door behind him. Clearly he wasn't happy, but Rose didn't care. Not now. Now, there were more important things to worry about.

"You're Teague Kendall's . . ." And she stumbled over her words, unsure how to define Kirsten. She had, of course, read Kendall's book, but that, too, had skirted around any specific definition. Was this woman a fiancé, girlfriend, or something more or less than either?

"I'm Kirsten Knelsen, and . . ." Kirsten glanced down at her bound hands, held them up in front of her as if to make sure Rose could also see them. ". . . I could really use some help, here."

"What's going on?" Rose asked the question, but made no move to help Kirsten.

"I don't *know!* Will you *please* cut me loose?"

Rose stayed silent, but her mind was racing a mile a minute. Obviously, Kendall's girl had been kidnapped, but why? And by whom? And—most important of all—how could she turn this situation to her own best advantage?

"You've been kidnapped." It was neither question nor direct statement, merely a verbal expression of the thoughts in Rose's fertile mind. "Yeah, that'd be it. But by who . . . whom?"

And she could have kicked herself. Among the baggage from Rose's brief marriage to Teague Kendall was an often subconscious awareness of proper word usage and grammar, and worse, it cropped up at the most unexpected times.

Damn you, Teague Kendall, for that too, why not?

Rose blamed Teague Kendall for a lot of things, not least his having dared to achieve his success as a novelist *after* their divorce and under circumstances that didn't entitle her to the financial share of it all she thought was rightfully hers. And then going back to Canada and striking it rich again—because of this woman here!

It wasn't true, of course, but even God could never convince Rose that she hadn't *earned* a share of Teague's financial success. Like sixty percent, maybe. Or more. Maybe even seventy-five percent. Hadn't she put her entire life on hold so that he would have the time in the evenings and early mornings and on weekends to work on his damned novels? Hadn't she given up parties, nights out with the girls from work (she'd been working as a psych nurse in Hobart then, where Kendall was employed as a journalist), and even fought to get her shifts regularized so they could spend more time together? Which *he* spent writing his damned novels!

Rose hadn't done any such thing, actually. Except in the very beginning, when the relationship was new and they spent as much time in bed as he did at his word processor. Almost from the moment he'd decided to try his hand as a novelist, however, the resultant restraints on Rose's lifestyle had galled and chafed like an ill-fitting halter.

By her own admission, Rose was a hedonist. She'd told Teague that, right from the start. Almost. She'd been honest. Almost. If she'd had his way with words, she might have more properly defined the word *hedonist,* might have gone beyond the clinical definition. Because it wasn't so much that Rose believed that pleasure was the chief good and proper aim in life—Rose believed that *her* pleasure was those things and more. Nobody else's pleasure was remotely relevant.

Nobody else but her was at all relevant in any way, by Rose's thinking. It was all *me, Me, ME!* She ought to have been an actress. Kendall had told her that, once. It was about as forceful a criticism as he ever ventured, even during those moments when she was slinging kitchen utensils at him and ripping his manhood to shreds with her tongue.

Kendall was a gentleman. Too much so. Rose was . . . Rose. A hedonist, an opportunist pleasure seeker with an eye to the main chance. Nothing wrong with that.

Ian was less charitable and far more accurate in his opinion of her.

Slut! Goddam bitch!

Ian was barely out the door before his mind began playing tricks on him. He knew it, too, but couldn't fight the situation and didn't really bother to try. There were higher priorities.

Almost without a pause, he strode over to Rose's SUV and peered inside.

Yes!

Gently, silently, his gaze flicking back and forth from vehicle to doorway, he eased open the door of the vehicle, reached in, and liberated the plastic baggie of drugs from where it nestled on top of the other things in her handbag.

You little beauty. And he wasn't referring to Rose.

His fingers trembled so much he almost dropped the precious cargo, but he managed to get it safely tucked into the front of his shirt, and heaved a huge sigh of relief at that small accomplishment.

Another glance at the doorway. Then take the time to rifle through the handbag and see what other goodies Rose might have secreted there—like the $500 she'd promised him. No such luck, but she had just over $100 in her wallet.

Down payment. Have to do, I reckon. Not enough, but.

I killed somebody? Never reckoned on that.

Should have asked for more money . . . more goodies.

And it was a judge! They'll go hard with me over that, should I get caught.

He finished ransacking the handbag, knelt to check under all the seats, in the glove box, crawled halfway into the vehicle to check behind the seats. Nothing worth a second look.

In the back, maybe in with the spare? Wouldn't put it past the conniving bitch! It was only a moment's work to unlock the rear of the SUV, rip up the floor mat to find only a spare tire and the minimal tools that came with such a ponced-up piece of Japanese junk.

Bugger-bugger.

A judge! Bloody oath—that's bad. I only aimed for that American's hat. Scare him a bit is all. Fucking jack-jumpers!

He glanced again at the closed door to the shack. Then patted the lumpy plastic bag under his shirt. *Good shit in here, I reckon. Wonder . . .*

He almost succumbed to temptation before he managed a desperate grab for self-control. Ian wasn't the swiftest cab off any rank, but he wasn't a complete fool, either. Yet.

They'll never find the bullet. Couldn't match it, any road, if they can't find the weapon. Easy fixed.

He reviewed the situation in his mind, replaying every step of the assassination, his escape, his trip north to Pyengana. Nothing there to worry about, and he was pretty certain, at least, that he hadn't shot off his mouth in the pub there. He already had a mental list of hidey-holes where he could secrete the Finnish rifle. Too good a weapon to just chuck it away into the bush somewhere, or dump it into the ocean.

And without the rifle, they'd have nothing on Ian Boyd. She'll be apples, mate. Not a thing to worry about.

Which left Rose.

And she can't tell. Not without getting herself in the shit with me. She wouldn't, any road. It'd be stupid.

Fucking bitch. I should shoot her, too. Serve her right.

Naw . . . I'm safe as houses. She wouldn't say nothing. Wouldn't bloody dare.

Would she?

He had a serious moment when he considered just shooting Rose, along with the weird woman chained up in the shack. She'd seen Ian, after all. But it went against the grain. Ian Boyd was of a generation brought up to respect women, even tarts like Rose. Sometimes, he even did.

Then he began to fragment again.

She's a bloody nurse, the cow. All the time acting like God, giving orders.

I wonder what's in the bag. Christ—I need something! There's a few tinnies under the seat of me truck . . . there should be anyway. But this stuff . . .

First things first, he decided with unusual resolution considering his choices. The drugs would wait. He had them, which was the important part.

Now he needed his rifle back.

CHAPTER FIFTEEN

Rose remained consistent in her crankiness with Kirsten. She knew there had to be something in all this that would be of value. To her. But what?

"You must have *some* idea what's going on," she said, glaring at Kirsten as if this whole situation was somehow Kirsten's fault. "Don't you bloody know anything?"

"What day is it?"

"You don't even know what day it is?" Rose's glare intensified.

Kirsten glared back. Obviously this weird woman had no intention of helping her . . . but why? "The last thing I remember it was Saturday night," she finally replied, choosing her words carefully. This woman must know *something* useful, but how to get it out of her . . .

"Where are we, anyway?" Kirsten said.

"Tasmania. Don't you even remember that?" Rose's voice was sullen, suspicious, dismissive. Angry.

Kirsten shook her head, not as a negative gesture but in utter futility. What was *wrong* with this woman? "Why won't you help me?" Kirsten asked again, this time holding out her bound wrists in a gesture of supplication.

The only effect of that was to have the woman lean the bolt-action rifle against the wall just inside the door. She made no attempt to free Kirsten, didn't even seem to notice the plastic wrist-bindings and the chain.

"So you don't know who kidnapped you, or why, or even where the hell you are? Not good for much, are you?" Which was true enough. Confusing, actually, but Rose wasn't about to admit that. Damn it! Even with Ian Boyd's somewhat questionable backup, it would be far better if she knew what to expect. And who! *Whom?*

She silently damned Kendall yet again, and because his face was now in her mind, said, "He won't rescue you this time, either."

Kirsten could only look at her, now totally confused by the abrupt dog-leg in the conversation.

"Who?"

"Kendall, you stupid woman. Who else would I be talking about? That's what it's all about, isn't it. You're being held to ransom for a slice of Kendall's royalties from that damned book."

How to reply to that one? Kirsten stayed silent.

"Well he won't rescue you this time, either." The dark-haired woman's voice was scathingly contemptuous. "Kendall's nothing but a wimp . . . a pussy. He couldn't—"

The tirade was cut off in mid-sentence as the cabin door flew open and Ian Boyd's tall, gaunt frame shouldered its way inside. He ignored Kirsten, glanced only briefly at Rose—his interest was in the rifle he immediately located. His huge hand reached down and grabbed the rifle while he held off a belated attempt by Rose to stop him.

"Right," he said. "I'm outa here." And, simple as that, he was. No time for argument, no discussion at all.

Kirsten watched through the now open doorway as the tall man stalked down the muddy track toward the vehicles, the dark-haired woman stumbling along behind him, screaming and swearing. Kirsten could hear the occasional word, things like ". . . money in this," and ". . . dare to walk out now," but the overall context escaped her.

She saw the woman catch up with him, saw him thrust her away with one hand, heard the sounds but not the actual words as the much smaller woman picked up a stick and rushed at him again. This time the big man was less gentle; he pushed her away so violently that she staggered into the brush beside the track and fell to her knees. Still shrieking.

"Shut up, you silly cow!"

"You'll regret this, Ian. I will hunt you down!"

Kirsten heard that all right. Just as she saw him reach into one of the vehicles, the shiny, relatively new SUV. He flung open the door, his arm reached in, emerged again, was raised near shoulder height.

"Go hunt *this* down." And Kirsten saw something gleam in the sunlight, heard the woman's shriek of anguish, realized the man had just thrown the vehicle's keys away into the thick surrounding scrub.

The woman scurried after the keys. The big man reached into the vehicle again, pulled out something else—*a cell phone?*—glanced at it only briefly, then tucked it away in his shirt pocket. Then he strode to a battered 4 × 4, fired it up, effected a four-point turn despite the narrow confines of the track, and was gone.

Kirsten didn't bother to follow the action after that. She turned her attention to the eyebolt and tried to focus on her original plan to somehow twist it free from the wall.

It was difficult, made more difficult because of having to keep half her attention focused on the open doorway. Kirsten had finally figured out how the leverage issue could be solved. She got one of the bent pieces of steel into the eye of the bolt—barely—then used two of the straight pieces to pry upward, using two other bits as a fulcrum to pry against.

It was tricky. She kept losing her grip on the smooth steel

and having both hands tied together didn't help, either. But slowly, eventually, it worked!

She got one half-turn with some difficulty, was more easily able to twist the eyebolt around so it was again parallel to the floor. Took the time to pause, listen, try and see what that weird woman outside was doing. Failed in that, but managed yet another turn before the sound of the woman's voice gave Kirsten warning of her return. There was only time to pry the eyebolt back to its original, vertical orientation, albeit three turns looser . . . the important part . . . before she had to stop, turn away, position herself so as to hide any evidence of her activities.

It wasn't loose enough to yank herself free, but each turn had come with slightly less effort. Kirsten knew she could get the eyebolt free. All she needed now was the chance to do it. And the time.

"Damn that Ian Boyd. I should have shot the bastard while I had the chance." The weird woman was damp, muddy, as disheveled as Kirsten herself when she stamped her way back inside the shack.

She glared at Kirsten, then turned her attention to the collected foodstuffs, cracking open a bottle of water and drinking in great gulps. She made no offer of a drink for Kirsten, hardly so much as glanced at her.

"The fucker threw away my car keys, damn it! Shit! If I can't find them it'll mean I'm stuck here with you, unless I want to walk it. Shit-shit-shit!"

"I could help you look, if you could figure out a way to get me loose."

The look the woman shot Kirsten was pungent with scorn. "You've got Buckley's," she replied with a sneer. And with that incomprehensible remark, she took the water bottle and stomped out again, leaving Kirsten no better off or wiser than before.

"I think we've got Buckley's, but let's run through it again. There isn't much else we can do." Constable John Small's voice revealed how cranky and frustrated he was as he sat with Kendall and Rex Henderson, staring at the hotel security tapes for what seemed the hundredth time.

Teague Kendall glanced at his fellow writer, instinctively preparing to translate the uniquely Australian expression, only to sit up in wonderment as Rex's voice emerged in a flat, obviously rehearsed monotone:

" 'William Buckley (1780–1856) had been convicted of a minor crime in England and transported to the then-new penal colony in Australia, but Buckley and two other convicts celebrated Christmas 1803 by escaping and fleeing into the wilderness. Faced with a lack of food and shelter, his comrades quickly changed their minds and turned themselves in, but against all odds Buckley managed to survive in the wild, living off the land and making friends with the local Aborigines. Incredibly, Buckley lived with the Aborigines for thirty-two years, and by the time he surrendered to a survey party in 1835, he had forgotten how to speak English.

"Buckley was pardoned and went on to work as an interpreter and guide, and when he published an account of his ordeal in 1852, his story became a national sensation. Given the amazing luck Buckley's saga of survival entailed, it wasn't surprising that by 1898 'Buckley's chance' had become a popular figure of speech meaning 'very slim chance' or 'no chance at all.'

"A curious coincidence, however, may have boosted the popularity of 'Buckley's chance' still further. The Melbourne department store of Buckley & Nunn (no relation to William Buckley) opened in 1851, and within a few years its goods were well known as the epitome of fashion. The popularity of Buckley & Nunn lent the phrase 'You've got Buckley's chance' the additional punning sense of 'You've got a slim (Buckley's) chance or none (Nunn) at all.' "

When the recital ended, Kendall found himself staring at the Houston author, unable to voice his astonishment with any words at all.

"I studied up a bit when I knew I was coming to Australia," Rex said, his voice almost but not quite apologetic. "That's from *The Word Detective,* I think. I'm fascinated by unique word usages, things like that. It's amazing what you can find on the Net."

"Unbelievable," Kendall replied. "I knew about the department store bit, there's something about tea, or tearooms, too. But not the original source."

"I did. Now can we pay some attention to this tape, please. Again." John Small's voice revealed more than he probably realized.

In a pig's eye, you knew. You're a shitty liar, little mate. I just hope you're a better cop.

What Kendall *said* was much more polite. He'd decided early on that listening to Charlie's advice, doing what Charlie said to do, was best. So if Charlie said this supercilious twit was "on our side," then . . .

"We have to be missing something," Kendall said. "But what?" All three men had reviewed the tapes a dozen times at least, but in fairness to all there wasn't much to be seen. But *again* was about all they could do. The alternative was to do nothing at all while they waited. For a ransom demand. For more information. For . . . something. Anything!

The relevant sections of tape had been copied and spliced into a tape that showed Kirsten's abductor—*At least there's no more argument about that,* Kendall thought—entering the hotel lobby, then the elevator, then the corridor where Kendall's suite was located. And then, of course, the same route in reverse, this time with Kirsten as his companion. The security cameras hadn't been able to provide significant details about whatever happened at the door to the suite.

The three men had watched the damned tapes so often they found themselves chanting the not-too-relevant details almost in unison. "He's six foot, maybe six-one. No more than six-three. Dark hair, looks like. Caucasian. Casual slacks, casual shirt, sneakers, or basketball boots, or some such. Or maybe boat shoes. The damned hat and sunglasses make it really hard to see his face."

The Mole Creek caving mob had reviewed them too, before eventually being given statements to sign and then sent home, but were unable to help in even the slightest detail.

"There's enough that I think I'd know if I'd ever seen him before. At least if I'd noticed him," Kendall said. "But there's nothing very distinctive." The man's sunglasses, given the late hour, had been one strong element in acceptance of the abduction theory.

"She isn't fighting him, that much is obvious." This from Rex, who was off to Hobart the next day and didn't dare seek a change of schedule. But he wanted to. Then it was a flight back to mainland Australia and eventually to New Zealand before heading home. "No sign of a knife, or a gun, or any indication of duress. He isn't talking to her, either, anywhere they've been caught by the cameras."

John Small's trained eye caught the only unusual aspect of the taped interludes, but it took him several viewings. "This bloke looks really light on his feet," he said. "Like a dancer, maybe? But the woman's not. She moves more like she's . . . what? . . . sleepwalking, maybe? That Mole Creek mob said she was properly buggered when they dropped her off, totally exhausted, but this looks . . . different, somehow. Might be just a matter of comparison, but she seems more than just tired. Drugged?"

"Not really time for it. He wasn't in the room more than about thirty seconds, if the tapes are accurate." Kendall sighed, shook his head in frustration, and tried to stifle the panic that was slowly eating him from the inside out.

They were doing all they could, *had* done everything possible. Everything logical. The knife had gone for fingerprinting, the tapes had been collected, collated, and copied and were being reviewed at police headquarters as well as here in his suite. The telephone in Kendall's suite was rigged to tape any ransom call (relatively easy) and steps were being taken to try and get tracing equipment hooked up to the hotel's telephone system (not so easy). Posters had been prepared for email and fax distribution to police throughout Tasmania. The media had been alerted. Kirsten's picture would be all over the state with the evening news. The most the police would commit to publicly was "Missing," but behind the scenes, abduction was no longer doubted.

And some things perhaps less than logical, at least this early in the game, were also being done. Kendall had already prepared a statement that he hoped would emphasize his willingness to meet any ransom demands, any demands of any sort. Stressing also the fact that until tomorrow, when the banks opened, collection of any ransom funds would be impossible. John Small had pooh-poohed that, saying it was stupid to offer what hadn't been asked for.

"We still don't know what's going on," he'd cautioned. That was hours ago, eons ago, in Kendall's stressed-out condition, and still they knew nothing.

"I need it all straight in my head," Kendall had replied. "Don't jerk me around on this; it's how I work . . . how I think."

As if thinking, alone, was going to help anyone. They'd all been thinking. And getting nowhere fast. Or slow.

So they watched the tape. Then they watched it again. Slowly, quickly, fast-forward, fast-back. Over and over and over. And learned, Kendall was positive, not one damned thing!

CHAPTER SIXTEEN

Kirsten managed to get two more turns on the eyebolt before the mad woman returned again, looking even more disheveled, more frustrated and breathless. And decidedly more angry.

"The rotten bugger," she cursed, meanwhile glaring at Kirsten as if all this, somehow, was Kirsten's fault, her personal responsibility.

"I offered to help you look," Kirsten replied, fighting to hold down her own anger, but using that anger to ride down her panic. To keep her sane. None of this was making any sense. This strange woman, apparently, had nothing to do with Kirsten's abduction, so why wouldn't she help her get free? Why, for that matter, wasn't she more intent upon getting *herself* free, the thrown-away car keys notwithstanding?

"I should get the hell out of here," the woman said, in an eerie parallel to Kirsten's thoughts. But she made no move to do so, instead began rummaging through the assorted foodstuffs and gear in the small shack.

Kirsten again asked for help in getting herself out of there, again was rebuffed.

"Not until I know what's going on," the woman said. Then added insult to injury by rummaging through Kirsten's fanny pack, carelessly dumping everything out, then pawing through it. She rifled Kirsten's wallet, checked through every pocket and slot, eventually came to, and opened, the folder with Kirsten's passport and travel documents.

It was . . . weird, having to sit and watch this performance, unable to stop the violations of privacy, unable to do anything. Except watch. Kirsten wanted to scream out her objections, but knew it would serve no purpose. This strange woman clearly had her own agenda, and without being able to comprehend it, there seemed nothing Kirsten, herself, could do.

Nothing except listen. Almost at once, her strange companion launched into a diatribe that fascinated Kirsten as much as it frightened her. The very first thing out of the woman's mouth was that she was Kendall's former wife!

Ian didn't make it to the first decent bit of track before temptation claimed him and he stopped to sample the goodies in the plastic baggie he'd filched from Rose's handbag.

He was actually in better shape than he'd been in weeks, so he was able to carefully select the pills he wanted most. Then he reached down to find there were indeed three tinnies remaining beneath his truck seat. He stopped, snapped open one of the cans, used the warm beer to wash down his chosen pills. Then he lit a smoke, leaned against the vehicle's door, one freckled arm out in the warmth of the afternoon sun as he waited for the rush.

After that, it was all just as he wanted it to be, expected it to be. Except for niggling suspicion and curiosity. That wouldn't go away. By the time he'd reached the main road, it had actually become obsessive; he couldn't get it out of his mind regardless of the drugs.

He finished off the second beer, threw the can out the window and into the ditch, then muttered to himself, added a string of obscenities, and turned the old truck around. But he didn't return to the shack—not directly. Instead, he drove further up the tier, past the turnoff, and took an even less-used track that he knew would bring him onto a ridge from which he could easily hike down and observe the shack from a safe distance.

Which he did, the Vaime sniper rifle in one hand, the remaining can of beer in the other, and the all-important collection of pills tucked safely into his shirt pocket.

It took him no time at all, really, to make the drive and hike to where he could snuggle down into a comfortable, sunny spot. Not a perfect viewpoint . . . he couldn't see as much of the track leading to the shack as he would have liked . . . but it would do. He carefully selected a few more pills, tried to focus on making the remaining beer last longer than usual, but the tinnie was well and truly empty when he heard the sound of a vehicle approaching on the road below.

CHAPTER SEVENTEEN

Stafford, on his best day ever, wasn't a tenth the bushman that Ian Boyd was on his worst, so he, too, failed to notice on his return the evidence of increased travel on the trail to the shack.

Also, Stafford was on a high. He'd actually found a knowledgeable publican . . . a publican with vision enough to have put aside half a dozen bottles of the finest Piper's Brook wine. Probably for his own use, Stafford thought, but it had been a joy to spend a few minutes' discussion with the man, a greater joy to be able to purchase the wine at something less than highway robbery prices.

He'd also found a new, to him, fruit and veggie mart, stacked high with fresh local produce. No fresh meat to be had, of course. Not on a Sunday. But meat wasn't that important, for the moment.

The only minus was his disappointment at not having been able to find Ian Boyd, but that had been a long shot anyway, and he accepted that. Maybe best that he hadn't, although it might have been good to know where Boyd was and what mischief he was getting up to. The last thing Stafford wanted was to have authorities chasing Boyd for something and investigating his own hideout in the process. Bad enough the unexplained case of the gundog judge who'd been killed, but although that had been all over the radio, he couldn't see it drawing attention to the east coast, where he was.

The shopping experience added to his anticipation during

the trip back to the shack. He drove carefully, with fine chamber music oozing from the speakers, paying attention to his driving, but not to the condition of the track he followed.

It didn't take a bushman to see the gleaming shape of Rose's SUV parked outside the shack, although it did, in Stafford's twisted mind, take his own definition of fate to let him see the SUV while he was still some distance away.

And Stafford, on any day at all, was significantly smarter than Ian. Certainly smart enough to find a place to get his own 4WD off the track and turned around to facilitate a speedy escape, if needed.

Who, I wonder? Not Ian . . . not with a vehicle like that. Not the police, either.

He turned off his engine, then sat there, warm enough in the afternoon sunshine, hidden by the scrub, reasonably certain that if there was danger here, he'd have seen evidence of it already.

He closed the door carefully, quietly, took a tire iron from behind the driver's seat, and began a long, cautious stalk, paralleling the muddy track, moving as silently as he could through the underbrush as he approached the silent cabin.

You shouldn't be doing this. You should be running. Now, while you can.

Without Kirsten? No—I was meant to have Kirsten. Why else would I have found all that splendid wine?

It could be a trap. Kirsten trapped you before.

In a cave. (Stafford visibly shuddered . . . couldn't help himself.) *This is my territory, now. My terms.*

He moved in on the fern-shrouded cabin with mincing, feather-light steps, once again the fearless pioneer scout. Flitting from one patch of cover to the next, he carried the tire iron like a tomahawk, entertained mental visions of himself as Daniel Day-Lewis in *Last of the Mohicans*.

Stepping high, treading lightly, he was halfway around the main clearing that held the shack, peering from behind a tall, towering eucalypt, his ears already straining, searching for sounds from within, when Stafford felt a hard, solid *something* poking him in the back.

"Drop it, little mate." The voice was a whisper as quiet as his own footsteps. A voice he knew?

The pressure at his back held, and Stafford opened his fingers, let the tire iron fall with a muted thud.

Yes, I know that voice.

"Now turn around . . . slow."

Which Stafford did, making no effort to hide the huge grin on his face.

"Ian!" he said, his voice soft, but positively vibrant with delight. "How wonderful to see you again. I looked for you in town this morning and couldn't find you, but here you are and isn't that wonderful?"

Stafford ignored the look of confusion on Ian Boyd's face. He dropped his voice another octave, added a conspiratorial wink to his next words.

"And you're just in time for dinner! How splendid is that?"

Ian was totally flummoxed. All he could do was stand there, slack-jawed, and stare at the familiar/unfamiliar figure before him. Reflective sunglasses hid the man's eyes, nothing about his face *looked* familiar . . . but that voice!

Ian knew the voice, had heard the dulcet, rich, chocolate syrup tones often enough that even half stoned he couldn't mistake it. Except that it was impossible for him to be hearing it now, here.

The muzzle of the rifle wavered, then began to quiver just as Ian's hands quivered. His mind quivered even worse. He wanted to run, didn't dare, was half-inclined to shoot but didn't dare do that, either. No sense in that!

"We need to talk," the voice said, whisper soft. And Ian was beckoned away from the shack by a confident wave and a, "Come, Ian," as the dead man, ignoring the rifle entirely now, turned away and marched to the relative privacy behind Rose's SUV. Ian, his mind blasted by the thought of having just tried to bail up a dead man, followed him, having little choice in the matter.

CHAPTER EIGHTEEN

Rose stopped in mid-rant, her gaze flitting from Kirsten to the shack's door.

"What was that?" she whispered.

"What was what? I didn't hear anything." Kirsten hadn't heard anything but Rose's ongoing tirade, but the other woman's attitude prompted her, also, to whisper.

"Voices. I thought I heard voices."

They stared at each other then in silence, both listening, both hearing nothing. Kirsten was half tempted to scream out, to call for help. Surely she wouldn't be any worse off than she was now, faced with Kendall's intransigent ex-wife who might turn out to be more dangerous than any kidnapper.

Kirsten had nearly laughed outright when Rose's diatribe got into high gear. Either she, herself, was the world's worst judge of character, or this exotic, undeniably beautiful but so-strange woman knew next to nothing about the man touched by both their lives.

Or did she? As Kirsten had listened, Rose's ranting highlighted the best things Kirsten herself knew about Kendall. He was kind, gentle, never had a bad word to say about anyone, was aggressive only in his writing. . . . The list went on, and on, and on . . . and Rose managed to twist and turn every pleasant aspect of Kendall's personality and character into something negative and carping.

In all their time together—*Does it count as together, I wonder, when it never gets together in bed?*—Kendall had only mentioned Rose once that Kirsten could remember, had never shown her a picture of his ex-wife or even indicated he had one. He'd merely explained that the marriage had "fallen apart in a screaming heap," said that Rose was a psych nurse, "and they're all crazier than their patients," but made the comment, she had thought at the time, so lightly as to make it seem a joke.

Some joke! You always were a master of understatement, my love.

Rose, once begun, had seemed to forget entirely about the potential perils of their situation. She seemed intent on discrediting Kendall in every way possible, seemed oblivious to her surroundings and situation in her need to vent. It was nothing short of incredible, bordering on being terrifying. Kirsten didn't—couldn't—forget about the immediate issues, but neither could she find space in the diatribe to insert her concerns and beg yet again for them to somehow get out of here, wherever they were.

I wish you'd just shut up about Kendall and think about US. Here, now! Damn it—I don't know what the hell's going on and you don't seem to either. Can't you forget about Kendall and think about getting us the hell out of here?

Until it was too late. Much, much too late. The words were there in her mouth, but were never uttered, choked into silence by the opening of the cabin door to admit Ian Boyd and another man, equally tall but younger, a man who glided into the gloomy interior with the grace of a dancer. Ian's rifle was in his hands, and he seemed vaguely familiar, although she couldn't figure out why.

A stranger.

Until he spoke.

His first words were to Rose Chapman. He greeted her like an old friend, honeyed words flowing through his smile. "Rose!

How utterly delightful to have you here. And a surprise, of course."

He paused briefly, only long enough, Kirsten thought, to savor Rose's bewilderment, taste the pleasure of seeing it change shape to become astonishment, then continued, handing the rifle back to Ian as he swooped forward to take both of Rose's hands in his own.

"And you've met our other guest, I see," he said, suave and casual as if they were all at a dinner party somewhere instead of crowded into this hovel in the Tasmanian wilderness. "Have you been telling Kirsten how you arranged to have her boyfriend Kendall shot?"

Rose's vocal, "But you're dead!" was echoed by Kirsten's silent, equally incredulous thought. But it was as nothing, compared to the cloud of horror that surged upward from Kirsten's gut, that took over her mind, her body, her very existence. She was only vaguely conscious of the *No . . . No . . . NO!* that thundered in her mind and ears just before her legs lost their strength and she sagged into a swoon. The steel rod she'd been holding became too heavy for nerveless fingers, fell, landed at her feet with a dull thunk.

It lasted only a second, long enough for the horror to smack her again as Stafford released Rose's hands and caught Kirsten on her way to the shack's dirt floor.

"Dear, dear, Kirsten. That was a trifle abrupt. How insensitive of me; I do apologize . . . honestly I do. And Kendall's just fine, I assure you. The bullet missed him, you see." He lifted her by her bound wrists, steadied her until she somehow—miraculously—got her feet under her and found a semblance of balance, then he released her and stepped back as if to admire his handiwork.

His gaze swept the cabin's small interior, pausing at the dismantled camp cot, swiftly cutting to the table, the tools,

Kirsten's emptied fanny pack. "Aah . . . I see you've been a busy girl, too," he said, the words emerging in that too-familiar voice with the flavor and texture of rich chocolate fudge, emerging through a smile of what appeared to Kirsten to be huge satisfaction, genuine pleasure. A stranger's smile on a stranger's face.

She couldn't recognize the face, but could never forget the voice. It floated through her nightmares, occasionally brought her bolt upright in bed, shaking, bathed in an icy sweat, eyes wide with a terror she could taste, feel, fear! The devil's voice . . . rich as chocolate, smooth as butterscotch, deadly as the grave.

Kirsten couldn't look at him, couldn't *not* look at him. The pleasure in his voice both terrified her and clamped her attention. Her tummy writhed and squirmed at the delicately sounded words, and she swallowed convulsively, praying she could keep from being sick. There, then, now.

"Ian! A chair for the lady," he demanded abruptly. And when the folding chair was brought, he directed Ian precisely where it should be placed, then gently but firmly moved Kirsten into it. She had a flicker of relief that the chair now partially disguised the point where the eyebolt was installed, but only a tiny relief compared to the terror that flooded her, the horror that Stafford's very touch created.

She could only sit there, shaking and shaken, her gaze flashing from one person to another, following the voices as Stafford directed Ian to reassemble the camp cot, drew Rose aside and began—could this really be happening?—chatting about the Birch clinic, about employees from Stafford's tenure there, about who'd quit, who'd stayed, about Dave Birch's reaction to everything as Stafford's infamy had unfolded. A strangely grotesque old home week reunion, made even weirder by the fact that both Ian and Rose fell right into Stafford's spell.

She could only sit there as Stafford sent Ian to fetch his

vehicle, bring in the wine, meanwhile focusing his attention on Rose, enveloping Rose with his presence, his aura. Seducing Rose, not sexually but intellectually, taking control by the sheer dominance of his personality as thoroughly as if he'd chained Rose to the wall, as if he'd bound Rose's wrists.

She listened, when Ian returned, as Stafford made apologies for having only two *real* wine goblets, as he insisted that Rose should have one goblet, Kirsten the other, as he opened a bottle with the flourish of a trained wine waiter, poured, offered it to Rose to taste, smiled hugely at her nod of acceptance.

She could only sit there, having been transferred from folding chair to camp cot so that Rose had somewhere to sit, as Stafford regaled Rose and Ian with details of his escape from Kirsten's cave, of his cosmetic, reconstructive surgery in Mexico, of his eventual return to Australia and, finally, Tasmania. Here. Now. Could only sit there, sipping at the wine because her befuddled mind couldn't think of what *else* to do with it. Throw it at him? To what purpose? Not drink it? Again . . . to what purpose?

So she sipped, and watched, and listened, feeling more and more like Alice in Wonderland as the surreal conversations ebbed and flowed around her. It was an amazing performance . . .

It is a performance. That's exactly what it is. He's performing! Yes, he is. The bastard's got an audience and he's loving it. That's what's happening, sure as shit.

Those were the first thoughts that made sense to Kirsten, the first signs in her own addled mind that she wasn't dreaming, that whatever was happening actually *was* happening. She hunched forward, elbows on her thighs, eyes closed, and clung to those thoughts, nurtured them, tried to use them to shut out the insanity of her surroundings, the peril of her situation. And Kendall's! Had his totally weird ex-wife *really* conspired to have him shot?

She heard Stafford's question, even understood it, but it somehow drifted inside her conscious mind, not demanding an answer, really. Just . . . there. But she heard the next one, and it did demand a reply.

"Cat got your tongue, Kirsten? It nearly did mine, but then you know all about that, don't you? We're waiting."

"I . . ."

"Oh, come now. Don't be modest. It isn't that difficult a question—how did you feel when you abandoned me in the bowels of the earth? Did you assume I'd get out eventually? Or did you fully intend me to rot in there? As I almost did."

Careful, Kirsten. He's leading you somewhere with his silver tongue, and you won't want to go there.

"I wasn't really thinking about you at all," she finally said. "I was just thankful to be free myself."

"So that you could rush back and rescue your lover." Stafford spat out the words, still in that honeyed voice, but with an after-taste of bile.

"Do you blame me for that?" The words emerged without conscious thought.

Idiot! Of course he blames you.

Now she was conscious of the attentiveness being shown by the other two people, realized that she was being drawn into the role of entertainer as surely as Stafford himself had stepped into it. He was sharing the stage with her, and the expression in his eyes told her he expected her to perform and do it well!

But not to upstage you—is that it? Yeah . . . I expect that's exactly it. Not enough for you to brag about your achievements, your miraculous escape—you want me to back you up. I'd back you over a cliff if I ever get the chance. Bet on it!

"I offered to help you rescue Kendall. Are you forgetting that?" And now there was a peevish tone in that seductive voice, a petulant little boy demanding . . . something.

Christ! You're starting to think in psycho-babble. Stop it, Kirsten. Stop it now before you're as crazy as he is, as they are.

"I didn't forget. I just didn't believe you."

And the truth shall set you free—and don't I wish it could?

"I very nearly died, did you know that? I *would* have died, I truly think, if that cougar hadn't dragged me free. Nearly died anyway . . . the brute fully intended to eat me. Me! What have you to say about that?"

"Everyone thought he had. The cops said there was enough blood around the cave entrance to account for you *and* the cougar. Speaking for myself, I'd have been happier if you'd stayed trapped in the cave and starved to death."

Get a grip, girl! You're not going to accomplish anything by deliberately provoking the bastard.

So she was surprised, almost amused, that her remark merely thrust the conversation off-track for a moment, into a monologue by her captor as he displayed his encyclopedic knowledge to his impromptu audience.

"Did you know that cougar—mountain lion, puma, painter . . . the name doesn't matter—was among the favored meats for mountain men and trappers in western North America? Along with beaver tail, which is extremely rich and was convenient, since most of the mountain men were there to trap beaver, so it was a natural byproduct of their profession. But cougar was even more favored. Said to taste quite similar to chicken, but I don't agree with that. It has a flavor all its own. Good, white meat. Succulent . . . but cloying after awhile, especially if you've nothing else to eat." He fixed Kirsten with a piercing glance, his eyes filled with a gloating satisfaction.

Okay, already . . . I got the point. Everybody assumed from all the blood that the cougar ate you, or at least killed you. Too bad nobody seriously thought it might have been the other way around.

Stafford went on, and on, and on, discussing esoteric meats

with a sort of abstract, almost clinical precision. Then ceased, abruptly. Turned to Ian with a confidential tone and said, "You'd understand, Ian. Of course you would. You've tried all sorts of exotic meats right here in Tasmania, as I recall you saying. Wombat, echidna, even platypus. A platypus tail is quite similar to that of a beaver . . . what does platypus taste like, Ian?"

Kirsten was among those who waited in silence while the tall bushman contemplated his reply, which he spent much longer thinking about than actually saying. And when it finally came . . .

"Like meat. Tough."

. . . Kirsten had to stifle her laughter, lest it break free and become hysteria. Especially when the other two listeners, Rose and Stafford, laughed almost gaily at the terse, unimaginative reply. Even Ian grinned through yellowed, tobacco-stained teeth, seemingly happy to have done the right thing even if he wasn't quite sure what he'd actually done.

"Food . . ." Stafford poured out the word slowly, as if tasting it. "It's a necessity, of course, but so much more . . . satisfying when it's delightfully prepared, when it's something unique. An experience for the senses as much as for the mortal coil." And he turned his attention once again to Kirsten.

"We've all, I expect, eaten oysters, and I doubt anyone would deny that fresh off the rocks is best. No surprise that Sydney rock oysters are known throughout the world. The ones they serve on Canada's west coast can't even compare. They're too large, coarse, nowhere near as succulent. You'd know that, Kirsten."

Then he turned to his other listeners. "Now Kirsten's eaten what are called prairie oysters, too. She's a child of the Canadian prairies, and that's what they call the calves' testicles they fry up as a delicacy after seasonal round-ups in Canada's cattle country . . . *prairie oysters*. In fact"—and he graced Kirsten with one of his broadest, most comradely smiles—"Kirsten and I shared that particular delicacy at a dinner party, once. Didn't we, my dear?"

He seemed to take her nod as a suitable reply, turned abruptly to Rose, and Kirsten fancied there was a subtle change in his voice as he questioned her.

"What about you, dear Rose? You've been very quiet, almost uncharacteristically so, if I may say. What esoteric and wonderful foods have passed your splendid lips?"

"Me? Uhm . . . well . . ." Rose seemed stuck for a reply, but Stafford didn't force the issue. He merely smiled and let the conversation lapse while he rose to refill all their glasses. Then he pounced.

"Forgive me, Rose. I forgot for a moment what a sheltered life you've lived, here in Tasmania, away from the wickedness of the wide world. Well, don't worry too much about it. I think we can remedy that."

Kirsten went cold inside.

Here it comes. Now we'll get a lecture about how nutritious human flesh is, or some other such nonsense. And then . . . ?

"But it does worry me just a tad that you've brought nothing to the party, really," Stafford said then, resuming the conversation with a twist that totally lost Kirsten. At first. "In fact, it's been worrying me a quite a lot, because I'm not sure what you *can* contribute, if you take my meaning . . ."

He let the sentence run out, but Kirsten could see that he held Rose transfixed by his gaze, like a deer in the headlights.

You stupid, stupid woman. You should have run when you had the chance. And taken me with you, or at least cut me loose. Well it serves you right, sitting here having exotic discussions about esoteric foods with somebody who eats girls like you for breakfast!

Girls like US. The amended admission was an ice block in her belly, and it created such cramps that Kirsten doubled over in the agony of it, staring down into the wine glass in her trembling fingers, trying to keep from being sick, or fainting, or going instantly, numbingly—maybe thankfully—insane. She almost missed Rose's reply, and wished instantly she could have seen the look on Rose's face when it was uttered.

"I can give you Kendall."

CHAPTER NINETEEN

Monday did not begin well for Charlie. His police vehicle chose it as a day to die, or at least become seriously wounded, so he had to call for the tow-truck before he could even begin his workday. A quick phone call to Launceston brought no good news. Kendall had received no ransom demands, knew nothing he hadn't known the night before, when Charlie had also phoned. But Kendall's discipline was slowly but surely being destroyed. Charlie could tell that much just by the tone of his friend's voice.

Nor would Kendall have Rex Henderson's steadying influence much longer. Rex was off to Hobart, then back to the mainland, then on to New Zealand, assumedly with the hat and boots he'd arrived in.

Too bad you couldn't take me with you. The way this day's shaping up, it could only be an improvement. Ah well . . . at least I'm not lumbered with that bloody evil dog.

There was some satisfaction in seeing the electronic posters featuring Kirsten's photo and one copied from the security tapes that showed both Kirsten and her assumed abductor. Not a good picture, by any means, but better than nothing. Maybe. Even more satisfaction that his efficient staff was out distributing the posters before Charlie made it in to work. Kirsten's photo, supplied by Kendall, was excellent, but the best likeness they'd been able to render from the security tapes was next to useless in terms of actually identifying her alleged abductor. So bad, in fact, that the local paper had ignored it altogether, choosing instead to stick just with Kendall's photo of Kirsten. Charlie was little surprised by this!

Which reminded him to make one more phone call, this one to a mate in the Hobart forensics division, giving him a heads-up about the fingerprints that should, by this time, have been lifted from the mysterious knife and sent from Launceston. Unfortunately, Charlie's friend was on leave, and although the person he did manage to speak to promised a quick check of the prints when they eventually arrived, he could tell from the bored tone of voice that there'd be no urgent priority. The knife had been involved in no crime, and there was nothing but the vaguest of circumstances to link it to the abduction, assuming there actually had been an abduction.

What else could it be? It wouldn't have been a publicity stunt. I'll grant Kendall that much. But none of it makes any sense. No ransom demand? No threats. It's a worry.

He was sitting at his desk, wondering whether to go out now and buy wine for tonight's dinner date, or wait until later, when Dave Birch entered the police station, looking like death warmed over. Charlie's psychologist friend had fared poorly in the aftermath of Ralph Stafford's infamous exploits. He and Stafford had been job-swapping to allow Dave—an avid skiing fanatic—to spend Tasmanian winters at home, then take over Stafford's Vancouver Island practice so he could trade Tasmanian summers for winters in Canada, and more skiing.

But in the aftermath of the Stafford affair, business at Dave's private, low-level mental health clinic had deteriorated visibly. He'd lost customers, lost staff, lost his enthusiasm for skiing. Today, he looked as if he'd lost all enthusiasm for anything at all.

"You don't look happy, little mate," Charlie said once greetings had been exchanged.

"I'm not," replied the psychologist. "I'm worried as hell, actually, and not even sure if I should be or not."

"What's happened? Lost one of your patients or something?" Charlie meant it as a joke, only realized after the horrid words were out that this was no time for humor.

"A nurse." Dave Birch regarded Charlie through eyes haggard with worry and fatigue. "And as I said, I'm not sure I should be worrying at all. Except . . ."

Charlie waited patiently. He'd learned long ago that silence was the finest prompter of all. Dave Birch was, from appearance, a beaten man. Charlie hoped not, but he knew how the Stafford incidents had damaged Dave's personal credibility along with his business. This was rural Tasmania, after all. Rumors and innuendo were quick to whelp and slow to die.

"I think there might be some drugs missing." The words emerged in a whisper, as if by reducing the volume the psychologist thought he might reduce the seriousness of the words themselves.

"Christ!" Charlie reached for a pad and something to write with. "Okay, let's start at the beginning with this."

"I . . . I'm really iffy about this, Charlie," said Dave Birch. "I really don't want to get anybody in trouble and I'm . . . I'm not really sure—"

"You're sure enough to be here in the first place. That'll do me for now. Give me the details, please. Then we can talk about the other issues."

"One of my nurses didn't turn up this morning," said Birch. "One of my . . . best nurses. And she didn't phone in sick or anything, and she's not answering her phone at home, or her cell phone, or . . ."

Charlie caught the original hesitation, also caught the fleeting expression of guilt in Birch's eyes. There was more to this than just a *best* nurse situation, that much was clear. As was the likely identity of the *missing* nurse.

"There could be all sorts of explanations for that," he replied. "But what's the drum on these missing drugs?"

"I'm . . . I'm not really sure yet if there's anything to it at all. She's the one who's been keeping the records, and I've sort of just, sort of, left it all to her." The psychologist's voice somehow managed to hold steadily low in volume and scream with guilt at the same time. "But I think there's some missing. Maybe. Not a lot, but maybe for quite a while, and if there is . . . well . . ."

Charlie shook his head wearily. This didn't sound good. Nothing to do with drugs *ever* sounded good, but this, coming from a friend and a doctor, no less. And . . . he shook his head again.

No easy way out, so why bother looking for one? Might as well ask the questions, even if you already know the answers, or most of them.

"Who's the nurse and how long have you been sleeping with her?"

Dave Birch reared back as if Charlie had smacked him in the mouth. "Damn it, Charlie," he said. "That's a bit rough."

"Not if it's true," Charlie replied blandly, knowing full well it was true, and had been true for quite some time, knowing Dave might try to deny it, but wouldn't be able to lie to him. Dave was an extremely poor liar.

The two regarded each other in silence for a moment. Charlie sat patient as a statue behind his desk. Dave Birch fidgeted and squirmed as he tried to summon up nerve for the admissions both knew had to come.

"Rose Chapman, but it isn't like you think." Dave spat out the words with machine-gun speed. Then he looked away, ostensibly to collect his thoughts but in truth, Charlie knew, because the psychologist knew all too well how the admission would look, must look.

"Rose Chapman? I know that name." Charlie did, had known

it from the beginning. But then recollection struck him in a bolt of surprise. It almost forced a smile, but he managed to maintain his police-sergeant poker face. It was a struggle. "Isn't she Teague Kendall's ex?" he asked, and immediately kicked himself mentally for being so abrupt.

"I . . . she's . . . been married before, I think." The confusion on Dave Birch's face was too thorough not to be genuine.

So you didn't know. Ah well . . . too late now. Jesus . . . I wish you hadn't used the word "before" like that. Bugger! If half of what I've heard is true, you should be glad she's gone, little mate. That one is pure poison.

Charlie knew more than he actually wanted to about Teague Kendall's former wife, although virtually none of it from Kendall himself. Kendall wasn't the type to bad-mouth any woman, or man, for that matter, except in fiction. Nonetheless, Tasmania is a small place in many ways. The "six degrees of separation" concept was usually reduced to about three degrees in Tassie, and Rose Chapman's reputation was a known thing.

"Psych nurse? From Hobart? Have to be the same one, I'd reckon," Charlie said. "How long has she been working for you?" He thought he already knew, but it couldn't hurt to clarify the timing.

"About two years, I think. I'd have to look it up if you want anything more specific. And she's been a godsend, Charlie. Especially after . . . well, you know the problems I had. Patients fleeing the place like rats from a sinking ship . . . staff doing the same, at least right after all that Stafford cannibalism stuff hit the headlines. She and Gladys Rainbird were about the only ones that stayed with me. I've been damned glad to have somebody with her experience."

"Yeah . . . I'd expect you would have been," Charlie said. "And she's worked out okay, up 'til this current situation?"

"Splendid. Excellent nurse, excellent . . ." The doctor's voice faded, sagging into silence.

Excellent at a lot of other things, too, judging from the way you're reacting, me old mate. But we'd best not go there, I reckon. Yet. You poor bugger!

"So you don't want to get into the missing drug thing yet, I gather?" Charlie knew the answer, still had to ask.

"No." The word emerged flatly, without emphasis. But it was what it was, effectively handcuffing Charlie. Without a complaint, without something that at least looked like evidence of a crime . . .

"There's naught I can do about her being missing. You know that? Legally, she's an adult, for starters. And it's not anything *like* an amount of time to create concern for anyone . . . except you, of course."

Dave Birch merely sat there, the defeat obvious in his entire demeanor. Then he reached into the pocket of his white jacket and came up with a folded bit of paper, which he handed across the desk to Charlie.

"She drives a white Honda SUV," he said, his voice and actions united in a plea. "This is the license number. I know you can't do anything officially, Charlie, but if you could just maybe pass the word . . ."

"Unofficially? Sure, Dave. I can do that and I will. Anything for an old mate. But it'll cost you. I want your promise that if you can't get this missing drugs thing totally, properly sorted out—and soon—you'll be back in here with everything you've got. Promise?"

"I do. But . . ."

"Good enough for me. Now you'd best get back to work and I should, too."

But when Dave Birch was safely out the door and visible driving off in his clinic's minivan, Charlie set out walking toward the other end of town, and he wasn't working.

Charlie had a date that evening. With a woman who interested him a very great deal, and had interested him for quite some time. It was the first time, though, that she'd invited him for dinner. Charlie was on the hunt for a good bottle of wine. Maybe two bottles.

The publican at the bottle shop Charlie favored most was a retired police chief inspector from New South Wales, who'd visited Tasmania for the trout fishing, fallen in love with the place, and used the proceeds of a healthy retirement package and some earlier wise investments to purchase a pub. The two men got along well despite their relative discrepancies in rank, but Charlie's visits to the pub were most often on business.

"Are you lost, Charlie? It's a bit early for you to be coming round here because of trouble; I've only just got the doors open," said Mike Findlay, the publican. Findlay was a man whose extreme fitness made him appear bigger than he actually was, and in point of fact he was more than capable of handling any trouble that his quality establishment might encounter.

"I'm after some plonk, Mike. Something really top-drawer," Charlie said.

"I have plenty of that, so long as you're not after Piper's Brook. I sold out of that yesterday. Six bottles, no less. My last six, and I'd been saving them for myself, if you want the truth.

Charlie laughed. "You can always order more, I reckon. But where'd you find six people who could afford it? That stuff's like liquid gold, and we're nearly out of tourist season."

"There's still a few about. And I didn't need six; these all went to the same bloke. Must be a tourist . . . American, from his voice. Nice feller. We had quite a chat about wines and such. Knowledgeable chap, too. Made for a change, I can tell you. But, as you say, something of a surprise. Haven't had a run on Piper's Brook like that since all the kafuffle last year about that

Specialist feller."

Charlie couldn't avoid a shudder of distaste. He truly detested the media's penchant for nicknames, and the choice of the Specialist for Dr. Ralph Stafford was so bizarre as to give him the creeps. Stafford, in his view, was a butcher, plain and simple, an evil malignancy better off dead.

Mike paused to wipe his forehead; it was warm in the bottle shop. "My God, but that was a bun fight and a half. When the media started on about how that bloke—what was his name again . . . Stafford?—favored Piper's Brook, I couldn't keep it in stock for about a month. Everybody wanted to try the stuff, and bugger the price. Went out as quick as I could order it."

He paused, but only briefly. "I never did meet the man himself. I had a manager here in the bottle-o, those days. But I heard all about him for months afterwards. Andrew Pirie must've been glad of the publicity, although I think they're heavier on export sales than local ones. Then the popularity died overnight and it was like nobody'd ever heard of the brand. The six bottles I sold yesterday were the last of it, although of course I didn't tell the bloke buying them that. Didn't stick with last year's prices, either . . . inflation and all, you realize." And he grinned almost sheepishly—if one could imagine a wolf in sheep's clothing.

"Just see that you treat me a bit more fairly," Charlie said. "And keep the cost down to a dull roar, too. I don't need to be taking out a second mortgage for plonk, no matter how good it is."

"Piper's Brook is the best, for my money. No question! But I didn't know you drank wine at all. Thought you were a beer drinker, at heart."

"Heavy date tonight," Charlie replied, and winced inwardly at this false show of bravado. Such a revelation wasn't an issue—Findlay could, and would, keep his mouth shut about something so obviously personal. But for Charlie himself, the worries kept oozing to the surface. He was inwardly confused, and he hated that.

"The widow McKay, I assume. Can't imagine what a fine woman like that would see in you." It was an observation, not a question. Findlay knew as much about who was doing what, and to whom, and with whom—and usually why, as well—in St. Helens as Charlie's entire detachment. "You're not involved in this abduction thing, then?" Findlay asked, reaching down to pick up a copy of the Launceston *Examiner* and show Charlie the front page spread with Kirsten's photo front and center. Charlie had already seen it, but dutifully took another look, knowing the publican would have read the article with interest and would want to talk about it.

"I should be," he said. "Teague Kendall's a good mate of mine. But there's nothing to connect whatever the hell's happened there to my patch down here, and I've enough on my own plate anyway. Speaking of which, just between us, like, have you seen anything of Rose Chapman, that sexpot nurse from up at the nuthouse? Who just happens to be Kendall's ex-wife—bet you didn't know that."

Charlie almost glanced around to be sure Dave Birch couldn't overhear the disparaging description of his treatment center. He knew Dave hated it, but everyone local used the term so regularly it was difficult not to.

Mike Findlay paused in silence for a moment, then replied. The question might be unofficial, but Charlie knew the former policeman was taking it seriously, reviewing his recollections before he spoke. "Not the last day or so," he said. "She's in and out on occasion, of course. Never a problem, not too heavy on the sauce or anything like that. Nothing . . . worrisome. Apart from being probably the finest looking woman on the east coast, but we can't hold that against her, although I've got something

I'd like to, no matter whose ex-wife she is. And no, I didn't know that."

Both men laughed, although Charlie had to force it. With tonight's affair on his mind, he didn't need such gratuitous chauvinism in there too.

The publican stopped laughing, a bit abruptly, Charlie thought, and appeared unexpectedly thoughtful for a moment. "One thing," he said. "She was in the pub last week . . . can't remember which day. But I do recall her going straight over to Ian Boyd. You know Ian, I expect. Not her type, for sure and certain. But they had their heads together over something, and she was buying the beer."

"Ian Boyd? That *is* one for the books," Charlie said. "Not my business though, unless she's taken up poaching or some such thing. Only reason I asked—unofficially, remember?—is that she didn't come in to work today, seems to have disappeared, and it's got Dave Birch all stirred up."

"Doesn't take much to stir him up these days, poor bugger. He's had a helluva rough go of things since that Specialist stuff. Did he tell you, by the way, that he's been rooting our Rose?"

Charlie had a brief mental glitch involving a birch tree attempting fornication with a rose bush, and had to stifle a grin. "He's in denial. I asked him straight up how long he'd been sleeping with her, and he tried to slide out from under it. How long do you reckon?"

"Since about two weeks after all the Specialist fallout started. Dave happened in here about a fortnight afterwards, and you could tell by the look in his eyes that he'd just been pussy-whipped into the middle of next week. Another few months and she'll have her name over the door. I've seen it before. So have you."

The publican snorted with bitter laughter, and this time Charlie couldn't help but join him.

"Half his bloody luck, say I," Findlay continued. "Although I reckon the woman is a ball-breaker, well and truly. She's got that *look*. On the other hand, she's stuck by him, which a lot didn't."

No argument there, either, but Charlie couldn't help but wonder how much power Rose Chapman might be wielding when it came to actually running the facility. Especially the drug dispensing elements of it all.

The publican went out to collect Charlie's wine, and returned a few moments later with two bottles of a quite acceptable vintage and a copy of the poster that was being distributed in connection with Kirsten Knelsen's disappearance.

"Nice looking bird," said Mike. "But the lads in Launceston want taking out and shooting if they expect anybody to make an identification from this shot of the alleged abductor. It could be anybody. It could be either one of us, it could be the bloke who bought me out of Piper's Brook, could be anybody. You can't see anything but the hat and sunglasses."

"I'm not tall enough and you're not thin enough," Charlie replied. "Best they could do, so that's what we have to work with. You know the drill, Mike. Real life is nothing like those American cop shows with all their high-tech equipment. Look at that sniper situation out at Ormley. There's half the police cadets in the state out there today, I'll bet, looking for the bullet that killed that gundog bloke. And for what? Unless they can find the rifle it was fired from, it won't tell them anything except the caliber, if that. And what do you reckon the odds are of them finding it in the first place?"

"Buckley's . . . at best. Complete waste of manpower, in my view, although of course it's something that has to be done. But not my problem. Most of the time I don't even think of police work and I have to say I'm glad of it, glad to be out of the field."

In a pig's arse. You miss it every day. You're as much in denial as Dave Birch, although probably for better reasons.

But Charlie didn't say that. One thing to twit Dave Birch, who needed it . . . quite another to get smart with a senior colleague, retired or otherwise.

"I'm just glad none of it's happening on my patch."

CHAPTER TWENTY

Rose almost immediately regretted her impulsive offer to "give" Kendall to Stafford, but it was a short-lived regret when she saw how much the suggestion excited the good doctor. He'd have had her off and away within minutes had it not been for the small problem of her missing car keys, and his obvious disgruntlement at that issue was almost a relief to Rose.

"Really, Rose. You might have mentioned it earlier, while there was still enough light for us to at least try and search," he'd said. Then taken the comment as a hint to light the lantern so they could actually see *inside* the shack, where the gloaming had subtly made its presence known.

With the lantern light came a flurry of activity. Ian was sent to bring down his vehicle from the upper road. He had his swag in the vehicle, and no objection to sleeping outside. Ian was also delegated the task of assembling the second camp cot, which resolved where Rose was going to sleep. Stafford, as host, declared he'd be quite happy with the chair where he'd spent what remained of the previous night.

But his quick acceptance of the idea that she could bring him Kendall eased whatever niggling concerns Rose had about her own place in the current scheme of things. If nothing else, it indicated she was going to be treated as a colleague . . . far preferable to what she visualized as Kirsten's fate.

It's nothing less than the stupid bitch deserves, though. All the shit they've been through and she hasn't slept with him yet? Well, I think you missed your chance, girl.

Not that Kirsten had deliberately provided Rose with the information that she hadn't slept with Kendall . . . at least not directly. But her facial expression when Stafford had asked something similar was sufficient to alert Rose to the state of play. All she needed now was to figure out how to make the best use of such knowledge.

The thought plagued her throughout dinner, intruding on the pleasure she took from watching Kirsten's reaction to that!

When Stafford announced his dinner preparations, Kirsten almost caved in right on the spot. It was just too easy to let her imagination—only *just* under control as it was—run riot with images created by the doctor while he'd pursued her through the inky blackness of the cave in Canada more than a year earlier. Images of her sister being slain, butchered, then eaten by this madman.

And yet . . . she was fascinated, couldn't stop herself watching his adroit handling of the utensils as he prepared the food. He peeled potatoes as if each one was a jewel in the process of being revealed, sliced up carrots and onions and some green herb she couldn't even identify—each slice a masterpiece of precision, each individual bit of food treated as a visitor to the table.

She, herself, was treated as a visitor to the table. Stafford blithely ignored her bound hands, the chain that linked her to the wall, the entire insanity of her being there at all. He carried on an animated conversation with her—with all of them—as if he was entertaining early arrivals while doing the preparatory work for a dinner party in his own home. Ian and Rose seemed blithely ignorant of the irony. Rose hung on the doctor's every word and Boyd was clearly under the influence of some drug or another. He functioned almost as some weird form of zombie, reacting only to direct commands, speaking only to answer direct questions, apparently uncaring of the circumstances, of Kirsten's plight, of the dangers and unspoken threat of the entire situation.

I doubt if he cares what the hell he eats, so long as it's meat of some kind. Preferably raw. He'll probably eat me, if it comes to that, and ask for seconds if he's still hungry.

Kirsten didn't know which of the two men she should fear the most, although she had to give Stafford top billing just on past performance. Rose, she thought, might be infinitely more dangerous than either of them.

It was impossible to know what Rose's grudges against Kendall were based on, or even if they actually made sense. What she did know was that Rose hated and resented her, and that Rose was likely crazy enough for this to be a serious problem. And Rose hated Kendall, too . . . maybe even more. There had been a savage little delight in her voice when she'd told Stafford she could get her former husband for him. Kirsten had a momentary flash of Rose sashaying into the shack with Kendall's head on a platter, like Salome's delivery of John the Baptist's head.

But she didn't take it too seriously until the subject of just how Teague Kendall might be delivered was raised. By Stafford. Even then she thought it only a ploy to torment her—until Stafford pointed to her and said to Rose, "She wears a ring on a chain around her neck. Show him that. It should be easy enough then."

Kirsten fought, but it was futile. With both hands bound she could only thrust and kick against Rose's assault. When Rose smacked her across the side of the face so hard it made her head swim and her eyes swim with tears, hearing Stafford chastise his former colleague did nothing to assuage the pain . . . or the loss of her sister's ring. The ring Stafford had discarded along with her sister's butchered body, the ring Kirsten had found. The ring that had led, inadvertently, to Stafford's being discovered to be a serial killer and cannibal.

"Your impetuousness will get the better of you one day, Rose," he said. "All you really needed to do was ask politely. Isn't that right, Kirsten?"

Kirsten didn't bother to reply. She merely glared at the both of them through a veil of tears.

I'm being stupid, trying to fight this. Now. I have to wait . . . there will be a chance, sometime, somehow. Maybe after Kendall gets here, if I live that long. He'll come if she shows him the ring . . . the damned doctor's right about that.

Then she lost her train of thought as Stafford finished off an admittedly splendid-looking salad, then turned his attention to a large camp cooler. "And for the main course," he said, "I must apologize in advance for not having something *really* fresh." And he smirked—actually *smirked,* throwing the expression in Kirsten's direction with terrifying accuracy. "So we'll have to take pot luck for today, although I can guarantee things will improve quite, quite soon."

If he pulls out any sort of raw meat I think I'll barf . . . even if it's straight from the supermarket and wearing a price tag. And if it's not . . .

Kirsten couldn't deal with that option. She closed her eyes and bent her head, fighting off the waves of nausea that roiled inside her. For months after her escape from Stafford, she'd had serious appetite problems, unable to deal with raw meat in any form. She'd had to avoid even the supermarket meat section, although she was, paradoxically, quite comfortable eating meat that someone else had cooked. Even steak, although certainly not rare.

Kendall, who usually cooked whatever meat she did eat, never once so much as commented on her reaction. He preferred *his* steak rare enough to get up and walk off the plate, as Kirsten knew very well. As she, herself, once had. But ever since her escape from Stafford, Kendall had cheerfully set aside his own preferences in favor of hers. He'd happily (she assumed) stepped down from his hobby-horse of saying that people who wanted their steak any more cooked than medium rare shouldn't be given steak in the first place, should be provided with hockey-puck hamburgers instead.

What would he say to this situation, I wonder? What will he say . . . more to the point?

Her nausea intensified just at the thought of Kendall being lured into Stafford's control. Part of her mind tried to focus on some way to warn him, or keep Rose from whatever plan she had conjured up to bring Kendall here, but the other part wanted to picture him magically riding to her rescue, the knight in shining armor, the hero.

"He won't rescue you this time, either." Rose's earlier charge echoed in Kirsten's mind. Obviously Kendall's ex-wife had read his book, where Kendall had been characteristically honest about the fact that it had—in fact—been a case of him being rescued by Kirsten.

But you tried!

That, to Kirsten, was the important thing. But hearing the sneering in Rose's voice, having seen the awe with which the Mole Creek cavers had regarded her own exploits with the Specialist, it was suddenly all too easy to see how Kendall might be intimidated. He was a man. Men don't just *try* . . . they succeed, they win, they conquer. And they don't talk about their fears, most especially to women, even more especially to women they care about. Not even Kendall, she realized, and he was probably the most liberated man she'd ever met. He'd always impressed her as being totally comfortable in his own skin, totally secure in his masculinity without having to flaunt it or play silly little macho games.

Or he's a great actor. We're all of us actors, really. Some are just better at it than others.

Kirsten didn't think she was one of them. When Stafford hauled out a large tin of processed ham, she couldn't hide her sigh of relief. Didn't even try. It was, to be fair (*Why in God's name do I care about being fair, here?*) a very expensive, top-of-the-line brand; even she could recognize that. But it was still processed ham, not raw meat that required cooking. Thank God!

Stafford made a show of pouring more wine, then began to dish up dinner, once again issuing mock apologies for the quality of their surroundings, the lack of proper tableware. It made Kirsten fume, inwardly, but she made herself even more angry because of what she desperately wanted to control—but couldn't!

She was ravenous. She hadn't eaten in nearly twenty-four hours, and it had been longer than that since she'd had a proper meal. And much as Stafford's performance fascinated and terrified her at the same time, the fact of the matter was that she was salivating like Pavlov's dog as her stomach growled along in unison. It was disgusting, maddening, embarrassing. And she couldn't stop it.

She was further angered when Stafford refused to release her hands so that she could eat like a civilized person. He insisted instead on making a great show of cutting up her food, as if she was an infant. He didn't, thankfully, also insist on feeding her . . . Kirsten was certain she couldn't have managed that, starving or not, but the psychological effect of having to eat so clumsily was wounding.

Which is just what you intended, you cunning bastard. And you've won Rose over by doing it. She's getting more sustenance from me being humiliated than from the food she's shoving down her gullet.

135

Sadistic bitch! I hope you choke on it. And I hope Stafford has you for dinner, once he's through using you.

Kirsten had no doubt in her mind that Stafford would do just exactly that. What she couldn't understand was why Rose couldn't see it, too. The woman was a highly trained nurse; she couldn't be entirely stupid. Or could she?

Kirsten got her chance to find out—or try to—when the meal was over. There was no way to avoid the inevitable effects, and within only a few minutes she found herself having to ask if she could be allowed some privacy.

"And soon, please. I don't know what spices you used, but they aren't agreeing with me."

She thought that with luck everyone would simply go outside and leave her alone, but Stafford surprised her.

"There's a dunny out back," he said. "That's an outhouse, Kirsten, if you didn't know. Rose can take you." And before Kirsten could even think, he'd reached into a pocket for some keys and was there, behind her, reaching down for the padlock that held her chain through the eyebolt.

Her first reaction was of total panic. How much had she loosened the bolt? And would it be obvious? She could only hold her breath and wait, eyes closed, praying he wouldn't notice what she'd done.

Rose exhibited great delight in leading Kirsten out behind the shack, to where a privy nestled so overgrown with bracken ferns it was almost invisible in the beam of the flashlight. Rose yanked Kirsten along like a recalcitrant dog, but at least had the decency to let her go into the sagging, decrepit outhouse alone. But she wouldn't free Kirsten's hands.

"You'll manage," she said. "You obviously did before we arrived."

Kirsten didn't reply, didn't argue. She was convinced there was no sense to that. Better to allow Rose the domination she so obviously relished. But once her business was done, she used the time spent struggling to get her jeans back up and tried to plant at least a seed of suspicion in Rose's mind.

"You do realize this guy eats people?" she asked. "Attractive young women, by choice. Which makes you probably even more tempting to him than I am. Have you thought of that?"

"If he'd wanted to eat me, he had plenty of opportunity when he was here in Tassie before," Rose replied casually. "I used to work with him, in case you weren't paying attention." If Kirsten's barb found a target, Rose was doing a good job of disguising it.

"That was then; this is now. Things are a bit different now, in case you hadn't noticed. Now he has nothing to lose, and you're going to end up being a witness, at the very least. Hasn't it occurred to you that maybe he doesn't plan on leaving any witnesses?"

"I know one he doesn't plan on leaving behind," was the abrupt reply. "Now get yourself out of there."

"Do you really mean you'd be a party to this . . . this craziness?" Kirsten said. "I find that hard to believe. Stafford is crazy as a loon, but you're not. Surely . . ."

"You don't know *what* I am," Rose said. "Now hurry up or I'll drag you back inside with your pants down around your ankles. Maybe I should, anyway . . . give him a chance to see his rump steak all laid out and ready for butchering."

And she meant it. No room for doubt. Kirsten scrambled to avoid that particular humiliation, but was, indeed, physically dragged back and into the shack with no regard shown for her inability to use her arms for balance. And then she had to endure the suspense of having Stafford reattach the chain, again the worry that he'd discover how she'd loosened off the eyebolt, the fear that he might notice but not show it, that she might simply be fooling herself with any hope of escape.

There was no chance of escape that evening, not even the hope of any chance. Nor was the next morning any more promising, but at least it brought some relief from Rose's sniping, which had continued throughout the evening until finally, thankfully, everyone else's tiredness matched that of Kirsten herself, and she was allowed to stop paying attention and just let herself escape into a sleep that was intermittently broken by the hideous, terrifying screams of Tassie devils somewhere out there in the night. Screams like those of souls in torment. Like her own soul in torment. Which it was.

CHAPTER TWENTY-ONE

Rose found that bringing Kendall to the party was easier than finding her car keys, and it took only marginally longer.

Finding the keys took her and Ian virtually the entire morning. Ian hadn't paid any attention to where he'd thrown them, and Rose's judgment was out by about twenty feet. By the time they did find the keys, tempers were hot, Rose was both hot *and* sweaty, and the relative pleasure of the breakfast Ralph Stafford had made such a production of was long gone.

Rose didn't stay for lunch.

She set out instead for St. Helens, went straight home and into the shower, then spent most of the afternoon napping. She had not slept well the night before. The shack was cold and dank, and she had not enjoyed the camp cot one bit. Rose had never liked roughing it and wasn't about to change her views. Beside her, Kirsten had been phenomenally restless—hardly surprising given her circumstances. Ian had rolled his swag outside, but he'd have needed to be fifty yards away if they were to ignore his chainsaw snoring, and he was only just outside the door.

Between Ian's snoring and the cacophony of screams from a nearby mob of devils fighting over something dead, sleep was a fleeting respite. And then there was Stafford.

Stafford was the worst element in the long, mostly sleepless night. Stafford spent his night sprawled in a folding camp chair. But his presence, his aura, seemed to fill the tiny shack like invisible, odorless smoke. Rose couldn't determine if he actually slept or not . . . but he *watched*. She knew that, could *feel* him watching despite the stygian blackness inside the shack, where it was darker within than outside. He watched both her and Kirsten, sometimes so intently that Rose imagined she could hear the wheels going round in his mind.

But in the morning, as he prepared them a breakfast of ham, eggs, even toast made in a nifty little rack over the fire Ian built, Stafford was the epitome of a gracious, even generous host. Not generous enough to help with the search for the missing keys, of course, but at least he didn't criticize the time it took.

Before Rose departed on her mission, he'd consulted with her about what must be done, and how, and when. They'd held that discussion in the privacy of her own vehicle and she'd been surprised, slightly, when he didn't jack up at her insistence on going home to shower and change before heading west to Launceston.

"It's probably best, actually, if you bring him here in the dark," Stafford had said. And after that, the rest was fairly straightforward. She rehearsed the details in her mind as she showered and laid out clothing for the mission. Nothing too showy or flashy . . . jeans, a warm wooly jumper—comfortable, casual clothes appropriate to the season.

She drove carefully, as instructed, never breaking the speed limit, so the trip took her longer than it might normally have done. At Kendall's hotel, she got lucky and was able to step aside into the gift shop as Constable John Small emerged from the lift. She noted his concerned expression, wondered briefly if he had anything to do with Kirsten's disappearance, quickly decided it didn't matter.

Stafford had prepared her with a plan for any eventuality, and in the end, it was the simplest one that was required: She knocked on the door of Kendall's suite, offered her warmest, most sincere smile when he opened the door, and held up one finger for silence.

If he's not alone, you must immediately get him alone. Tell him you simply MUST speak with him in private.

"Are you alone?" Whispered so quietly she could hardly hear the words herself.

Kendall nodded. "Rose? What—"

Explain nothing. Nothing! Just show him the ring and insist that he go with you. He'll object, perhaps, but he'll do it in the end. But you must tell him nothing!

She cut him off quickly with a gesture. "You have to come with me." And then clinched the demand by lifting Kirsten's ring from beneath her sweater and thrusting it into his field of vision. The effect was suitably dramatic, Rose thought.

"What? You? What the—?" And Kendall stammered into silence, could only stand there in the doorway, staring down at Rose, at the ring, and flapping his lips soundlessly. It was actually funny, she thought, if you could ignore the horror in his eyes. She could.

"You have to come now," she whispered, forcing urgency into her voice, feeling the urgency herself. This would be the tricky part, getting him out of the hotel, into her vehicle, and on the move.

"But . . . but . . ."

"She is all right," Rose assured him. "But she needs you. And I can't explain it to you—I have to show you. We have to go. Now."

"But—"

"Now, dammit! Can't you see I'm trying to help you, here?" She reached out, grasped his wrist. It was the first time they'd touched since well before their divorce, and the last time she'd physically touched Kendall it had been to slap him across the face as hard as she could. He'd never retaliated, never attempted

141

to defend himself. Damned sissy, that's what he was.

Nor did he this time. Rose wasn't surprised. She had plenty of experience dealing with recalcitrant patients, *crazy* patients. Kendall was, she could tell at a glance, not quite crazy . . . merely fatigued by worry and the lack of sleep, right at the end of his tether, almost at the point of physical and mental collapse.

Easy to handle. She'd done it before; Kendall was a pussy.

Under her direction, he gathered up his wallet and room key, then followed her down the hall to the lift, docile as a lamb. Every time he tried to speak, she shushed him. By about the fifth attempt, he gave up asking questions.

Until they were on the road. Even exhausted and worried as he was, Kendall could see they were headed east, out of Launceston and toward the coast. But again Rose was able to follow her instructions to tell him nothing. She just kept insisting that she didn't know anything, couldn't tell him, had to *show* him. And that Kirsten was all right.

So long as you can convince him that his lady love is unharmed . . .

"Why don't you try and get some rest?" she finally said. "I need to concentrate on my driving. This road is a proper bitch at night."

And, somewhat surprisingly, he acquiesced. The combination of stress and lack of sleep—he hadn't slept at all since noon the day before—combined to have him slumped in the seat beside her even before they reached the start of The Sideling, and he stayed asleep until Rose turned off the bitumen onto the first of the bush tracks leading to Ian's cabin, waking only briefly once before that when she paused at one point to get her bearings.

Kendall came awake abruptly to the sound and feel of the gravel road Rose had turned onto. At least his body came awake. His mind was somewhat slower. His eyes followed the headlights into the night, his body instinctively wanting to steer the car, since he was on what was, for him, the driver's side. Then he looked to his right, saw Rose's profile, and the earlier events of the evening came back to him with a rush.

"Rose?"

She ignored him, all her attention focused on keeping the SUV from drifting off the skittery surface of the deteriorating track.

"Rose! Will you please stop?"

This gained him a brief shake of her head but no vocal response. Rose had both hands firmly on the wheel, either didn't or wouldn't look at him.

"Dammit, Rose—what the hell is going on?"

"It's all right, Kendall. Your lady friend is fine. You'll be seeing her soon . . . quite soon. Just . . . trust me. You have to trust me."

Not in this lifetime.

The problem was, he couldn't do much of anything else. He didn't dare try to wrest control of the vehicle from her. Not on this rugged track . . . they'd end up in the ditch for good and certain. But actually trust her? Rose?

He tried again to get some useful information out of his ex-wife, but each attempt was met with a rebuff or an excuse. "You're distracting me." . . . "I have to concentrate." . . . "Just be patient."

Be patient? Kendall found himself clenching and unclenching his fists, fighting for control, for any semblance of sanity in all of this. The simple fact of Rose's involvement was warning enough—it had to mean trouble, couldn't mean anything but trouble. Some sort of kooky kidnapping? He wouldn't put it past Rose—wouldn't put anything past Rose. But it made no sense.

Neither did this journey through the night on a maze of bush tracks that deteriorated more and more as they progressed. This wasn't Rose's thing . . . Rose hated and loathed and detested the bush. Which meant . . . ? Kendall pondered the options as the vehicle lurched its way along, Rose fighting the wheel. Her bush driving skills were such that he found himself worrying whether they'd finish their journey at all, or end up stuck for the night in some bloody ditch!

And some bloody ditch *where?* He had only the vaguest of notions where they might be. Somewhere south of the Tasman Highway, obviously. He'd wakened at the turn, knew that much. And somewhere back in from the coast, for all that told him. Not much. During his earlier career as a journalist in Tassie, he'd seen most of it, but there were whole regions so remote that hardly anyone ever saw them.

And damned sure not Rose! No way known she'd be out here by choice. She must be hooked up with somebody, then. But who? And why?

"Not long now," Rose said, once again fighting the wheel, then stamping on the brakes as her vehicle slewed from side to side, climbing out of one set of ruts only to fall into worse ones. They skidded one way, then the next before she finally got a semblance of control.

"Jesus, Rose! I don't suppose you'd like to let me drive," Kendall said, unable to bear it any longer. Wherever they were going, wherever Kirsten was and why, he wanted to be sure of actually getting there!

Rose's response was to flash him a determined, savage grin, then a shake of her head.

"Don't be stupid."

This whole thing is stupid, dammit!

Kendall braced himself against the lurching of the vehicle and tried to focus his thoughts. It was hard. He kept trying mentally to control the vehicle, his subconscious mind creating reactions that made his right foot stamp on a brake pedal that wasn't there, his left foot reach for a clutch that also wasn't there.

Chapter Twenty-Two

Kirsten spent all of Monday watching for some opportunity—any opportunity—to escape this madness that seemed only to grow with the passage of time. But she got few such opportunities, and none of them worth anything.

The morning, during which there was the relative distraction of listening to Ian and Rose squabble as they trampled through the mud and bracken fern searching for Rose's keys, was endurable only because it also diffused Ralph Stafford's focus on Kirsten herself.

Then, once Rose was off on her mission, Stafford spent time in a huddle with Ian Boyd, the two of them involved in an occasionally heated discussion, but doing it just far enough away that she couldn't hear them properly or follow the thread of their conversation. Something about an old man and a dog, she thought. They stayed close enough, however, that Stafford could look back through the open door of the shack to check on Kirsten.

Which he did. Constantly.

She didn't dare even try to further her attempts to free the eyebolt, and wasn't sure she ought to, now, because if it became obviously loose, he would notice, and do something to thwart even that tiny chance of escape.

It's loose enough that I can force it. I'll damned well have to, somehow. Assuming I ever get the chance. Maybe when—if—Kendall gets here? But what can either of us do against a gun? And what if

Rose can't make him come with her? What if they chain him up more securely than I am? What if Stafford just shoots him? What if . . . ?

She tried to quell the second-guessing in her mind, but it was impossible. Tried to figure out what evilness lurked in Stafford's mind, but that opened too many doors to the kind of speculation she couldn't face. Didn't dare face. Not until she had to.

Whatever was going on, she realized, it was all escalating. Stafford was clearly on a roll and enjoying the sensation. Kirsten found herself wondering if he was doing drugs of some kind, or merely in a manic state that was normal, for him. His eyes were bright with the excitement and his speech, chocolate fudge voice notwithstanding, also reflected his mood.

And as Stafford's moods escalated, so did Kirsten's panic. No matter how hard she fought to control it, no matter how many deep breathing exercises, no matter how much useless plotting and scheming she did in a vain bid to find some hope of escape, it was all overshadowed by the presence of this evil man she'd thought was dead . . . who *should* be dead.

She listened as he and Ian Boyd argued, wishing she could learn from the words she couldn't quite hear, wishing they'd move further from the shack to have their discussion, wishing it could somehow give her a chance to free herself.

And do what? Run? Get a grip, Kirsten. You don't know where you are or how far it is from anywhere. You don't even know where to run. Or how to outrun a bullet. That bastard would shoot you as soon as look at you.

Then, the argument apparently over, Ian Boyd shambled over to where his battered truck was parked, clambered inside and departed in a cloud of oily fumes. Kirsten had learned nothing—except that Boyd didn't take his rifle with him.

Ralph Stafford didn't make a big show of having the rifle when he returned inside. He didn't have to; merely propping the weapon conspicuously just inside the door was sufficient. Nor did he mention it. Instead, he started in immediately on a subject obviously closer to his heart—Kendall's book.

Not a good subject for Kirsten. She'd never read the book, didn't need to, didn't want to. She knew she was in it, knew her words were there, even her thoughts, but even Teague Kendall's skill with words couldn't approach the reality of the nightmares that had plagued her both sleeping and awake.

And even they couldn't quite match the reality of here, now, being bound and chained and forced to discuss with this madman the details of his previous attempt to capture her, kill her, eat her. As he'd eaten her only sister.

But Stafford had read the book. Many times, judging from how he seemed able to quote from it almost at random. Chapter and verse, just as some learned scholars could recite from the Bible or the Koran—and equally capable of twisting, skewing meanings and interpretations to suit his own agenda.

He continued the conversation—if it could be dignified by description as such—throughout what remained of the afternoon, hardly paused for breath as he prepared a tasty evening meal. (*Credit where it's due, the man's a dab hand in the kitchen. He'd have made somebody a wonderful wife if she didn't wake up some morning to find herself being served for breakfast. My God— did I actually think that?*) Delicately sliced cold ham, tiny roast potatoes, ears of corn wrapped in tinfoil and baked in the open fireplace.

Kirsten ate. She hated to, in some ways, but common sense said she must.

Even if he's fattening me up for the slaughter, I'm no use to myself so damned hungry I can't even think. Have to rest . . . have to keep my strength up . . . have to THINK, damn it! There must be something I can do. If not now, then maybe when that slut shows up with Kendall. There has to be!

And Stafford was an experienced, skilled interrogator. He used his rich voice to probe and explore with questions, ideas, suggestions, all with the skill of a fly fisherman casting delicate lures into the rills and runnels of her imagination, her memory. He would begin with an innocuous query, flicking it out to lie floating, an enticement that could be resisted but never quite ignored. Then he would twitch it, just a little bit, and somewhere, somehow, a part of her mind would respond, couldn't help but respond despite her best intentions.

Kirsten's husband had been a violent man. Not at first, obviously, but as their brief marriage progressed it deteriorated in direct proportion to his need to control her, dominate her. First the control freak part, then the cocaine use and an escalation to physical abuse. By the time he died as a result of arguing the right-of-way with a moose on the Banff–Jasper Highway, the widow he left behind was an emotional wreck whose self-confidence was too low to be measured.

Time had worked to resolve much of that issue, but she was still hand-shy, still easily spooked by sudden movements of any man's hands. It had complicated her early involvement with Teague, but even worse—with hindsight—was the fact she had actually discussed these problems with the self-same psychologist who now took such delight in keeping her captive.

Captive? No question. But for what purpose? Kirsten could only assume he still harbored dreams of tasting her flesh. He'd alluded to it while pursuing her through the cave on Vancouver Island, seeming then to think she should feel privileged that he meant to compare the flavor of her flesh with that of her sister Emma, whom he'd already killed some time earlier.

"Did you have some part of Emma stashed away in a freezer or something? Were you planning to compare us bite by bite, or something?"

That earlier Kirsten would never have dared to ask, never

149

have dared to even think it. But Kirsten had survived this man once, and it had made her stronger . . . far stronger than she wanted him to know. Stronger than she herself knew, Kirsten sometimes suspected. When she bothered to think of it at all, which wasn't often. The awed curiosity of her Mole Creek caving group had made her think of it, though. Now Stafford's subtle trolling did so, too.

"I wish I had," he replied. A quick reply, one he hadn't had to formulate. "But of course I didn't know when Emma and I were . . . together, that you could become . . . available, much less that I would have such a fortuitous opportunity to meet you." And now Stafford paused for a moment, his eyes flicking downward to the copy of Kendall's book he'd been thumbing through as they spoke. And when he spoke again, there was a different quality to his voice, somehow.

"By the time you and I had our little adventure in *your* accursed cave, Emma was, unfortunately, merely a delicious memory. I think. My goodness, Kirsten—I truly can't remember. Except the delicious part, of course." And he licked his lips, not suggestively but more as some unconscious gesture not aimed at Kirsten but a genuine residue of a fond memory.

"Would it have made any difference? No, I suppose not." He asked the question, answered it himself, not even bothering to look up from the book. "What I had in mind at the time, if memory serves, was sampling you and *Kendall* for comparison, actually. Of course, I didn't realize then that you two hadn't been . . . intimate, yet. So it really wouldn't have worked very well as an experiment, would it, Kirsten?"

Stafford clearly expected a reply. Kirsten couldn't think of one that would satisfy either her captor or anything even approaching logic and common sense. She half expected some show of anger, perhaps disappointment. But not . . .

"And you still haven't been intimate, have you? Why is that, I wonder?"

No . . . no . . . no! Do NOT let yourself be dragged into this one. NOT!

Outside in the darkened wilderness, not all that far away, either, or so it seemed, a Tassie devil screamed, the challenge echoed by another devil screeching in reply, their guttural, squabbling cries piercing the night.

And Stafford, a cunning, more sophisticated, more truly evil devil than any of those outside, abruptly changed the subject. In the blink of an eye, he moved the conversation halfway around the world and into a totally different realm of food discussion.

"Did you know that the Tasmanian devil is considered an absolute world-class scavenger?" he asked. "World class! Right up there with the hyena and the vultures. A devil can consume nearly half his own body weight in less than half an hour, and once a mob of devils get onto a carcass they eat it all . . . hide, hooves, fur or feathers, the bones—everything! Nature's vacuum cleaners."

He sighed. "Absolutely amazing creatures. So totally efficient, so perfectly adapted to their role in nature. And they were hunted like vermin for more than a hundred years before somebody finally realized how much *good* they were doing, especially for the very sheep farmers who were trying to obliterate them. Without the devils to keep the carrion down, it's estimated early graziers would have lost incredible numbers of their flocks to fly-strike, for instance.

"But they are ugly, of course. And so eerily, beautifully noisy at what they do. Two devils feeding together sound like a dozen; a dozen sound like hell itself must."

"So is that your plan for me—to feed me to the devils?" The words were out even as she thought them, and once said could not be retracted. So she plunged on, reckless with an anger that stirred in her belly, souring the taste of that excellent dinner. "Too bad we didn't have them on Vancouver Island," she said with a sneer. "They might have done a better job on you than the cougar did."

Kirsten closed her eyes briefly, fearing for an instant that she'd gone too far, but Stafford only laughed.

"Goodness, Kirsten. I didn't realize you were quite so fierce. Now please, settle down . . . relax. I have no such plans for you. Nor for your boyfriend Kendall, who should be arriving fairly soon, by the way."

And you lie in your teeth, you bastard!

Again he switched tack, back to the Tassie devils he so admired, leaving her to wonder whether she was being lied to for some specific reason or merely . . . accommodated, pacified. Not that it mattered.

"The early settlers in Tasmania actually used to eat the beasts," Stafford mused. "Hard to imagine, but I suppose times were . . . quite different back then. Some reports compared them to veal, although I've never thought so. I must remember to ask Ian Boyd when he returns what he thinks of that. He'll know, I suspect. Although . . . maybe not. A wombat or platypus is one thing, but even Ian might draw the line at eating a devil."

The implication was too obvious. Stafford was losing his subtlety, positively smacking her in the face with the fact that *he* had eaten a Tassie devil at some time or another. And liked it.

Kirsten wanted to scream. Would have screamed, had she thought it would do her any good. She was strung tighter than a guitar string, close to snapping if she wasn't careful, and she knew that too. The problem was, so did Stafford, damn him!

"I could open some wine," he suggested. "It bothers me to see you so tense, Kirsten. Not good for you . . . not at all."

"You could let me go. That would resolve my tension problems."

He smiled, but Kirsten noticed the smile never reached his eyes. "True," he said. "But it would cause tension problems for me. So I'm afraid we'll have to keep that situation as it is, at least until Rose arrives with Kendall. Which should be soon, I'd expect. I just hope she doesn't get herself lost trying to find this place in the dark. I don't think Rose is much of an outdoors person, do you?"

"I try not to think of her at all." Honest answer; it came easily to her lips.

"Because she was married to Kendall? I would have thought you far too mature to let a little thing like that bother you. You're actually quite a stable individual, Kirsten. Far more so than Rose, who is extremely juvenile in many ways. She is nowhere near as . . . complex an individual as you."

She's a fool to trust you . . . I know that much.

But Kirsten didn't say it. Never had the chance. And Stafford wasn't listening in any event; his attention, she could see, was now focused outside the shack, into the night where the faint sounds of an approaching vehicle grew slowly but steadily more audible.

"Speak of the devil," he said. And smirked. "I expect that'll be Rose now, although I suppose it's possible Ian might have accomplished his assignment more quickly than I anticipated. Doesn't matter, really."

Stafford reached into one of the containers that crowded the folding table he'd set up and brought out a syringe and a small bottle of some clear liquid. His fingers nimble from long practice, he carefully drew off a measured amount of the liquid, put the vial away again, and rose from his seat.

"I'll just go and welcome our new arrivals, shall I?" And, rifle in one hand and syringe in the other, he was out the door, which he left wide open behind him. He stepped out into the glare of the headlights when the vehicle lurched to a halt outside.

Kirsten watched as, first, Stafford was silhouetted by the headlights, then, once the headlights were extinguished, backlit only by the glow from the light inside the shack. She saw Rose step from the driver's side, and only realized she was holding her breath when it soughed out of her in a whoosh at the sight of Kendall emerging from the other side of the vehicle.

"Kendall—how lovely to see you again," she heard Stafford say as he gestured with the rifle and Kendall halted in midstride. "You know Rose, of course, and I expect you'll be happy to know that Kirsten's here, too."

She saw the confusion on Kendall's face, then—frighteningly, horribly—the recognition of the distinctive voice. The disbelief, the dumbstruck, jaw-dropping astonishment, and then the narrowing of her true love's eyes as he recognized the insane truth and turned his eyes away from Stafford and peered straight at the cabin's open door, straight at her.

And she saw Rose's expression, too. One of gloating self-satisfaction that changed only slightly as Stafford gestured her over and handed her the syringe. "If you'd do the honors, please, Rose," he said, and his protégé practically glowed with her desire to assist.

Rose had years of experience administering sedatives to patients far more difficult to handle than Kendall, who was still in the shock of trying to sort out what was happening. Kirsten could only watch in stunned silence as Rose took the syringe, spun back to her ex-husband, and, with a look Kirsten could only think of as pure, savage joy, plunged the needle into his upper arm before he even knew what she was doing.

Kendall flinched, turned long enough to glare at Rose, then stepped forward, ignoring the threat of Stafford and the rifle. "Kirsten?" he called. Then again, louder. He managed one step, then another, before he began to sag. A few more steps before slumping to his knees. It was only Stafford's strong grip that saved him from landing face-first in the mud.

Kirsten couldn't stop her mind flashing back more than a year, when there, in the darkness of her cave, Stafford had done almost the identical thing—stepped forward to assist Kendall . . . and then flung him into the pit of knee-deep, icy water. So quickly that Kendall never had the slightest chance to resist.

To Kirsten, it had been like watching a well-rehearsed routine, and this situation had a similar flavor. Stafford hands off the syringe, Rose spins to administer the sedative, then back to be in position when Stafford hands her the rifle as he catches the victim in mid-fall. Smooth as silk, deadly in its simplicity and unexpectedness.

Do they practice this sort of maneuver in mental hospitals? Hold regular little "stick it to the patient" classes? It wouldn't surprise me, but then nothing this pair does should surprise me much. Stafford's crazy and she's insane. Must be.

So she never even got to speak to Kendall before Stafford lifted him and carried him into the cabin. Tenderly, gently, laid him on the camp cot where Rose had slept the previous night. Whereupon Kirsten was blatantly, almost brusquely ignored as Stafford took the rifle from Rose and propped it back in place, then went outside to his own vehicle, where he fumbled around for a few moments. When he returned, it was with a handful of the same electrical cable ties that held her own wrists and a length of chain just like the one around her waist. Kendall's hands were bound, the chain closed snugly around his waist and held with a cable tie.

Then Stafford picked up the other end of the chain, fumbled in a pocket for a set of keys, and knelt to where the eyebolt was screwed into the wall at floor level. The eyebolt she had so slowly, agonizingly loosened. Loosened . . . how much? Too much? Kirsten held her breath, tried not to watch, couldn't manage that, so she tried to conceal her dismay from Rose, who she desperately hoped was too busy gloating to notice that dismay.

Please, please, please don't twist on it, don't yank at it.

She was able to force her attention elsewhere, didn't dare to say a word, lest Rose notice her concern and speak out. Rose knew Kirsten had been working with the sections of disassembled cot frame, surely was bright enough to realize what Kirsten had been trying to do. But Rose's attention had switched to Kendall again, Kirsten saw, and again there was that gloating smirk on the woman's lips.

Then Stafford grunted, straightened up, and Kirsten felt the tension go out of her like a flood.

"I fear you've lost your bed for the night, Rose," he said with a gracious, mine-host smile. "Not to worry; we'll find somewhere for you to cool your heels. Why don't we go outside and discuss that . . . leave these two to get reacquainted?"

Then he paused, cocked his head thoughtfully, his gaze flitting between the two women. "But first, I think it's only fair that you give Kirsten back her ring," he said, smiling hugely, the inference being that he'd caught Rose out, somehow.

Which might have been the case. Rose shot him a scurrilous glance as he reached out to lift the ring and its chain from Rose's neck, then step over to replace it around Kirsten's.

Thank you . . . I think. But she didn't say it out loud. Couldn't.

He gallantly waved Rose out through the door ahead of him, stepped through behind her, then paused and looked back, first at Kirsten, then at the rifle propped against the wall. She could see him measuring with his eyes, calculating the risk. Kirsten measured too, in her mind, knew she couldn't reach the rifle no matter how hard she tried. Unless she could free the eyebolt. Could she even do it? She had yet to try and unscrew the damned thing using only her hands and there would be no time to dismantle the camp cot. Would she have time? If Stafford caught her at it, he'd find a more secure way to hold her . . . to hold both of them.

Stafford looked from Kirsten to the rifle, then back again. Then he smiled and followed Rose. But he took the weapon with him, so it didn't matter that he was gone for what seemed a surprisingly long time. With Kendall, also chained to the eyebolt, unconscious, it wasn't worth even trying to free them from the wall. What could she do—carry him?

And Stafford knew that, the bastard. Knew she wouldn't try to escape without Kendall, thus confining her effectively even if she wasn't bound and chained.

She heard a vehicle start up, listened as it slowly moved away. Then, to her utter surprise, heard the sound of a second engine firing up, that one, too, rumbling away over the rutted track outside.

Dammit! Are they both going? Maybe I should try and get us loose. I can't do anything with Kendall, but I could get a weapon of some kind, surely. There are knives everywhere if I could just reach one. Everything would be a lot easier if my hands were free.

Which brought her to a different thought pattern. They hadn't searched Kendall, hadn't emptied his pockets. Didn't he always carry a pocket knife? A tiny one, a mini Swiss Army knife on his keychain? Kirsten turned swiftly and struggled to investigate the possibility. Not an easy task with both hands bound so tightly together . . . all she could do was pat him down clumsily. Finding nothing but loose change in one front pocket and nothing at all in the other. Then remembering, with the clarity of hindsight, his complaints before they'd even left Canada about the idiotic airline rules that prohibited anything sharp, even the smallest of pocket knives.

Typical. They worry about a man having something to clean his fingernails or slice open a letter, but they can't stop a fiend like

Stafford from traveling halfway around the world.

She could only sigh with the frustration of it all and kneel there beside Kendall, trying not to dissolve into hysteria as she looked into his calm, sleeping face.

My poor, innocent love. Will we both be dead before we get our shit together and make some sense of our lives? I'm sorry, Kendall . . . truly I am.

She stared at Kendall for what seemed hours, occasionally reaching out with her clumsy, bound hands to stroke his cheek, to touch at his lips. He never moved, showed no sign whatsoever of coming out of the chemical-induced sleep.

Then the sound of vehicle doors slamming filtered through, and she realized that Stafford hadn't actually *left,* but was apparently shifting the vehicles around out there for some purpose or another. One of them, anyway; she couldn't hear the other one at all anymore. Then everything went quiet again, and stayed that way for another five or ten minutes. Not long enough to *do* anything, to actually accomplish anything useful to them in their dilemma, just long enough for Kirsten's spirits once again to flag.

And then suddenly, he was there. Stafford, no rifle in his hands now, stepped through the doorway with a broad, cheerful smile on his lips, his voice rich with satisfaction when he spoke.

"Right. That's all taken care of," he said, as if sharing some momentous news. "And now it's bedtime. Do you need to go outside, Kirsten, because now's the time to ask?" Even as he spoke, he was reaching the keys that would unshackle her from the wall.

And risk you finding out how loose that eyebolt might be . . . had damned well better be? No thanks. Any chance is better than none at all.

"I'll just use the bucket, if you don't mind giving me some privacy," she replied.

Stafford merely shrugged and opened the door to return outside. "Holler when you're done," he said, obviously driven by thoughts of something he considered far more interesting than Kirsten's primitive toilet arrangements.

When he returned, Stafford spent a few minutes sorting and resorting the various foodstuffs he'd brought, shifting things from one container to another, reading labels.

"I might try flapjacks in the morning," he said. "It's been a long time since I did flapjacks. Or I could do omelets . . . we have eggs and plenty of ham." Then he shrugged, a strange, rather perky little gesture, Kirsten thought.

"Plenty of time to think on it tomorrow, I guess. There'll only be the three of us to feed unless Ian surprises me by arriving early with his contributions. Rose won't be with us for breakfast, of course, but she'll be here for dinner."

CHAPTER TWENTY-THREE

The biggest of the Tasmanian devils had once been a giant among his kind, but he was old now, and had lost conditioning. He now weighed only about eleven pounds, but in his prime he'd weighed nearly twenty, and he was still taller than the others who were also moving through the dense forest around him. He was scarred all around his graying muzzle, the scars reminders of mating battles over many seasons. And scarred even worse in the thinning fur around his rump. Those scars were from ruckuses over food . . . not exactly battles, but the jostling for position that devils engaged in when there wasn't space for all to eat comfortably. Instinct provided a marginal protection from such constant strife—a devil's usual practice was to back into the fray, using its rump to shove an opponent away from the goodies. Bites nonetheless resulted, but a devil's rump is far, far tougher than its nose.

And a devil needs its nose. This old stager had first smelled the carrion from more than a mile away as the slow night breeze carried the scent through the dense temperate coastal forest with its pockets of genuine rainforest hidden away like jewels.

Carrion, but fresh carrion. The scent told him that. It held the hot, coppery taste of blood in it, the delicate odors of entrails already cooling, already beginning to decay. The old devil yawned, stretched, shrugging powerful shoulders as he did so. Then he moved out of his den in a hollow beneath a windblown forest giant and began to amble his way down along the ridge.

Around him, others of his kind also drifted through the night, following their noses, their instinct to scavenge, their hunger. Black pelts with occasional splotches of white flowed in and out of the moon-shadow beneath the hulking eucalypts as the devils congregated, eventually, around the gut pile that still steamed beneath the overhanging branch of a gigantic blue gum.

The first arrival snuffled, searching the air for danger, although Tasmanian devils have no significant natural enemies. Protected by law for more than fifty years, they are seldom if ever shot at, nor trapped. Their biggest threat to survival comes from within . . . from the natural instinct to scavenge. It takes them out onto roads and highways after road-kill, and lures them to share that fate.

But here there was no road with speeding trucks and blinding headlights. There was a track, to be sure, but it was merely two uneven ruts chewed into the forest floor, and while those ruts smelled of petrol and oil and rubber, they flagged no obvious danger, no threat. Not far away, but silent, totally nonthreatening, a vehicle slept beneath a tall stringy bark. The devils didn't fear it, nor were they concerned about the person inside.

Their attention was focused entirely on the coils of entrails there before them, the heart, lungs, liver. Steaming . . . not yet cooled. First one devil, then another rollicked in and bent to the feast, fearsomely strong jaws agape but not really needed to crush this soft food. There were only three there, in the beginning, but another soon arrived, then two more. It was enough to crowd the spoils, and soon the night was rent with the devils' piercing, eerie screams and growls. There was pushing and shoving and snarling and caterwauling.

When the oldest devil swaggered in, there was a momentary hiatus, but it was brief. He shouldered his way to the feast, screaming his defiance and superiority over the smaller, younger animals. Who backed off at first, at least a little, then returned to make their own claims for dominance and food.

Sensitive noses, too, had detected new scents, potentially more lucrative ones, and piggy little eyes stared up in the moon's pale glow to consider the carcass suspended above them. Far out of reach, it was. Pale in the moonlight, cooling quickly, no longer dripping anything tasty onto the ground where they squabbled over its insides. Hardly worth even considering. One of the youngest devils made a clumsy, half-hearted effort to climb the tall blue gum, but adult devils climb seldom and not well. He barely got above his own height before slumping down and rejoining the feast.

When the headlights of the vehicle came on, they squinted momentarily, but without fear. Most of their feast had been consumed, now. Final helpings were of more significant consideration than harmless lights. Already the stronger, wiser devils were scurrying away with whatever remnants of the gut pile they could carry.

When the vehicle lights went off again a few minutes later, only the oldest devil remained and he, too, belly filled for another day, was losing interest even in the carcass strung high in the tree above. He couldn't reach it, couldn't climb to it, but he wasn't hungry anymore either. For tonight.

CHAPTER TWENTY-FOUR

Charlie's dinner date began well enough, considering that he was distracted right from the start by something but didn't quite know what it was. Something he'd seen, or heard, something that had lodged in his mind and was demanding to be processed.

It annoyed him out of all proportion, because Charlie had his own agenda for the evening and didn't need to be niggled and distracted. He had enough to worry about right there on the personal front. Right there in front of him, directly across the tidy expanse of the dining room in Linda McKay's bed-and-breakfast establishment. In the form of Linda McKay herself, to be precise.

Linda was a tidy, attractive blonde, a bit younger than Charlie but not too much younger. An intelligent, mature, and desirable woman. Highly desirable. A woman whom Charlie thought just might be as attracted to him as he was to her. A woman he was more than half convinced he wanted permanently in his life. A relationship, much as he loathed and hated and detested the word and all its implications.

Thus far, their relationship had been limited to occasions that barely even qualified as dates—a couple of drives in the country, two Monday night meals . . . counter meals at local pubs, coffee together when they happened to meet in the main street and both had a few minutes to spare. Linda was a busy woman with a busy life. She ran her bed-and-breakfast profes-

163

sionally, competently, and with a serious eye to detail. The place was, after all, her home as well as her business. And it kept her very busy indeed, to the point where about the only nights she could reasonably be sure of any free time were Mondays, and sometimes not even then in a busy tourist season.

Linda was a police widow; she knew and understood the complications of being married to a cop. Which was the good part. The bad part was that Linda's husband had been a bad cop, a bent cop, a narcotics officer poisoned by the very substances he was charged with policing. The worst part was that Charlie had been a major, if behind the scenes, personage in the sting that eventually caught Alan McKay and then, to everyone's gratification, saw him die of a heart attack even before charges could be laid. Which meant no huge publicity issues, no media feeding frenzy, no political bun fight in which the state police got kicked from pillar to post with no visible means of defense.

McKay's situation was no secret within the police community, and Charlie was all too aware that Linda would have known . . . *must* have known her husband was bent, but as to his own involvement . . . ? Charlie was reasonably certain Linda didn't know that, knew he would eventually have to tell her, didn't know how to do it, or when, or even if he truly, logically, should.

What Charlie did know was that he should never—could never—tell Linda that her husband had died cursing Charlie to hell and back, even accusing Charlie of setting him up because Charlie was infatuated with Linda. And that he would *have* to tell her. Tonight. Because he couldn't *not* tell her, not if their fragile situation was to have a chance of thriving.

At the time of the accusations, Charlie had only ever met Linda once. At a police function in Launceston several years earlier. And had spoken no more than five words to her. Five words—no more.

But—infatuated? The truth of that was never in doubt . . . then, or now. Charlie had taken one look at Linda McKay, upon being introduced to her all those years ago. And had been attracted, no doubt of that. Had said, "A pleasure to meet you," listened to her polite response in a husky, contralto voice that somehow reached out and *touched* him. And had become infatuated, done like a dinner, as they say.

Alan McKay's accusations, nonetheless, were nonsense. Charlie hadn't seen or spoken to Linda after that initial meeting until long after McKay's death, and Linda's move to St. Helens. Which didn't explain why he somehow felt strangely guilty when he thought about those fateful words, uttered as Charlie was leaving McKay in custody, less than an hour before the man's heart attack and death.

Others had heard the accusations. Other policemen, most of them more directly involved with McKay than they were with Charlie. They were stationed in Launceston, as McKay had been, while Charlie, even then, had opted for the existence of a country cop. He didn't do politics well, least of all office politics.

Still, he'd wondered then as he did now—had one of them told Linda? Or told his wife and *she* had told Linda? It was a worry, despite his own moral certainty that he'd done the right thing. Charlie was a thoroughly decent man. He had his faults and they were legion, but he knew right from wrong and always at least *tried* to do the right thing.

He'd immediately put his unexpected lust and infatuation away in an emotional bottom drawer. And left it there, although he was honest enough to admit he'd taken it out occasionally over the years, dusted it off, fantasized a little, even. And then returned it to the drawer, slammed the drawer. Done the right thing, dammit!

And all these years later, he wasn't much better at subterfuge and subtlety, at least in his personal life, which was why he'd decided that tonight, this very night and pretty damned soon, too, he would bring the whole sordid mess out in the open. The issue was one of *when*. He'd already lost the first opportunity, when Linda had handed him a goblet filled with the wine he'd bought earlier in the day.

Then she'd lifted her own glass in a silent toast, and her eyes had glistened with mischief as she smiled and looked at him over the rim of her own goblet. And he had been dumbstruck, had wanted only to drown in those eyes, never to return again to the real world. It was like being fifteen again, suffering from that first adolescent crush.

Charlie sat down at the dinner table, followed Linda with calf-eyed attention as she brought in the platters of potato, vegetables, finally the crown roast of pork with its decorative little doily caps on the ends of the ribs. He rose, politely, when it became obvious she was about to seat herself, rushed around the table to hold her chair. Once again basked in the warmth of her smile as he returned to his own seat.

And then his cell phone—which he thought he'd turned off, given the circumstances—chirped like a demented sparrow that promptly shat all over everything.

Chapter Twenty-Five

The chief fingerprint techie in Hobart was not a happy camper. She'd had a rough weekend, a pig of a Monday already, and she'd hoped to knock off a bit early. Quite a bit early. Also, her period was due and she knew, usually to her later regret, that she could give PMS a whole new definition if she wasn't careful. So did her coworkers, which is why the one who brought in the package from Launceston merely dropped it on the desk and fled.

Her first inclination was to leave it for the next morning. There was no PDQ or ASAP notice attached, nothing except a scrawled note indicating that the sergeant at St. Helens had called about it earlier in the day. Which stirred her curiosity. Why would Charlie Banes be interested in fingerprints obtained from a knife found at Mole Creek?

Seven fingerprints, to be exact. Thumb and first three fingers of a right hand, and thumb and forefinger from the left. Exactly what you'd expect from somebody opening a stock knife in the usual way. Two of the prints ever-so-slightly smudged, but the rest as clear as the proverbial bell. Good lifts—somebody had taken the proper care to do it right.

A little curiosity can be a dangerous thing. Almost before she realized it herself, the techie was started on the process that would see the prints run through the scanner for checking by the national computerized data bank.

So much for an early day of it.

Other work came in to keep her busy during the wait, but she was bored and restless and busily clock-watching when the results finally arrived. The techie looked at them, slowly digested the information that accompanied the matches—perfect matches. No mistake!—then took a deep breath before reading it all again.

This can't be happening. It is not, NOT possible. Somebody's having a lend of me, here . . . this is all some sort of practical joke. It has to be! And it is not, Not, NOT funny!

Whereupon the PMS crankiness evolved first to a flurry of mind-fucking, then became a raging storm and whirled into a tornado before it took on a life of its own and upgraded to a full-scale cyclone of truly astonishing proportions. E-mails were sent, received, replied to. Phone lines sizzled and snapped and crackled with the intensity. Harsh words were exchanged as the storm raged up the Tassie police food chain like a new strain of botulism.

And then down again . . . ending with Sergeant Charlie Banes of the St. Helens police station. Charlie Banes, wine goblet in hand, lust in his heart and an emotional dilemma to deal with. Charlie Banes, who picked up his cell phone to hear his commanding officer's angry, impatient, unhappy voice.

"Have I disturbed you at something important, Charlie? I certainly hope so, because I've just had *my* evening ruined on your behalf."

"I . . . can you hang on a tick, Sir?" Charlie didn't wait for a reply. He shot an apologetic glance at Linda and another toward the meal that he knew instinctively would surely be cold before he got back to it. If he got back to it.

Linda clearly knew the drill. She opened the sliding glass door to the balcony, waved Charlie through, then shut the door behind him to provide privacy.

"What the hell are you and John Small playing at, Charlie?"

No preamble, no conventional exchange of greetings—just straight for the jugular.

"I'm not sure I know what you mean, Sir," Charlie replied, brain wide awake now and whirling as he tried to figure out how he and the cowboy constable could be linked in anything at all.

"You don't *know?*" The voice was scathing, bitter. "Then let me refresh your memory, Sergeant. Did you not insist that Small arrange to have some fingerprints sent to the forensics lab in Hobart? Fingerprints from a knife that was *found* in some bloody cave or another? Not from any crime scene. Not from anything that involved a crime or even looked like a crime scene. And did you not also personally request a hurry-up from Hobart on the identification of those prints?"

Bugger-bugger! But why such a bloody great flap about it?

"I didn't actually ask for a hurry-up, Sir. I merely asked to be kept in the loop," Charlie replied. "It . . . sort of involves this woman who's apparently been abducted. Or at least I thought it might, Sir. Seemed proper strange that the knife would be found right where she was on a caving trip, and then have her abducted . . . apparently abducted . . . only a few hours later."

"By a dead man?" Who couldn't have been deader, flatter, more obviously road kill than the voice that uttered those four words. And Charlie's career with it, perhaps. A funereal tone, the tone that in police circles almost inevitably preceded a demotion, if not worse.

Charlie cringed, inwardly, but tried to keep that out of his voice. "Dead, Sir? I don't think I understand."

"Well I do, Sergeant. I understand that the fingerprint technician in Hobart is right royally pissed off as a result of you and that cowboy Small playing silly buggers—sending her a dead man's fingerprints to examine. As if they aren't busy enough in the forensics lab. As if the woman doesn't have enough to do—

except raise a ruckus that went right to the upper echelons of the department, Sergeant. And you know what that means, don't you?"

Indeed Charlie did. It meant his superior was even more royally pissed than the fingerprint techie, having been shat upon from dizzying heights—hence this unloading of the cumulative shit storm at he and Constable John Small. But why?

"I want an apology to the technician in Hobart. Personally, first thing tomorrow morning. By telephone . . . none of this email shit. In person would be even better, but I do recognize the time factors involved in that. And I want a written report on the whole matter. In detail! Is that clear?"

"Yes Sir, except that—"

"Except nothing! So far all I can see is that our entire department's been suckered into some sort of bizarre publicity stunt and you and John Small are playing games. Alleged abductions are one thing, Sergeant, but fingerprints from a dead man are something else again."

"But—"

"Just do it!"

The phone went silent and Charlie was left no wiser than before. He snapped his phone closed, returned inside, and sat down again at the table, where he was able to stare at the plate in front of him, but couldn't remember for the life of him whether he—or Linda—was expected to carve the cooling crown roast of pork that graced the center of the dining room table.

"Bad?" Linda's voice was soft, unobtrusive. Her demeanor showed no impatience, merely a knowledgeable and genuine concern. She'd been married to a cop, knew how suddenly things could come up to change one's plans.

"I don't know," Charlie replied. "It makes no sense at all. Am I supposed to carve this roast?"

Her smile warmed up the room. "Are you safe with a carving

knife when you're this distracted? I gather whatever's up doesn't mean you have to dash off without eating. That's a bonus."

"I don't know what it means," he said, repeating himself, speaking to himself as much as answering her question. "Okay . . . I'll carve."

He picked up the carving utensils, reached out to draw the platter over to his side of the table, then nearly dropped it when his cell phone chirped again. Louder, this time . . . the dreaded sparrow now poised to dump another, bigger, load. Or maybe that was only his imagination.

"Now," he said, nodding sagely at Linda as if about to impart some great wisdom, something truly profound. He managed to get the platter safely down again, then handed Linda the carving utensils. "Now it will be bad."

It was Constable John Small's petulant, whiny voice, which was bad enough.

Then it got worse.

Chapter Twenty-Six

"What's going on with your little mate Kendall?" Small asked, but didn't wait for a reply before whining on, his voice screeching in Charlie's ear like fingernails on a blackboard.

Linda half-rose, one arm waving toward the balcony door, but Charlie waved aside the gesture with a grimace he intended to have been a smile. He planted himself firmly in his chair and stared at the abandoned, cooling pork roast while Small's voice whined in his ear.

"I tried to warn you it was all some sort of publicity stunt. Well now we've got the proof, I reckon. Fingerprints from a dead man? Jeeesus! We're in the shit over this one, Charlie. They're talking about sending me to Burnie, for God's sake. Burnie! Nothing but endless domestics and mind-numbing paperwork guaranteed to turn your brains to tapioca, Charlie . . . you know that. And once you're there, they never let you go. There's fifty guys ahead of you on the transfer list, and you'd have to kill them to get out."

"Settle, damn it. The way you're rabbiting on, I think your brain's already tapioca." Time enough later to commiserate. Charlie did, indeed, understand John Small's concerns. Small was a country copper—having been posted to Launceston must have been tough on him. But Burnie? Charlie had known good, experienced career cops to go white and trembling just at the thought of being transferred to the Burnie city watch. From a policing point of view, the small city on Tasmania's northern coast was boredom personified. And once there . . .

Charlie shuddered, forced the thought from his mind. Small's whine droned on in complaint until Charlie once again called for calm, reason, *answers!*

"I've just had my rocket from the brass too," he said. "Which told me precisely two-thirds of five-eighths of sweet fuck all. Typical, but I expect better from you, John. What's the story on these damned fingerprints and why is everybody so stirred up about them?"

"They didn't tell you?"

Charlie could only sigh heavily, grit his teeth and throw a helpless glance across the table at Linda, who was unashamedly eavesdropping. Maybe *she* could make some sense out of this, Charlie thought.

"All I got was some blather about the prints belonging to some bloke who's dead," he said, keeping his voice level, hiding his frustration, fighting to keep his temper.

"Not just *some bloke.*" John Small's voice rose a full octave as he added in a heaping tablespoon of smugness, or so Charlie imagined. "That Stafford bloke—the *Specialist* in your mate Kendall's book? That's whose fingerprints they were."

Kendall's book—and Charlie's storehouse of nightmares. Charlie's mind flashed to the abandoned mineshaft on Blue Tier, the charnel house where Stafford had disposed of the pieces of his dismembered victims.

"But he's dead!" The words emerged before Charlie realized that he'd just voiced the crux of the problem. *Talk about stating the obvious!* The fingerprints on a knife found only days before were those of a man who'd been dead for more than a year.

"Dead or not, it was *his* prints on the knife that Mole Creek mob *said* they *found.* The prints *you* insisted I send in for testing. Somebody's playing silly buggers, Charlie. And if I catch up with them, they'll wish they hadn't. That mob from Mole

Creek are mixed up in this somehow, but I'm damned if I can figure out how. I'd have sworn they were fair-dinkum about their part of it. Bloody oath, Charlie—Burnie? It's bad enough being posted to the Launceston watch, for God's sake."

"Put Kendall on the phone." Charlie wanted to reach through cyberspace and throttle away Small's whine.

"Can't. He's gone. While I was in getting fitted for a new asshole, your little mate did a runner on us, Charlie. Not surprising, now that we know this whole thing's some sort of publicity stunt."

"What do you mean he did a runner? And how do you know? Maybe he got a ransom demand of some kind. Maybe . . ." Charlie's mind whirled, trying to make sense of it all. He stared fixedly at the pork roast in front of him, trying to focus. But all he saw was the rotted remains that had emerged from Stafford's grotesque disposal bin, and he floundered up from the table, choking back sickness.

"He's scarpered, Charlie. I've already talked to the desk, and he left not five minutes after I was called away." Charlie heard the words as he rushed out through the balcony doors.

"Wait!" Charlie gasped, leaned over the balcony rail, then found he had nothing to be sick *with*, save for the one glass of wine he'd consumed. He gulped, swallowed a few times, then— thankfully—found his equilibrium returning. Still, he gripped the balcony rail tightly with one hand as he continued the discussion.

"He left? But he was supposed to be waiting for a ransom demand. Did you find out if he left alone, or—?"

"Way ahead of you. I asked at the desk, then I double-checked on the security tapes. He left with some woman. And it wasn't under duress, either, he was twice her size and she was practically running to keep up with him, in some shots."

"And you're sure it wasn't Kirsten?"

"Short, with long dark hair, about the same age as Kendall's bird, but definitely not her. Really good-looking Sheila, though . . . great figure, built like a brick shithouse. They drove off in what must have been her vehicle, a white or light-colored SUV. Honda, I think."

Rose! I'd bet my soul on it. But why?

"They'll be pulling you off this, then, I expect," Charlie said. "But if they don't, nose around and see what else you can find out. This is no publicity stunt—I'd stake my career on that. There's something totally amiss, John, and I fear it'll be serious."

"Okay. And you promise you'll speak up for me, Charlie? I mean . . . Burnie? Jeeeezuz!"

"The way this is shaping up, you mightn't be there alone if it all falls apart in a screaming heap, but yes, I'll speak up for you. For both of us, I reckon."

Charlie hung up, then returned inside and sat down again, unspeakably grateful to find that Linda had carved the roast herself, and the neat slices were tidily interspersed with potatoes, green beans and baked carrots. Just normal food, arranged to titillate his taste buds, not torment his imagination. He sighed.

"I'm sorry about . . . that," he said. "I just . . ." There were no words to describe what he'd felt, or at least none that belonged at the dinner table. All he could do as he stared across the table at his hostess was to try and look properly abashed.

"It isn't a problem, Charlie," said Linda. "Now please, try to get some of this tucker inside you, where it belongs." She paused, gathered succulent pork and bits of potato onto her fork, forcing Charlie to follow suit. One forkful followed another as she guided him through the dining process in a delicate, unobtrusive but deliberate dance.

Charlie felt about ten years old, being instructed by Mum to eat all his veggies or forfeit dessert. Only this experience, for some reason, felt . . . more comfortable. So much so, that he opened up while enjoying his lemon meringue pie dessert and explained to Linda why the whole issue of Kirsten's abduction had his mind in such a twist.

"And now this fingerprint thing! Bloody oath, Linda—think on it. If this abduction thing is some sort of prank or publicity stunt—and I damned well don't think it is; Teague's not the sort to play silly buggers like that—then how the hell could anyone manage that fingerprint trick? It's beyond me."

"Maybe it isn't a trick. Did that occur to you?"

"Well, it has to be some sort of scam. The bugger's been dead for more than a year."

Charlie's lovely hostess thought for a moment, then strode over to a bookcase, where she consulted a well-thumbed copy of *Bartlett's Familiar Quotations.* After a minute, she returned and placed the tome open in front of Charlie, one lacquered fingernail guiding his eyes to the quote she obviously wanted him to read.

Charlie would have preferred to concentrate on the exotic scent of her, the quickening stir he felt from her leaning over his shoulder. Then he looked at the quote, more than a century old and originating halfway around the world, and something *pinged* in his subconscious. It *pinged* and *pinged* and kept right on pinging as Linda put the research book back on the shelf and returned to her place across the table from Charlie.

"*When you have eliminated the impossible, whatever remains, no matter how improbable, must be the truth:* Sir Arthur Conan Doyle: The Sign of Four. 1890."

"It's impossible, never mind improbable," he sighed. "It can't be possible."

Linda raised an eyebrow, but said nothing for a moment. And when she did speak, it was to change the subject entirely.

"I've been meaning to mention this, Charlie," she said, and her tone might have sounded ominous but for a lightness, a sort of buoyant tone Charlie couldn't identify.

"It's about Alan," she said. "I know the role you played in getting him caught, Charlie. I've known it right from the start. And I didn't hold it against you then or now. He was a bent copper and he needed catching!"

Charlie was struck dumb, unsure whether he should reply, even less sure what he should say if he did. So she'd known all along, which meant he'd been worrying about nothing for months. Or . . . ? Thankfully, Linda didn't keep him in too much suspense about that.

"You've been so careful to avoid mentioning him, Charlie," she said with a slight grin. "It wasn't hard to figure out what was bothering you. I also know, just so that you know I do, what he said to you when you . . . when you nailed him."

"The bastard accused me of—"

"I said I know, Charlie. It's over . . . let it lie." Then she smiled, and it was the usual warm, genuine smile Charlie had always associated with Linda. "Besides, it's sort of . . . nice to think you've been lusting after me all these years." She said it in a voice that was velvet soft, then her grin dissolved into helpless laughter at the look on Charlie's face.

Chapter Twenty-Seven

Charlie tried his best to stave off having to phone Hobart on Tuesday morning and apologize about the fingerprint issue, but it niggled at him. Worse, it kept him from concentrating on the other things that niggled even more. Such as Kirsten's disappearance and now Kendall's. Like how such a thing with the fingerprints could have been accomplished. Where had the fingerprints on the knife come from . . . and how? Important things . . . maybe, although he couldn't quite make enough sense of them all to actually know why.

But he hated the notion of apologizing. It hadn't been him who'd sent the prints through the system, hadn't even been him who'd suggested it. Or had it? Now he wasn't sure. Therefore, he was suitably grateful for the reprieve provided when old Viv Purcell dropped by to have a yarn. If nothing else, it gave him an excuse to put off the call for another few minutes.

Viv, atypically, was direct and to the point, marching into Charlie's office with a mental list of what he wanted and foregoing his normal habit of beating around the bush for half an hour before getting to some obscure point or another by such a roundabout track that the point got lost in the process.

"Give us your cell phone number," he said as he approached the front counter, his disreputable dog trailing at his heels and already—in Charlie's mind—looking around with his evil yellow eyes for some place to sprinkle.

Charlie was about to ask why Viv wanted the number, had

his mouth half opened, in fact, when the old man whipped out a shiny new cell phone of his own and stood there, poised like a grotesque caricature of a garden gnome playing stenographer, not looking at Charlie but clearly prepared to key in the number when it was given him.

"My God, Viv . . . *you've* got a cell phone?" Charlie couldn't resist the jibe. In his mind, the old reprobate was the antithesis of the modern world, a throwback to a slower, totally different era in Tasmania's often turbulent history. To Charlie, Viv belonged in the nineteenth century, not the current one; he was a character straight out of a Banjo Patterson poem about drovers and ne'er-do-wells and cattle-duffers and sheep thieves.

"And why not? I'm not getting any younger, you know. Might need it for an emergency or some such."

"Fair enough." Charlie recited the number, watched as the grizzled old bushie punched it in with surprisingly agile fingers. "What's next," Charlie asked then. "I suppose you'll be getting a computer, too, so you can surf the Net? And maybe a fax machine?"

Both ridiculous suggestions, on the face of it. Old Viv—unless something had been changed and he hadn't bothered to tell Charlie—was still camping in an abandoned shepherd's hut on "Misery" bush run, in at the foot of Blue Tier on the extreme edge of a huge sheep station. With no electricity available for miles and no proper tenancy agreement that would have allowed him get the power in if he'd been able to afford it.

Viv had been living there when his dog Bluey had found the bones that started off the hunt for Dr. Ralph Stafford, the Specialist of Teague Kendall's book, and Bluey, referred to by Charlie as *that damned dog,* had been instrumental in finding the abandoned mine shaft where Stafford had been dumping his victims' body parts and gear.

The old man had made the most of his moment of glory, but

Charlie doubted even that would have convinced the landowner to bring in the power for a squatter he'd be at loggerheads with over some damned thing or another every other month. Much as Charlie liked old Viv, he considered him famous for his temperament—Viv was cantankerous all the time.

"Don't be stupid," was the old man's sneering reply. "Not that I haven't thought about it. A nice little laptop would be nice. I could write me own book about my dog's adventures. Or my memoirs, maybe."

Charlie struggled to hide a grin. The old man was reputed to have spawned children all over Tasmania and even on the Australian mainland during his younger, more productive years, although he maintained no familiar association with any of his descendants or the women who'd birthed them. He had the paternal instincts of the average tomcat, and any memoirs he might produce would be likely to get him lynched . . . or worse.

"I didn't even know you could read," Charlie said, the words out before he could stop himself. And could have kicked himself. Old Viv appeared genuinely wounded by the sarcasm. But before he could reply to the jibe, a question far more serious popped into Charlie's head.

"You mind where we found the abandoned shaft that solved the Specialist case?" Charlie asked, now abrupt in his own manner as niggles of bad memories plagued his mind. "I don't suppose you've been up that way recently?"

"The place where *me lovely dog, here* solved your case for you? Not for a while. Why?"

"And no unusual activity up there on the tier above you? No strange lights, or things going bump in the night?"

"Jeez, Charlie. Have they put you on UFO patrol now? There's been nobody at all up my way except me and Bluey and the usual mob of devils and roos and wallabies. Oh," he added, slyly wrinkling his lips over such teeth as remained, "and the Tassie tiger I saw the other night."

Normally, Charlie would have granted the old man a smile at that remark. Viv, like an amazing number of old-time bushmen in Tasmania, remained firmly convinced that isolated pockets of the allegedly extinct Thylacine—the Tasmanian tiger—still existed. Most claimed sightings of their own, and each year in Tasmania *somebody* would claim to have seen a tiger on some isolated bush road. Viv was good for such a claim about every two years, in Charlie's experience, and the veteran policeman wasn't about to tell Viv he thought it was all bull dust. Partly, because he wasn't sure if such reports mightn't be more real than not. Charlie didn't know if the Thylacine was extinct, but he did know that he *wanted* it to still exist, despite the odds. There was something comforting about the thought, however ridiculously romantic.

But now wasn't the time. Now that he'd asked about Stafford's killing ground, his mind did a U-turn back to the fingerprints, and he was suddenly impatient to make the requisite phone call and get it over with.

"Is there anything else, Viv?" he asked. "I've got a lot on my plate this morning, and—"

"What about me book?"

It was the last question Charlie could have anticipated, and it took him a moment to bring it into context.

"Kendall's book, you mean? I know he'll have one for you, Viv, but he's not likely to be down this way until—"

Old Viv interrupted him. "He hasn't stopped to see you, then?"

"I told you—he's in Launceston. There's a bloody great manhunt going on up that way, Viv. Or was. Somebody's snatched Kendall's girl. Why would you think . . . ?" And suddenly he realized that Kendall wasn't in Launceston. Kendall was . . . somewhere. With . . . ? "You've *seen* Kendall, then?"

Charlie demanded, and focused his attention on the old man with the intensity of a spotlight.

"Last night. Thought I told you that," the old man replied in a tone that told Charlie that Viv knew damned well he'd mentioned no such thing. "He was with that really beaut-looking nurse from the nuthouse . . . the one that Dave Birch is shagging, the one with the big tits."

"You saw Kendall and Rose Chapman? Together? Last night? Where, for God's sake?"

"On the highway, headed toward town here . . . I thought. 'Twas this side of Goshen . . . nowhere else they could have been headed. Going real slow, they were . . . probably looking for a place to pull off and have a bit." The old bushie snorted an evil laugh. "That'd be right. His girl's gone off and left him, so he's *consoling* himself with his ex-wife."

Christ on a bloody crutch! Talk about knowing who's up who and who's paid the rent! Is there anything you don't know about anybody, old man? You're a wonder . . . a fair dinkum wonder.

Charlie didn't know why he was surprised. Old Viv quite regularly astonished him with his encyclopedic knowledge of things he had no business knowing anything at all about. On his own patch, Viv was the grand master of gossip.

"You're a dirty old man," Charlie said. "And you're sure about this? What the hell were you doing up that way . . ." He paused to consider the time frame, couldn't compute it in his head. ". . . at that time of night?"

"None of your business." In point of fact, the old man had been en route home from the pub at Pyengana, got caught short by his geriatric bladder, and had to make a pit stop. He was a touch sensitive about mentioning it, then condescended. "I was taking a slash, if yez must know. And of course I recognized him. Seen his picture often enough, haven't I? And yez couldn't miss *her*. I might be old, Charlie, but I'm not dead yet. Half his bloody luck, I say."

Charlie's head was spinning with the effort to process this new information. None of it made any sense, at least on the surface, but he had alarm bells going off all through his subconscious.

"Okay," he said. "Now listen—you've got my number. If you see them again, if you see either one of them, I want you to ring me up straight away." He paused, then rushed in with his next thought, knowing he might well regret it, but knowing also he might regret not asking, even more. "And keep your eyes and ears open up your way," he said. "Let me know if you run up against anything . . . weird. Okay?"

He gently but firmly hustled old Viv out of the place, then poured himself a fresh cup of coffee and started formulating the words of his apology speech to the fingerprint techie in Hobart.

"There is no need for any sort of apology, Sergeant Banes." The techie cut Charlie off in mid-speech. "Or at least not from you. I should be thanking you, actually, because without your hurry-up these prints could have sat here for days or even weeks, and, well . . ."

"Well what? My boss was fair beside himself when he called last night," Charlie replied.

"Perhaps. But last night I hadn't completed my tests. Today . . ."

Charlie sighed, then forced himself into the game. "Today . . . ?"

"Oh," said the techie. "I guess you haven't got the latest." And she snorted, audibly. "Typical that you'd be the last to be informed. The Brass here are all over the moon about it. Imagine—having a chance to get one up on the famous Royal Canadian Mounted Police. Not often a little force like ours gets that, I can tell you."

I don't give a shit about the goddamn RCMP. Tell me something that makes some sense.

"You've lost me, love," he said, forgetting about rules involving sexist protocol in his haste to try and make some sense of this discussion, to force the woman to just get to the point!

"You're the one who broke the Specialist case, aren't you? And they haven't told you yet? Well, I can't say I'm surprised."

"Haven't told me what?" But Charlie knew what. He knew it in his very soul, knew it by the shiver of dread that flowed down his spine, by the quaver of disgust he could feel knotting like a mob of worms in his guts. He *knew!* And wished he didn't.

"It's all about the prints, Sergeant. I only finished up my tests this morning, and believe me, I double-checked—*triple*-checked—just so as to make damned sure. But those prints are *fresh,* Sergeant. And they're not a hoax, either; I'm staking my career on that."

"They're real? So Stafford is still alive. And here in Tassie?" Charlie blurted out the questions, already knowing the answers. Worse, already knowing the common thread that somehow, insane as it appeared, seemed to bind together all the disparate incidents of the past few days.

He heard the techie's reply, but his mind was already racing ahead of it, making lists of things he must do, and do quickly. If he wasn't already too late.

CHAPTER TWENTY-EIGHT

When Kendall didn't regain consciousness by late morning, Kirsten began to seriously worry. He lay on the camp cot so totally still that if she couldn't see him breathing it would have been all too easy to imagine him dead. Especially under these conditions.

"He's fine. He'll come out of it in his own time," Stafford said after a cursory glance at his other captive. "The sedative affects different people differently, dear Kirsten. That's the truth of it."

"The truth of it is that bitch probably *wanted* him dead," Kirsten replied, trying to hold her voice calm, knowing she wasn't doing so at all well. "You've already said she tried to have him shot!"

"It was a mistake. Ian was only supposed to frighten him, not actually hurt him."

Whereupon Stafford pointedly ignored them both and returned to his perusal of Kendall's book, studiously underlining passages and occasionally muttering to himself in undertones she couldn't follow.

It was utterly, totally maddening, because she couldn't do anything until Kendall recovered consciousness, and was now starting to worry that Rose, or Ian . . . or both . . . would return before that happened. If she and Kendall had any chance to get out of this, it had to be under circumstances that would somehow allow them to take Stafford by surprise.

And Kirsten was starting to question her own effectiveness when and if such an opportunity arose. She was haggard with exhaustion after a night in which the little sleep she managed had been fraught with nightmares and broken by the squabbling of Tasmanian devils right outside the door. Or so it had seemed. The screaming of the ugly little scavengers could have been coming from half a mile away, for all she knew, but it had been enough to bring her bolt upright, wide-eyed in terror.

And it must have disturbed Stafford's rest, too. She'd seen him ease out of his chair when the chorus of devils started out, and he'd left the cabin and stayed outside somewhere until the devil feast was over.

You were probably out there hand-feeding the damned things. Is that what you did with the remains of your victims here in Tasmania—hand-fed selected morsels to the devils before you ate one of them, too?

The thought was a torment, the mental picture it created even worse, not least because it all seemed quite plausible, totally believable. Ralph Stafford was clearly crazy as a loon and slipping further and further, Kirsten was certain, from any semblance of reality or normal thinking.

By mid-afternoon, even he was apparently concerned about Kendall. Or so she thought. He came over several times to inspect Kendall, take his pulse, raise an eyelid to check for . . . something.

"Isn't there something you can give him?" Kirsten asked. Only to be ignored, at first. Stafford looked up from his inspection of Kendall, looked at her with eyes that held no expression she could read. And he smiled, a slight smile so cold it could have frozen hell, she thought. It made her shiver.

Then he slapped Kendall across the face so hard it nearly tipped him off the camp cot. A brutal, solid, open-handed slap that left a quickening red mark on the cheek of the man she loved. Kendall never moved, never so much as changed the pace of his slow, steady breathing. But Kirsten was forced to hold her rage, to subdue the urge to retaliate somehow, any way she could. Because Stafford was expecting that, waiting for that. She could tell by the way he poised to step quickly out of range, the way he broadened that icy smile into an even worse smirk.

"He's not faking it," Stafford said. Almost sadly, she thought. "I rather thought he might have been."

And Stafford smiled again, only this time it was the warm, soft smile of his *mine host* persona. The abrupt change was incomprehensible, and all the more fearsome because of it. Stafford's mood swings were becoming, she thought, more and more erratic and more and more severe.

"He should come right fairly soon, now," the doctor said. "Not in time for lunch, unfortunately, but we'll have an early dinner. He'll be ready for that, I expect, and so will you. I know Rose will be." And again there was that beaming smile, the voice that fairly dripped bonhomie.

"Speaking of which, I'd best go and check on a few things, if we're going to be dining early."

As soon as the door closed, Kirsten knelt beside Kendall's cot. She was shaking with pent-up emotion, and knew it, but couldn't stop the shivering, couldn't keep the tears from welling out. All she could do was stare down at his unconscious figure. And worry.

"Is he gone?"

The words were barely audible, and at first she thought she'd imagined them, because there was no movement of Kendall's lips, no sign of movement from him at all.

"Is he gone, Kirsten? Talk to me, dammit!"

"You're okay?" She had to ask that first, could hardly believe the relief she felt when he opened his eyes and then, magically, smiled at her. His smile somehow lit up the room, dispensing the gloom of the dying daylight, instantly restoring her sense of hope, her belief that somehow, some way, they could survive this. Now that Kendall was awake, there was renewed hope.

"I've been better. Now, quickly . . . fill me in on what the hell is going on."

Kendall was rolling over even as he spoke, so that he sat slumped on the camp cot, his bound hands between his knees and his head bowed as he listened to her outline the situation.

"Okay," he said when she'd finished. "I think we have to wait until we can somehow overpower the bastard before we try anything at all. No sense getting loose in here when he's outside there with a gun. But how loose *is* that eyebolt? Could I yank it out of the wall?"

And this time he didn't wait for an answer, but stood up, grabbed the chains linking them to the wall, and tugged. Hard. And with no discernible result.

"Dammit! Okay . . . let's try it this way." Kendall spoke over his shoulder as he knelt and grasped the eyebolt in his hands, twisting it entirely free, then thrusting the eyebolt back and forth to loosen the fit of the threads within the wood of the wall. It took only moments for him to make the eyebolt *appear* solidly in place while actually loose enough to snap out of the wall with ease.

Kirsten, her attention focused on the doorway as he'd demanded, listened then as he outlined *The Plan*.

"Which bloody well better work," he said, "because I haven't got a better one."

"Ah . . . you're awake at last. Good. Dinner will be ready soon."

Stafford smiled hugely as he entered the cabin to find Kendall sitting slumped on the camp cot, elbows on his knees and his head resting against his bound wrists.

Kendall's breath was labored and he was moaning softly, his

entire upper body swaying in tune with his moans. Kirsten stood beside him, her hands on his shoulders. She turned to look at Stafford, her own bound hands outstretched in supplication.

"You have to do something," she said.

Stafford had stopped just out of reach, but—as they'd prayed—he wasn't carrying the rifle, nor any other obvious weapon. But he was free, unfettered, and fit. And in psychological control, which was what they were banking on.

Kirsten saw his gaze flicker from their bound wrists to the loops of chain behind them to the eyebolt in the wall. Stafford paused briefly, as if to assure himself that his preparations still held good, then stepped toward them. One step, only. Not enough.

One more, damn you. Just . . . one.

As Kirsten tried to will Stafford into taking that extra step, Kendall swayed upright, his moans louder, now. He didn't look up, didn't seem aware, even, of Stafford's presence. From his throat emerged a horrible, choking, gagging sound, then *he* staggered forward a single step, collapsing to his knees as he did so, his outstretched wrists, bound together with cable ties, barely halting his fall.

Stafford reached out to halt Kendall's fall, both hands extended to grasp Kendall's shoulders.

Kirsten stepped forward too, as if to try and halt the fall, but even as Stafford reached forward and down, she was turning, reaching behind her, her fingers groping for a decent grip on the twin chains that held her and Kendall to the eyebolt.

Kendall's fists clenched and his moaning changed to a mighty roar of anger and anguish as he thrust upward to smash with hands and wrists at Stafford's testicles. Once. Then again and again.

Stafford gasped with the first impact, his eyes widening in pain. By the third blow he was swaying over Kendall's shoulders, his mouth open in a soundless cry. He found his voice as Kirsten swung herself around, the chains a flexible, clumsy metal lash that she whipped forward to snap around Stafford's head and neck. The chains themselves had a serious impact, but the eye-bolt added to that, especially when she dragged the improvised whip back for a second blow.

A line of blood opened across Stafford's forehead as the chain ripped loose for Kirsten's second blow, which almost hit Kendall, too, as he flung up his head to smash against the doctor's chin with an audible, solid, thunk. Then he thrust a shoulder into Stafford's gut and heaved upward, lifting the doctor up and back to slam against the cabin wall before they fell in a twisting, writhing heap on the floor.

After that, she didn't dare try to strike at Stafford because Kendall emerged on top of the doctor, his voice a roar and his hands locked, now, on Stafford's throat as he slammed the man's head against the floor.

"Bastard . . . bastard . . . BASTARD!" Over and over again as Kendall, kneeling on his opponent, tried to throttle Stafford and smash his head open at the same time.

Kirsten could only watch, horrified and fascinated at the same time, as the man she loved did his best to kill the man she hated and feared so much. Until . . .

"Stop it, Kendall. You'll kill him," she cried.

"Good!" And he managed two more thumps before he suddenly sagged and slumped over the doctor's now unconscious body. Kendall was gasping, his shoulders heaved with his attempts to draw breath, and when he finally spoke his voice was more a whisper than a roar.

"You're right. Enough. Find something. Cut me loose. And hurry," he gasped, not moving his fingers from the doctor's throat, although he seemed to have released the pressure.

Kirsten managed, by stretching to the limit of the chains that still held her tied waist-to-waist to Kendall, to reach a knife on the folding table. But her fingers shook so much when she tried to cut Kendall's wrists free that she had to use both hands, and nearly dropped the knife when Kendall reached out to take it from her.

"Hold steady," he said, as if she could actually control the tremors that shook her entire body. And his fingers, too, trembled as he slid the knifepoint along to snick the cable ties that joined her wrists.

Kendall still knelt on Stafford, and once Kirsten's hands were free he turned quickly as if to ensure that his opponent remained comatose. Or to finish the job—Kirsten could see the impulse even as it formed in Kendall's mind, as his gaze locked on the doctor's exposed throat.

"No," she said. "No . . . please."

When Kendall turned to look at her, she was shocked by the bleakness in his eyes, by the apparent lack of any and all emotion. His eyes were hard as river stones, blank of any expression she could read. It was, indeed, all she could do to keep from reeling back, away from those eyes, away from the iciness in them.

Then he sucked in a huge breath, sighed, and she saw the lights come on again inside him. He glanced once more at Stafford, but this time it was only a cursory glance, thrown back as he lurched to his feet and reached out to turn Kirsten around.

"Free . . . first," he said, his voice strangely soft after the rage she'd heard in it only an instant before. "Then hugs."

Quickly, easily, he slashed through the cable tie holding the chain around her waist. Handed her the knife so she could do the same for him, watching, she knew, to make sure that Stafford wasn't about to magically awaken and spoil things.

And then, indeed, came the hugs. Kirsten flowed into his

arms, barely able to breathe, barely able to think. Content just to wallow in the ocean of relief that surrounded her.

CHAPTER TWENTY-NINE

Ian Boyd was angry. He'd been angry even before setting out on the doctor's little errand, and it got worse once he was alone and could think more or less at his own speed.

The bastard kept me rifle! I shouldn't have let him do that. Why did I?

Ian truly didn't know why, only that—as on the various occasions he'd been treated at the Birch clinic during the summers when Ralph Stafford was in charge—he'd found the Canadian psychologist a presence difficult to ignore or disobey. Not like the officers in the military, not like the various police and legal authorities he'd faced in the many years since. Stafford had something they didn't, and while Ian couldn't define it and couldn't bother to try, it gave the doctor power over him. He recognized that, even as he detested it.

Not fair I should have to be the one to get him that stupid old man and that bloody evil dog. Shoulda sent Rosie. Maybe she could handle the mongrel without getting her balls bit off. Fuckin' dog hates me . . . always has. Old Viv doesn't like me much, either.

By the time Ian reached St. Helens, he'd worked himself into a fair snit over the entire exercise, so he fell into the logic of habit and stopped for a beer. Then two. Then . . . more. Many more. By the time he left the pub, far into the night, he was so pissed he could hardly walk and it was too dark to search for the clandestine Ruger 10-22 he had stashed away safely. It, like the Vaime, was an illegal weapon under Little Johnny Howard's draconian gun laws, but Ian cared naught for that. The Ruger was his possum gun, although he'd also shot a stag or two with it. Fitted with a six-power scope and a custom-made silencer. Not much range, but it uttered only a whispered *phfffft* when used with subsonic rounds. A handy, efficient weapon for a poacher.

He'd also scored a few pills to top up the hoard he'd filched from Rose's purse, and between the pills and the grog, lapsed into a stupor that lasted him well into this day and clouded his mind when he finally did waken. Three beers into the morning, he felt better. Well enough, at least, to be able to address and then ignore the warning signals his addled mind kept flashing.

Bring them both alive, the man said. S'pose he thinks it'll be easy, but he don't know that damned dog. Mongrel bastard of a thing. I get anywhere within cooee of the bugger and he'll go spare . . . yapping and carrying on like a pork chop. Old Viv's not much better—the old fart's rough as guts, he is. Dunno why the doc wants either of them . . . too old and tough to eat, that's for sure.

By the time he'd remembered where he'd stashed the Ruger and then actually found it (he'd been sober when he hid it, and had done so carefully and well), Ian was well on the way to talking himself out of the entire concept. Except . . . Rosie would have more drugs that he'd like for himself, and the doc would also have plenty, for sure and certain. He'd said so, and Ian believed him. No sense letting the chance go by.

There's an old chunk of trawl net I put away somewhere, if I can just find the damned thing. Might work to get the damned dog under control. If I can manage that, old Viv'll be easy enough to handle, I reckon.

Remembering that he was supposed to have brought man and dog back to Stafford the day before did not help Ian's addled brain to formulate anything like a sensible plan for the operation. Not that it would have mattered much—Ian was the sort who always favored a direct approach to problems.

So once he'd eventually found the scrap of trawl net, having devoted half an hour first to disassembling the Ruger, cleaning it thoroughly, then reassembling it, it was time for another beer. Then another. By the time he set out for the shepherd's hut where old Viv lived, the day was pretty much shot and Ian wasn't much better.

He drove straight up the highway from St. Helens, oblivious to his condition at first, then smartening up a trifle when three motorists in a row beeped at him for his erratic driving. So he swung off on the road through Priory, in behind the heights of Gentle Annie, across Dead Horse and Mother Logans creeks and eventually, working westerly through the maze of bush tracks he knew so well, around the back of Platt's Lookout and on to the old man's hut on Misery bush run.

And throughout the tortuous drive over rutted, often barely navigable tracks, Ian gave free rein to his growing indignation at having to do this at all. By the time he reached Viv's hut he'd worked himself into a proper snit.

The only good thing was knowing what to expect, and in this Ian wasn't disappointed. The instant his vehicle came to a full stop outside the hut, Bluey rollicked around the corner of the building, already yapping and snarling and showing his teeth. When he realized it was Ian, whom Bluey thoroughly disliked, the yodeling intensified.

And when Ian opened the door of his bush ute and stepped out, the length of trawl net in hand, the silly dog ran straight into it, en route to his attempt to take Ian's leg off one mouthful at a time. It was so easy as to be laughable, and Ian did laugh. Then he cursed as the damned dog got a fang through a hole in the net and nicked Ian's thumb.

"Get out of it, you bloody mongrel," he cursed, and kicked at the dog, who thrashed around in the net more actively than any fish ever had. Bluey growled, snapped ineffectively, and returned to his writhing attempts at escape. Ian ignored him, reached into the truck for the Ruger. He'd just smack the silly bugger across the head, he thought. Calm him down a bit.

But there wasn't time. He turned to find himself the object of attack from a different front. Old Viv, twenty years older and half Ian's size, was on him with a ferocity that matched that of the old man's dog. Fists and feet flying, the old man was in a frenzy, but doing little actual damage, not least because his attention was divided between fighting Ian and checking to see that the dog was all right.

"Give over, Viv," Ian snarled, holding the oldster away with one hand. "I'm just trying to keep the bugger from eating me, is all." As well to talk to a pesky mosquito; the old man continued to swarm Ian, all flying fists and thrashing feet, but doing no significant damage. Annoying, though. Ian finally lost his patience and used the rifle butt to smack the old man away, hoping that if he could quiet the master he might have a decent chance to subdue the dog.

Viv went down, a thin line of blood tracking across his brow where the rifle had struck him. Ian turned and made a grab for Bluey, still held by the length of trawl net but not far from getting loose. The dog growled, snapped, and thrashed around, all four short legs scuttling as he fought for purchase and tried to escape the net and eat Ian Boyd at the same time.

The entire situation had become, in Ian's eyes, a farce. One that exhausted his slender trove of patience very quickly indeed. *Bugger this for a joke. I'll just shoot the mongrel, and maybe old Viv, too, while I'm at it.*

He charged toward the writhing dog, intent now on kicking the beast into submission, and had his foot raised for the first kick when he caught movement in his peripheral vision and realized the old man had staggered away and into his dwelling.

Ian had only seconds to process this information when old Viv emerged again, and this time he had no intention of laying into Ian with fists and boots.

This time he was going to run him off—or kill him.

"Get out of it!" he shouted, raising a double-barreled shotgun and peering along it as the weapon trembled in his hands. An old hammer gun, probably—Ian thought—loaded with black powder cartridges, to boot. The twin muzzles looked like cannons to Ian, who reckoned the ancient weapon was older than the diminutive man holding it. The muzzles wavered in a huge circle, testament to the fact that Ian's blow had left old Viv unsteady; the old man could barely stand upright, was having trouble holding the gun.

But no trouble firing it. He gave no further warning before pulling one trigger, and Ian leapt in alarm as flame spewed from the shotgun. Flame, and a cloud of smoke that momentarily obscured the old man behind the trigger. Pellets scoured the area between Ian and his vehicle, sending up gouts of sod and twigs and leaves. None touched him, but the edge of the shotgun's spray pattern was too close for comfort.

"Jeeesus!" Ian cried, and raced for the safety of the nearby scrub, leaping over the net-enmeshed dog as he high-stepped through scrub and bracken fern, aiming for safety behind the first decent-sized tree he could reach.

Boom! A second shot, and this time the pellets thrashed the tree branches above him, showering Ian with leaves and bark as he fled. Behind him, the old man's curses were echoed by screams of outrage from that fuckin' dog, who was, Ian could see, almost free of the trawl net. The old man scuttled back into his hut, breaking the shotgun as he moved, obviously looking for more ammunition.

It was a worry. He could outrun the old man, and his Ruger gave him a serious advantage over the ancient shotgun, but the dog . . . ? Ian didn't think about it very long. Sliding down into a seated shooting stance, solid, totally controlled, he lifted the Ruger and peered through the powerful scope at where Bluey writhed against the strands of trawl net.

Ian's piercing whistle stopped the dog for an instant, which was all Ian needed. The trigger was already half-squeezed, he completed the gesture, and the possum gun spat a single round toward the animal. Hardly a sound, it made. Just a *phfffft*, and Bluey, voice cut off in mid-yelp, sagged into a silent heap beneath the edge of the net he'd so nearly escaped.

CHAPTER THIRTY

It all looked exactly the same. For anyone who didn't know the horrors that had been inflicted in this place, it was merely an abandoned mine site—three old shacks that perched high on the escarpment of Blue Tier, snuggled under towering eucalypts that shadowed the area even at mid-day, their tortured, twisted branches shedding bark like diseased skin.

It was well past mid-day now, pushing toward the evening of a day in which Charlie had nearly gone crazy trying to get on top of an investigation that hadn't even been assigned to him, officially. Or at least not specifically to him. Every cop in Tasmania was now alerted to be on the lookout for Dr. Ralph Stafford, infamous serial killer, cannibal, believed until this very morning to have been dead for more than a year and half the world away.

The Specialist. And this had been his operations center. While working half-yearly stints at Dave Birch's clinic, the Canadian psychologist had spent his spare time stalking, capturing, killing, and eating young women. Bicycle tourists, usually, girls he somehow lured under his control, then brought to this shadowed, lonely spot for butchering. Charlie shuddered inside just at the thought of what they'd found when *that damned dog* and his geriatric master had shown them this place.

Bluey had, to give the beast his due, been responsible for them finding out any of it. Scrounging, or chasing some forest vermin into a chasm in the rocks far below here, at the bottom of the steep escarpment, Bluey had found bones. Human bones. He'd taken one to old Viv. Viv had brought it to Charlie, and eventually the old bushie had guided Charlie to this place, where investigation of an abandoned shaft led police to a veritable charnel house.

Charlie didn't need Teague Kendall's book about the incident to keep the memories fresh. Too fresh. Which is why he hadn't come near this place again once the investigation was finished. Not once. There were ghosts here. Charlie knew it.

Ghosts. But no sign whatsoever of Dr. Ralph Stafford. No sign anyone had been anywhere near the place in weeks, maybe even longer than that. Charlie wasn't the world's greatest bushman. Old Viv could probably have told him to the day when the last human was here, but that didn't matter. It wouldn't have been recently.

So where else? Where the hell would you go, I wonder? The area round St. Helens was your only patch, far as anybody knows. Christ! Why come back here? Why HERE? It makes no bloody sense.

Once again Charlie shivered, then shook himself as if by doing so he could rid himself of the ominous atmosphere here in this place. Why here? Why *anything,* when it concerned a man crazy enough to slaughter and eat people in two countries ten thousand miles apart? A man who should damned well be dead!

They'd find him, of course. Eventually. But it might turn out to be more of a problem than The Brass anticipated, Charlie thought with a rueful half-smile. The Brass had flooded the state's police offices with photos of the cannibal doctor, along with copies of the Kirsten abduction photos. Nobody, however, had bothered to recognize that the fuzzy shots from the hotel security system were of a man who didn't look anything like Ralph Stafford. Except for the occasional very alert policeman. Most of them weren't sure, from the information they got, if they were to be looking for one man or two.

Finally taking that issue of Kirsten's alleged abduction seriously, they'd called upon the media for help, flooded the media, too, with the grainy, indistinct photos. And, for good measure, they'd poured photos of Kirsten and Teague Kendall—separately and together—into the mix.

Charlie had also distributed the information and photos to his own people. He couldn't do otherwise. He instructed everyone on duty to devote their time to prowling the town and district, looking, talking to people. He had first searched Dave Birch's mental health facility, then put people in place there to watch for any sign of Stafford. Or of Rose Chapman. Charlie was certain in his soul that she was somehow part of whatever was going on.

He had rushed through the day, making telephone calls, guiding his troops, although, in point of fact, they needed little guidance. Charlie's people were well trained, worked well together, and worked well for *him,* because he ran a tight but comfortable ship. Most had been in St. Helens long enough to have developed independent sources of information. It was a small town, strangers were noticed even during tourist season, and suspicious strangers were reported. Charlie knew that sooner or later, if Stafford was in the area, he would be seen and word would get back to the police.

But would that happen in time? And how could he speed the process? Charlie knew it was all somehow intertwined . . . all of it. Stafford and Rose Chapman and Kirsten and Teague. There was simply no way it could be otherwise, even though none of it yet made much sense. Yet.

He'd been hoping to find some answers here, certain somehow in his instincts that Stafford would return to this place. To gloat, if nothing else. Or perhaps to collect something he might have left behind the first time? Something they might have missed, despite the amazingly thorough search that had been done of the area?

But the aged shacks were just as Charlie had last seen them, huddled beneath the trees and staring out over the forest below with unseeing eyes. Like Stafford's victims, Charlie thought, and shuddered inside despite himself.

No sign at all that Stafford might have returned. No sign that anybody had been in the vicinity for weeks, perhaps months. No fresh tire tracks, no evidence of the shacks having been opened by anyone. Curtains of spider-webs revealed that much.

So where the hell are you, you bastard? It's somewhere here on my patch . . . I'd bet my soul on it. But where? Talk to me, dammit!

But from the gloomy silence surrounding came not a single word. Charlie couldn't stay here, didn't want to, truth be known. What he'd been after was some sort of *sign,* and he was pragmatic enough to recognize the silliness of that type of thinking. So he turned the vehicle around and headed back through the maze of bush tracks that eventually brought him to the highway again, and from there, steadily eastward and down, past the Pyengana turnoff and eventually to the wide spot in the road that some maps said was Goshen.

Here again Charlie paused, halting on a broad section of highway shoulder, and wondering why Kendall and Rose would have halted here, wondered even more seriously if old Viv had perhaps had one too many beers at Pyengana and if the old curmudgeon had actually seen anything significant at all.

Why would they stop here? There's nowhere they could go except on to the town, unless . . . Charlie hauled out his own map of the region, a highly detailed topographical map that had been over-written with various notations over the years. Roads altered, bridges out, dangerous curves, and creek crossings. Nobody but Charlie could begin to interpret it, and even he sometimes had problems. He'd inherited the map on his posting to St. Helens, and there were still places on this map he'd never seen.

But the map wouldn't speak to him, either, not this time. There were too many options, most of them with no logic whatsoever. If Kendall and Rose hadn't gone on into town, they could be anywhere at all.

Viv would probably know, the cunning old bastard. Where are you when I need you, Viv? Where the hell would they go?

Viv wasn't there to respond, at least not directly. Charlie's cell phone, however, was more cooperative. The instrument chirped, Charlie flipped it open, hit the appropriate key, replied, and heard the ghastly whisper of his old friend's voice.

Chapter Thirty-One

It took Sunday, Monday and most of Tuesday—nearly a hundred and fifty man hours working four metal detectors through all the daylight hours there were.

But the Tasmanian police forensics people found the bullet that had smashed through the retrieving trial judge, ending his life in a heartbeat and spawning a murder investigation with no clues, no suspects, and even less logic that anyone could figure out.

At least they thought it was the bullet . . . only extensive DNA testing could confirm that. It was a 7.62 NATO projectile—.308 caliber by American designation—and it was in excellent condition for ballistics testing, hardly damaged at all in its deadly flight.

But there was no rifle to compare it to, no information that could guide them to such a rifle, or to the shooter, no apparent reason for the assassination, no suspect. Nothing.

They also found several .22 slugs, a few of larger caliber from more conventional deer rifles, an assortment of shotgun pellets, empty shotgun cartridges, a vast assortment of bottle caps, ring-pull tabs from old-style soft drink cans, a surprising number of coins both recent and predating the country's changeover to decimal currency, several dozen fish hooks, a few lead sinkers, one wristwatch, and four pocket knives. And a dead cell phone.

CHAPTER THIRTY-TWO

"We have to get out of here. If that other man comes back . . ." Kirsten shuddered just at the thought, and her final words were muffled as she tried to bury herself deeper against Teague Kendall.

"Not before I sort out our friend here," he replied, and the grimness in his voice was almost a living growl. Kendall thrust Kirsten away, gently, then turned his attention to the cabin's interior and the various supplies scattered throughout.

"Hah! This'll do the trick," he said, grabbing up a handful of the cable ties Stafford had brought in after Kendall had been sedated by his ex-wife. The same cable ties that had bound them both until only moments earlier.

Kendall knelt over the still-unconscious Stafford, roughly turned the doctor over on his front, and quickly manufactured handcuffs and ankle-shackles from the sturdy plastic material. Once locked, they would be impossible to remove without being cut. Not a perfect confinement system, but it would do nicely.

"And just for good measure," he muttered as he bent Stafford so that he could use even more ties to fasten the hands bound behind the doctor to the circles of plastic joining his ankles. It was an effective but almost tortuous way of doing it, since it forced Stafford into a back-bent arch that would be painful, Kendall suspected, when the man awoke.

If he awoke. The impact of Kendall's head butt appeared to have made Stafford bite his tongue, so there was blood trickling from his smashed lips. And the head wounds caused by the chain and eyebolt, although superficial, really, had spread a mask of blood over much of the doctor's face.

"How badly is he hurt?" Kirsten couldn't avoid the question . . . Stafford looked truly awful.

"Not badly enough," Kendall replied. "I should have killed the bastard while I was at it. No death penalty here in Australia—he could spend forty more years in jail . . . if some silly bloody judge doesn't take the easy option and just stick him in a mental hospital."

Kendall's years as a journalist had left him vividly cynical about the workings of the justice system. To him it seemed to be getting less and less effective all the time, with worse and worse offenders getting more and more leniency while innocent victims suffered.

"I think *I* could kill him. Easily," Kirsten said. But she lied and they both knew it. She couldn't do it any more than Kendall could. Not like this, not in cold blood while Stafford was totally defenseless.

"Let's just get us to hell out of here before that mate of his comes back. Or Rose does, although I think we could handle Rosie if she doesn't have a gun. Right now I'm not sure I could do much of anything, the way my head feels. That bugger's got a helluva hard chin." Kendall grabbed up one of the full water bottles and the bottle of pain killers while Kirsten gathered her belongings and flung them hurriedly back into her fanny pack. They were halfway out the door when Kendall stopped short, turned abruptly, and knelt over Stafford's unconscious figure.

"Keys," he muttered. And straightened up a moment later with the doctor's key ring in his hand. He looked at them, grunted, then reached out to pick up a flashlight as well. Then he led Kirsten out into the near-dark of the evening, and after a brief pause to look around and listen, they made their way through the mud to where the doctor's 4WD squatted just off the track.

"Do you have any idea where we are?" Kirsten asked as Kendall flung open the driver's door and waved her around to the other side.

"Vaguely," he said. Which was true enough. Somewhere in the hills more or less above St. Helens and south of the Tasman Highway. Exactly where didn't matter . . . the track from the shack would lead to some other road, sooner or later, going somewhere, sooner or later. Downhill and to the east lay the ocean and better roads and people, assuming he could find his way in the imminent darkness.

"We only have to follow our noses and keep angling downhill," he said as Kirsten moved around the vehicle. "If we drive into the ocean we'll know we've gone too far."

It was meant to be a joke, but Kirsten's scream wasn't at all funny.

Already halfway into the driver's seat, Kendall flung himself out again and rushed around to where she stood, shock still and white-faced, her lips moving soundlessly and her eyes wide with shivering, soul-shaking terror.

The tailgate of the 4WD was down, spread with what appeared to be an old sheet or tablecloth that was stained with black, irregular blotches. And atop that, covered with a flimsy layer of cheesecloth that did nothing to disguise it, nothing to soften the horror of it, was a human thigh.

Kirsten gagged, turned away, and promptly lost the little she'd managed to eat that day. She heaved and heaved and retched until her head was light and she was near to fainting, but nothing could dismiss the images from her mind, nothing could relieve those other images—those mental pictures of her own dear sister Emma—that crowded in to add to this mental scrapbook of horror. Emma, beautiful, vibrant, alive. Emma the actress. And now, startling in the imaginary detail, Emma the victim, the corpse, the carcass. Emma—like this!

The edges of the cheesecloth were held down by a trinity of carving knives with razor edges that gleamed in the fading light. And the thigh itself had been surgically, tidily sectioned at the thigh and knee joints, a task done so neatly only tiny scraps of cartilage clung to the rounded knobs of bone at each end of the thigh.

This puts the term "tailgate party" in a whole new light.

The thought, obscene as it was, snuck into Teague Kendall's mind before he could shut the door on it, but he did manage not to voice it out loud as he strode forward to enfold Kirsten in his arms. Only to have her stare at him, wild-eyed, her lips firmly closed with a fierce, rigid determination before she opened them to shriek at him.

"I'll kill him!" she screamed, then broke free of his embrace and bolted past Kendall to snatch up one of the knives, repeating, "I'll kill him" over and over, like a mantra, as she tried then to duck past Kendall, to run back to the cabin and . . .

"No!"

The shouted word halted her just long enough for Kendall to grab her wrist and twist, hating himself for the pain he knew it must cause, but certain that it was something he had to do. They stood there, locked together in that grip, and watched the glimmering knife fall from Kirsten's fingers to the muddy ground on which they stood.

Kendall turned, tugging Kirsten along like a recalcitrant child, ignoring her half-hearted attempts to twist free of his grip. Ignoring Stafford's vehicle—how could they take it without somehow dealing with its grotesque cargo? Striding forward instead through the rutted mud of the track, Kendall's mind focused only on getting away from this. Kirsten's not focused at all.

It was nearly full dark now, but he could see well enough to move along the rutted track, even to see the outline of another vehicle parked beside it, huddled beneath a high, spreading blue gum. It was newer, shinier, more modern than the one Stafford had used as a butcher's block. Rose's SUV, he thought, and they were right up to it before Kendall could see that it, too, had been put to unorthodox use by the mad doctor.

Worse, he didn't see until it was too late to turn away, too late to somehow shield Kirsten from the sight of Rose's body—now one-legged and naked—suspended high in the tree. Held there by a length of rope that ran from the vehicle's front towhook up and over the tree limb to where it held Rose's remains high off the ground, encased in more cheesecloth, a hunter's game bag of the stuff. Safe from the ubiquitous blowflies, the Tassie devils, and other vermin.

But not safe from the devil himself. Too late for that. Bloody oath, Rosie—what have you done?

The rope had been passed around her body under arms and breasts, then twisted and knotted under Rose's neck just above the gaping wound that had opened her throat to death.

He turned, hoping somehow to shield this second horror from Kirsten. But it was too late. Even as he threw his arms around her, gathering her into what he hoped would be a protective hug, he felt the tremors of terror that vibrated in his love, heard her choking, terrified sobs.

And was strangely grateful when she abruptly sagged in his grip, her mind and body both giving up the fight against the obscenity of it all.

CHAPTER THIRTY-THREE

"Ian Boyd's just shot my dog. I'm going to kill the bastard if I can. But I'm outgunned, Charlie, and I'm hurt. You've got to help me."

The connection was bad, the voice so tremulous that Charlie could only just make out the words. And he only got time to ask, "Where are you?" and hear a quavering, "Home" before the connection was lost.

Home. For the old man, home was an isolated shepherd's shack under Blue Tier, at the end of a truly primitive bush track. No electricity, no piped water, nobody else living within miles. But through this curious quirk of circumstances, Charlie could be there in fifteen minutes. Even in the dark. Maybe less, if he hurried.

He did. Charlie threw the police vehicle into four-wheel-drive and used every driving skill he had to keep it moving forward and out of the ditch as he lurched and rocked his way along the constantly deteriorating track. Old Viv regularly used the road in an ancient two-wheel-drive vehicle held together by faith and fencing wire but Charlie had no time for slow, careful driving. He relied on memory to navigate, on reflexes to follow his bouncing headlight beams as he slewed through puddles and slithered through boggy sections without even bothering to check them out first.

If Ian Boyd was there at Viv's, he'd got there the same way Charlie was doing it, and if Ian had driven this track, Charlie knew he could also get through, provided he was careful and at least reasonably sensible.

His vehicle soared over the final rise in the terrain, skidded through the last of many bogs that had already painted it with mud, and Charlie had to leap on the brakes as the lights picked up the shape of the discarded trawl net with Bluey's unconscious form lying still and unmoving, half under the net and half free.

Dead? You'll pay if he is, Ian Boyd. Mark my words, you will! And when you get out of the crowbar hotel you'd best leave this island, because that old man will hunt you down and kill you. Slowly.

In the headlights, Charlie could also see Ian's abandoned four-wheel-drive and the door to Viv's shack, and as he watched, the door opened slightly and a gnome-like visage peered out at him, a face still smeared in blood from a wound on the old man's head. Then the head retreated and emerged again a second later, this time followed by the old man's arm, triumphantly waving an old double-barreled shotgun.

Waving a bloody shotgun that's older than you are, and standing there in the headlights making a right proper target of yourself. Bloody oath, Viv, what are you thinking?

Charlie quickly killed his headlights, then sat for a moment, letting his eyes adjust to the relative darkness. It wasn't quite full dark, so after a moment he could see reasonably well. Well enough. He could see a shadowy Viv gesturing to a patch of stringy barks, where Charlie assumed Ian Boyd might be bailed up.

Only one way to find out, and I'd best get to it before that silly old trout goes after Ian again with that shotgun.

Too late. Even as Charlie slid cautiously out of the police vehicle, BOOM! The shotgun erupted with a roar and a mighty gout of flame.

"Yez might as well give it up, you mongrel bastard." The old man's voice was a triumphal screech. He sounded like a parrot in heat.

BOOM! Flame spewed from the shotgun's second barrel, and Charlie wondered what on earth the old man had been using to load his shot shells.

Black powder? Too much of it, whatever the hell it was.

Leaves and bark fluttered down from the trees as Charlie cautiously moved to his left, hoping for a better view.

"That's enough!" he said, filling his voice with an authority he didn't quite feel. "Put that shotgun away and leave this to me."

No way to be sure if the old man obeyed, although Charlie doubted he would. *It'd be a world first if you did, you silly old bastard. But I don't need you complicating this now, so just bugger off out of it.*

He kept moving slowly forward and to his left, his gaze locked on where he thought Ian Boyd was, and soon enough got confirmation of that.

Phffft. And a tiny gout of dirt flew up a few feet to Charlie's left. Ridiculous as it seemed, even to him, Charlie was reassured by the width of the miss. To him, it meant Ian wasn't serious about shooting him, and that matched his own assessment of the man.

For all his faults, Ian wouldn't shoot me. He just . . . wouldn't.

He took another slow, measured pace. Then another.

"Get away out of this, Charlie. It's nothing to do with you."

"It's over, Ian. Time to put the gun down." Another step, slightly more to the left. He could see Ian Boyd clearly now, or as clearly as the faded light would allow.

"So that silly old bastard can blow me in half? Not on your Nellie!"

"Viv! Take that shotgun back in the shack and stay there!" Charlie shouted the command, but didn't take his gaze off the tall, rangy figure ahead of him. Too far ahead for any sort of accurate pistol shooting, but that wasn't the reason Charlie hadn't even bothered to draw his gun.

Ian Boyd could shoot the buttons off Charlie's epaulets with that .22 at this range, and both of them knew it. If he was going to shoot—seriously shoot—it would have been done by now. Or so Charlie believed. Had to believe, or else run.

"It's time to put the gun down, Ian." Spoken slowly, calmly, as Charlie took another step, then another. In his peripheral vision, he saw the old man, shotgun still in his grasp, reeling as he hobbled over to kneel beside his stricken dog.

Charlie took another step to the left, well out of the direct line between old Viv and Ian Boyd.

I'm not sure which of you is the most dangerous. Damn it, Viv—why can't you ever just do as you're damn well told?

Ian Boyd was losing it. The cocktail of drugs and alcohol in his blood was foaming into utter confusion and he shook his head, trying to clear his vision and his mind.

Charlie Banes was a policeman and policemen were authority and he hated authority and he hated policemen. But this was Charlie. Charlie had always played straight with him. He actually sort of *liked* Charlie. But he didn't like that cantankerous old man, and the feeling was mutual and that old man would shoot him soon as look at him. Had already tried.

Ian wanted to run, but there was nowhere to run to. Charlie was between him and his vehicle, and so was the old man.

"It's over, Ian. Put . . . the gun . . . down."

Charlie's voice was steady, calm, almost convincing. Almost. Ian looked down at the weapon, then at Charlie, then over to where old Viv was crouched over the dog.

"No."

"Put. The gun. DOWN!"

"I'm warning you, Charlie. No closer. Just . . . just go away and . . . and . . ."

Charlie was close enough now to see the hesitation, could feel the indecision and confusion in Ian. Close enough, almost, to be in pistol range. But he didn't draw his weapon. That would only exacerbate the situation, might too easily tip Ian over the edge.

Couldn't hit him anyway. I'd be better off throwing the damned gun at him. Come ON, Ian . . . give it away, damn you.

He watched as Ian turned, took two quick steps, then slipped on some forest floor debris and stumbled to his knees. Watched Ian abandon flight as an option, saw him turn, saw the wavering muzzle of the .22 as Ian struggled to regain his footing and his bearing on Charlie at the same time.

Please, God.

A silent prayer to one known to act in mysterious ways. Charlie caught the flicker of motion off to his right, half turned to it, afraid old Viv might be launching another assault.

But there was no time to do anything but watch as a small, scruffy-coated Jack Russell terrier rollicked across the clear ground between Charlie and Ian. His little feet merged in a blur of motion as Bluey caught proper sight of Ian. The dog's panting changed to a harsh, guttural spasm of sound as he charged.

Charlie could only watch. And wonder.

CHAPTER THIRTY-FOUR

All Kendall could do was flatten some relatively dry bracken fern and lay Kirsten down on it while he did what had to be done and hoped he could finish the grisly chore before she came out of her stupor.

The keys were there in Rose's SUV, and it fired up, thankfully, to exhibit a quiet, modern engine that didn't rouse Kirsten as he eased the vehicle ahead far enough that he could get out and deal with the rope by hand.

Which meant lowering his ex-wife's mutilated body enough so he could free the rope from the SUV, then hoist her back up into the damned tree. Because what else could he do? They needed the vehicle, and better this one—marginally better, anyway—than the one Stafford had used for his obscene tailgate party. But Kendall could not and would not simply abandon Rose's mutilated body to face further mutilation from scavengers, so hoisting her back into the tree was the quickest, most logical option.

It took all his strength, not least because he'd been two days now without eating and the exertion made his head swim. And the situation itself made his empty stomach churn and seemed to shut down his mind to everything but essentials.

You're a big boy now. Don't look at her. Don't think about it. Just do it. You have to. Do it . . . do it . . . do it.

The words were a chant inside his head as he forced slack into the rope, freed the end from the vehicle's tow hook, then dragged Rose back up into her macabre roost. Despite his shaking hands and bursting lungs, he managed it somehow, although he was forced to tie the rope off to a sapling smaller than he would have liked.

He straightened, stretched, dared not even look to see the effect of his efforts, couldn't look, didn't need to. He would, Kendall realized, forever hold that initial picture of his ex-wife hung up like a butchered doe.

He did have to watch his footing, did have to be careful not to tread in the thrashed-up underbrush directly beneath Rose, where he knew instinctively the devils had already been, had already cleaned up after the master devil.

Kirsten's right. I should go back and kill the bastard. Now. God would understand. God would probably thank me. Rosie sure as hell would. And Emma. And the others.

The thoughts rolled around in his mind as he leaned on the SUV to catch his breath, to try and think sanely, try to plan, try to understand. He didn't know where they were, didn't know what other threats lurked out there in the now-full darkness of the Tasmanian night. He needed to keep safe the woman he loved, a woman already half-destroyed by what had happened, never mind what might happen yet. But all he could do was think about how easy it would be, how *right* it would be, how *satisfying* it would be, to go back and kill Stafford. In cold blood.

Here. Now.

"And you can't do it and you can't let her do it either," he said half aloud, trying to use words, his favorite tools, the chosen tools of his trade, his life, to protect him from inner demons he hadn't known he possessed. But he knew it now, and feared the knowledge even more than he feared this night and its uncertainties.

Could he go back there and kill Dr. Ralph Stafford? Deliberately? In cold blood? Teague Kendall wasn't entirely sure, and didn't really want to know the answer, but he couldn't help asking himself the question. He knew without any doubt that he couldn't allow Kirsten to do it, didn't dare allow himself even to think that she could . . . or would.

If it was Rose, I wouldn't be all that surprised, I guess. But Kirsten? No. She couldn't and she wouldn't and even if she wanted to I couldn't let her. Didn't let her!

It was the first conscious comparison he'd found himself making between his now-dead ex-wife and the woman he couldn't help loving, but Kendall found the circumstances of it too bizarre for comfort.

And this wasn't the time for it.

As carefully as he could, hoping to manage it without waking Kirsten, he gathered her up and deposited her in the SUV's passenger seat. Managed to reach around and get the seatbelt closed. She muttered, stirred, but slid back into unconsciousness as soon as he moved away from her.

"Right. Time to go."

He walked around to the driver's seat, got in, and eased the vehicle ahead, turning sharply into the rutted track as he avoided Rose's gibbet and the devil-thrashed ground below it. After that, things got easier, except that he still wasn't entirely certain where they were, or which direction to turn—if and when he got the chance. It didn't matter, Kendall decided. What mattered was getting Kirsten away from this place of death and blood and madness.

Kirsten almost sent him into the ditch when she finally did awaken and freaked out at finding herself confined by the seatbelt. One flailing fist caught Kendall squarely across the eyes before he could skid to a halt and reach out to try and control Kirsten.

"It's all right," he said. Over and over and over, keeping his voice low, soft, nonthreatening despite the fact he was holding both her wrists to keep her from smacking him again. Her eyes were open, but strangely vacant, and he thought that wherever she was in her mind, it wasn't here with him. Nor was it anywhere even remotely pleasant, he thought.

"Emma?"

Her first recognizable word confirmed that. It was a plaintive plea, a whimper more than a question. But he tried to answer it anyway, hoping it might somehow calm her.

"It wasn't Emma," he said. "It was . . . Rose." And he felt himself choke on the name, the reality of what he was saying.

"Yes." Kirsten replied in a whisper. "Rose."

"We have to keep going, Kirsten," he said. "I don't want to be caught out here by . . . by . . ." He didn't have a name to put to the threat he feared, but Kirsten didn't appear to notice. Nor did she object, so Kendall sent the SUV moving again down the track.

"I warned her," Kirsten said.

He couldn't tell if she meant that she'd warned Rose, or her sister Emma, one of Stafford's earlier victims. Or maybe someone else entirely—she didn't seem to be tracking all that well.

"I did. I told her he'd have her for breakfast. She didn't listen. She was happy enough that he was going to eat *me*, though."

"Rose?" It was out even as he thought it. "But why?"

"She hated me. She hated you even more, I guess. She tried to have you shot." And suddenly Kirsten reached out to put her hand on his knee. "You're all right? You didn't get shot, did you?"

"No. I'm fine. But how could Rose . . . ?"

"She thought I'd been kidnapped for ransom, until she saw who'd done it." Kirsten's bark of laughter was bitter. "Then I think she was even happier, thinking of what he was planning."

Kirsten sighed, seemed to relax slightly. "He told me about the shooting. Stafford, I mean. Rose was there and she didn't deny it. It was that other man who shot at you, I think."

"Tell me about this other man," Kendall said. "I'm a bit confused about it all. I mean, I know why Stafford kidnapped you, or at least I can guess, but the rest is very weird stuff. Nobody tried to shoot me."

"He's a local, I think. Whatever you'd call a redneck here in Tasmania. He's tall, pretty old, I think his name is Ian . . . something. He looks like one of those evil hillbillies in the movie *Deliverance*. It was Ian that shot at you, I think, but it was Rose who got him to do it."

Kirsten sighed again, and looked across at him with a wistful, ethereal expression Kendall couldn't quite interpret.

"I'm glad he missed," she whispered.

Suddenly it all came together in Kendall's brain, facts and theories and pure speculation colliding in a realization so mind-blowing that he nearly lost control of the vehicle.

"My God!"

He let it all percolate for a moment, then told her about the shooting of the gundog judge on Saturday, which seemed like a month ago, given all they'd been through since then.

"The bullet burned Rex Henderson's ear on the way by. Went right between the two of us and into the judge. He never knew what hit him, poor bugger. Rex thought it was a bee, or a hornet. And this joker was shooting at *me*? Because Rosie convinced him to do it? It's too insane not to be true, I guess, but it makes no sense at all."

"She was jealous of your success," Kirsten said. "She ranted and raved at me a lot, but it was you she had the hate on for. She didn't make a lot of sense half the time, but I gather she feels . . . felt that she should be sharing in your wealth. That she'd earned it."

"That'd be right, for Rosie. Never mind that we were already divorced about two years before I struck it lucky with that first book. The first one that actually made any money, I mean. And I wrote that after we were divorced too, although she wouldn't . . . didn't . . ."

Kendall had to slow down, then halt the vehicle entirely as tears welled up to blur his vision. He could only sit there, gripping the steering wheel with fists that trembled from the emotions raging inside him. The two of them waited it out in silence.

"I'm sorry, Teague," Kirsten said once Kendall returned to being in at least some semblance of control. "Whatever Rose did, she certainly didn't deserve what happened."

"No, but dammit, anyway . . . getting herself involved with that monster . . ." Then he glanced at her and forced what he hoped would emerge as a grin.

"Charlie is going to absolutely *freak* when he hears, though. He was standing right there when the guy was shot, you know? In fact, he lost his entire Saturday having to be The Man in charge of the situation. And he'll freak even worse when he finds out Stafford is still alive. My God!"

They lapsed into a contemplative silence as he rolled up to a T-intersection with what appeared to be a somewhat better class of bush road, and Kendall didn't hesitate before turning left and increasing his speed to match the improved conditions.

"This other guy you mentioned . . . Ian? Are we likely to run into him out here somewhere, I wonder? Where the hell did he go? Or do you know?"

"Stafford sent him somewhere. Something to do with that old man with the dog, I think. The old guy whose dog found the bones that led them to Stafford and what he'd done here."

"Old Viv? That's a worry. The old guy's eighty if he's a day, I think. He'd be no match for somebody like this hillbilly bloke. We have *got* to get to a phone and alert Charlie about this. Or at least alert *somebody.*"

"Get to a phone?" Kirsten leaned forward, peering out into the cone of the headlights. There wasn't a sign that even suggested approaching civilization. No fence, no power poles, no . . . anything. Only the rough gravel of the narrow track ahead of them and the stark loneliness of the surrounding bush. "Are we actually getting anywhere?" she asked.

"I sure as hell hope so. But there isn't much out here until you get right close to the coast and I don't know how far away that might be. All we can do is keep on driving and hope for the best. At least we're away from *there*—that's the important thing." He didn't have to explain what he meant by *there*. "I don't know how long it'll take us to get to somewhere there's people, and a phone," he said. "But we're not stopping until we do. Not for anything or anybody unless it's a police car."

Whereupon the engine began to falter, coughed consumptively a few times, then died entirely. No warning lights had come on, but the inference was obvious.

"Or unless we run out of goddamn petrol, which I think we just did," Kendall said, peering at a fuel gauge that confirmed his worst suspicions. If there was a low fuel warning light, and there surely would be one, it wasn't working, that much was clear. Kendall killed the lights and made a cursory attempt to start the SUV, but the problem was frighteningly obvious.

He didn't even know why he was surprised . . . his ex-wife was the worst person he'd ever met for ignoring routine vehicle service until something actually broke down and died. He'd once changed a tire for her, then found out almost a year later—when she had another flat—that she'd never bothered to get the first flat fixed. He told Kirsten as much, then banged out his frustration on the steering wheel.

"God damn you, Rose!" He regretted the outburst immediately, but faced with having to spend the remainder of the night in the middle of nowhere, with the possibility that the first person to show up might be a man who'd already tried to shoot him, Kendall kept his regrets to a minimum.

"It's all right," Kirsten said, then rattled on, her voice brittle with fatigue and, he thought, approaching hysteria.

"Poor Teague. You haven't had much luck with the women in your life, have you? I nearly got you killed when you came to rescue me in my cave, your ex-wife tried to have you shot, and now . . . this."

Kendall had slouched back in his seat, left arm stretched across the back of the seat beside him. Not touching Kirsten, but there, right where it should have been when she suddenly snuggled in against him.

When he looked down, her eyes glimmered in what light there was, and she reached up to touch her fingers to his cheek, then draw his head down to meet her kiss.

"I really thought you were too grown up for this old *Gee whiz . . . we're out of gas* ploy," she said. And then snorted out a nonhysterical chuckle. "Ten thousand miles from home, with a perfectly good hotel suite, and you want to make out like teenagers in a car that's run out of gas?"

CHAPTER THIRTY-FIVE

Bluey regained consciousness slowly, painfully, and cranky as only a Jack Russell can be cranky. He shambled to his feet, stumbled, fell, reeled up again, his vision obscured by the blood from his wound. His flicking tongue could taste the blood, but couldn't reach far enough to clear his half-blinded eyes, no matter how hard he tried.

He was thoroughly disoriented, barely able to keep himself upright as he shook himself, half fell, then deliberately lay down and tried to wipe away the blood with his paws. It didn't help much, except to exacerbate his crankiness. He shrugged out from beneath the arm of his semi-conscious master, eventually reached his feet, where he reeled unsteadily, then plodded forward. Following his nose, following his rage.

He trundled through the darkening scrub, his nose lifted to any useful scent, his ears flicking as he listened. Being half deafened by the wound didn't help; there was a ringing inside his head that made hearing of any sort difficult. Which was why he smelled Ian Boyd's presence before he saw him.

Bluey knew that scent, could have selected the rancid, stale odor from a hundred others, a thousand. Knew it, didn't like it, knew he didn't like it. Hated it!

Boyd was just getting to his feet, his attention focused on Charlie, the Ruger at the ready, when Bluey rollicked into the small clearing. Boyd wasn't in much better shape than the dog, but his disorientation came from the chemicals inside him. Not that there was time to evaluate the difference.

Not time for Bluey to heed Boyd's squeal of angry terror as his peripheral vision caught sight of his nemesis charging out of the scrub. Not time for Charlie, only paces away from the dog but off to one side, to either warn Boyd or try to call off the dog. Not time, as Charlie's report would say later, for him to do one damned thing—merely watch and wonder.

Time only for the shrill yodel of Bluey's battle-cry as the animal flung himself out of the scrub, all four legs pumping in a blur of motion as he flew toward Boyd, then leapt.

High. For the throat. Charlie later said the dog's fangs flashed like swords, knives, mirrors, as he flew toward his target, mouth agape, yodels of outrage pouring out between those teeth. Outrage, anger, hatred!

Bluey had been struck by this man. Shot by this man. Kicked by this man. But—worse than that—this man had dared to harm his beloved master, had struck old Viv down with a casual violence and then actually dared to laugh. It was all there in the dog's mind; Charlie said later he could literally *hear* it in the yapping, yammering yodels as Bluey darted across the clearing and launched himself like a missile.

An old missile. Lame and hurting and incapable of the youth and strength and accuracy he needed to match his fury. He aimed for the throat, possibly envisaged the joy of sinking his blunted fangs into Boyd's jugular.

But he couldn't manage the altitude, the trajectory. He only got half the height he'd intended. Still, it was enough. The tissue that his bloodlust found was equally soft, if marginally sheltered by moleskin trousers and a zipper.

Bluey's yodeling muted as his jaws clenched in a fierceness that would have put the nastiest pit bull terrier to shame, would have made the hardiest Queensland pig dog step back in awe. Ian Boyd screamed, the rifle flew from his hands, and he fell backward beneath the dog's assault.

"It was terrible," Charlie said later in his report. "I didn't dare shoot the dog lest I hit the man, and when I grabbed the dog by his hind legs and tried to drag him off . . . well . . ."

What actually happened at that point was that Bluey growled at Charlie and—if anything—tightened his grip, either oblivious to Ian's shrieks or reveling in them. Charlie, who'd put away his gun, didn't even think to draw it again. He merely listened to Bluey, released the dog's hind legs, and politely backed away.

"Get the bastard off me!" Ian squealed.

"I can't. It'll be worse for you if I even try," Charlie replied, not sure whether to laugh or cry at the insanity of it all. "You'll have to wait until the old man gets here. Nobody but him can handle this brute."

And he called for Viv, half thinking the old bushie wouldn't be able to hear him over the cacophony of screams from Bluey's victim. But come he did, scrambling through the scrub, blood dripping from the cut on his forehead, to stand there beside Charlie, panting, puffing, staring in apparent astonishment.

Still carrying his antiquated shotgun, which, thank heavens, he made no attempt to use. But he also made no attempt to call off the dog.

"Serves the bastard right," he growled. "Let the dog have his reward, so long as he doesn't eat it. Probably poison him. I wouldn't fancy the vet bills."

"Fair go, Viv," whimpered Ian Boyd, faint with the pain of it, the effect of his drug use driven out by the shock and fear.

"Really, Viv," said Charlie. "He's had enough, don't you reckon?"

Even then it took a minute before the old man condescended, whistled cheerfully, and fell to his knees to cuddle the vicious beast when it lurched toward him, limping, blood still oozing from its own wound. They stayed like that, perhaps comforting each other, but equally likely to be sharing in the triumph, Charlie thought, as he knelt to handcuff Ian Boyd, then dragged the renegade to his feet, where Boyd stood hunched over in obvious pain.

"Not too much blood. That's a surprise," Charlie said after a cursory inspection of the damage caused by the dog. "You'll live, I reckon."

"I need a doctor," whimpered Ian. "Jesus, Charlie, but it hurts. What's the bugger done to me? I'm afraid to look."

"Nothing that shouldn't have been done at birth. Or at your father's birth, best yet. Just thank your lucky stars the dog's old and his teeth are a bit blunt."

"I shouldn't have missed the bugger when I shot at him," Boyd said, glaring at the dog. Bluey glared back, his eyes yellow, glowing, as if daring the tall bushman to start a rematch. "I should have shot you too, Charlie, when I had a chance the first time."

A quick search turned up the expected wallet, stockman's knife, Ian's vehicle keys, a small plastic bag nearly emptied of pills . . . not all of which Charlie could even begin to identify, and a cell phone.

"Bloody oath," muttered Charlie when he found it. "Is there anybody left on earth without one of these damned things? Not your style, Ian, I wouldn't have thought."

"Course it isn't mine," was the reply in a voice still shaking with shock. "I took it off Rosie Chapman to . . . to pay a debt, that's all."

"Why the hell would Rose Chapman owe you money?" Charlie asked. "She was supplying you with drugs, not the other way round. What the hell could you provide that'd be worth her paying for?"

Then the incongruity of Ian's earlier remark came to him. "And what did you mean about not shooting me the first time?

You could have shot me ten times over today, if you'd really intended to. What's this *first time* you're on about?"

Ian looked up, his bloodshot eyes weeping tears. "It doesn't matter now," he said. "Just get me out of here and get me to a doctor. Please, Charlie."

"It does matter," Charlie said. Paused. Then added, "Maybe I should get the dog to ask y—"

"At the gundog thing on Saturday." The words emerged in a whisper, urgently spoken to avert Charlie's suggestion, but now Ian wouldn't meet Charlie's gaze. His voice grew even more faint as he mumbled.

"Lucky I didn't shoot you. Could have been anybody . . . didn't get the guy I was aiming for. Fuckin' jack-jumpers."

Charlie was dumbstruck, if only for an instant. "You?" he asked. "Jesus, Ian, are you saying it was *you* who shot that gundog judge from Canberra? But why, for God's sake?"

"Never shot at him," Ian mumbled. "Told you that. I was aiming for that other bloke, the writer. Rosie wanted me to scare him. I was only aiming to knock his hat off or some such. Never meant to hurt anybody, never mind kill anybody. Jack-jumper bit me . . . told you that . . . hurt like buggery it did . . . made me flinch. Now please, Charlie . . . get me out of here. Get me to a doctor."

Charlie mulled over the surprising information all the way back to his vehicle, not too awfully surprised when most of the questions answered themselves merely on the strength of being mentally voiced.

Rose hires Ian to put the frighteners on Kendall. Why? Jealousy, I reckon. Or maybe some baggage left over from when they were married. Okay? But why would Ian want to mess with old Viv and that damned dog? Jesus, Charlie . . . you're losing it.

He waited until Ian Boyd was safely installed in the rear of the police vehicle before he asked that question, half afraid of what the answer might be, half afraid old Viv, who'd followed on out of the scrub with them, might welcome an excuse to sic Bluey on Ian again. Or shoot him. He didn't know what to expect for an answer, except for almost anything but the one he got.

"It wasn't nothing personal. I kind of like old Viv, Charlie. Well, mostly. We've had our differences, but usually . . . well, you know." The words came through clenched teeth. Ian was hunched over in the rear of the vehicle. He'd have been clutching at his ruined genitals if he could, Charlie knew, but Charlie had no intention of releasing the handcuffs that kept Ian's hands behind him.

"Cut to the chase, Ian, lest I open that door and turn the dog loose again," Charlie warned. "There had to be some bloody reason. What was it?"

"The . . . the doc wanted me to get them is all. Said he wanted to have a wee chat to 'em. It was something about that damned book, but I don't know what, Charlie. Honest. I wasn't really paying attention."

"And you're not making any sense, either. What doctor? What damned book?"

"The doctor that was *in* the damned book," Ian whined. "You know him—the guy from the clinic in town. The cannibal bloke that American I shot at wrote about."

"Stafford?" Charlie couldn't believe what he'd heard. It made no sense.

And then it did.

Charlie yanked open the door of the vehicle and half dragged Ian out again, now oblivious to his prisoner's howls of pain.

"Where?" he demanded. "Where is Stafford? Has he got Kirsten Knelsen with him? Has he got bloody Kendall with him? Rose Chapman? Talk to me, Ian, and do it damned quick smart, too, or—"

He was only marginally aware that he was shaking Ian, slamming him again and again into the side of the vehicle as he screamed the questions at him, over and over and over. That Ian was whimpering, then screaming, trying to answer but being given no opportunity. Until old Viv rushed in, shouting, grabbing at Charlie, screaming at him to stop. Until *that damned dog* rushed in and grabbed at his pant leg.

"Stop it, Charlie. He can't tell you anything if you kill the bugger."

Charlie let Ian go, saw him slump against the side of the police vehicle, was so shaken by his own loss of control that he couldn't even reach out to steady the man before he fell in a crumpled, fetal ball at Charlie's feet.

The three men lapsed into a momentary silence that was broken only by the furious yapping of the dog, who had fixed his gaze on Ian Boyd and was clearly only one command from resuming his assault on the man's testicles. And Ian knew it.

"Please, Viv," he whimpered. "Keep the bugger off me. I'm sorry . . . fair dinkum I am."

"Not as sorry as you'll be if I don't get some answers," Charlie snapped, his composure back in place, if barely, and only partially subdued.

"Rose was supposed to bring in that writer fella, whatever his name is," Ian said. "That was . . . yesterday, I think. Not sure. I was supposed to bring in Viv and the dog, but I stopped off in town . . . needed my rifle; the doc's got my Vaime, the bastard. So I stopped off to pick up the .22, then stopped at the pub . . . got pretty wasted . . ."

"Where, Ian? Where the hell are these people?" Charlie could scarcely contain himself, but knew he must. Ian was in pain, coming off a drug high, and never totally coherent at best. Push him too hard now and . . . Charlie shook his head sadly, angrily, wearily. It didn't bear thinking about.

"Jeez, Charlie, I told you. Didn't I tell him, Viv? They're at that old shack of mine up behind Loila Tier. You know the place, Viv . . . you go in along that track beside the river and then . . ." The rest dissolved into what sounded to Charlie like utter gibberish.

Charlie snarled with anger, hoisted Ian to his feet and once again thrust him into the rear of the police vehicle. Then he scrounged around in the front until he found the map he wanted, his detailed topographic map of the territory around St. Helens, amended here and there with hand-drawn additions.

"Show me, Viv," Charlie demanded. "I've got to get some people up there, and quick."

The old man looked at Charlie's map, but only briefly. Then he snorted with contempt and turned his attention to the prisoner.

What followed was an exchange of information Charlie could make little if any sense of. The two men spoke not in terms of miles and road names and numbers, but in the context of incidents that had happened, or so it sounded, when both men were still in their active youth. In terms of where some log truck driver Charlie had never heard of had lost his load, where someone else he'd never heard of had found a tin deposit, where some mighty forest giant had crashed too quickly, in the wrong direction, at the wrong time, and someone had died, where a particular bridge had gone out, where so-and-so had got bogged for a week with no tucker and no grog. It went on and on in a litany that might have been a foreign language for all the sense Charlie could make of it.

Yet it seemed to make sense to them, and Charlie realized it had better, because Ian Boyd was thoroughly losing it. He'd come down from his drug-induced high and now was floating into the abyss of withdrawal and the pain of his ruined testicles.

He'd be of little use to anyone, including himself, before too long.

But finally: "I think I know the place," said old Viv. "Fastest way is if we go in from this end. You drive and I'll try to reckon it out as we go along." He didn't wait for Charlie to reply, much less object. With startling agility he ran to the passenger side of the vehicle, whistling up the dog as he clambered inside.

Charlie devoted only seconds to wondering how he could explain attending at a crime scene accompanied by a geriatric bushman, an evil renegade of a dog, and the prisoner from yet a different crime. In the dark. After a cannibal armed with a Finnish sniper rifle.

Bugger it! If I start arguing with this old fart, I'll lose time. If I take Ian to the hospital, I'll lose even more. And there's no way known I can get any backup if nobody'll explain to me where we're going and why.

There was, however, one thing he could do, that he *had* to do, for his own peace of mind if nothing else.

"Give us that blunderbuss," he demanded. "I won't have it inside with us . . . that damned dog is bad enough."

The look the old man shot him would have frozen hell, although Charlie wasn't sure if it was on behalf of that damned dog or just Viv's usual irascibility. Whichever, he gave up the weapon, if grudgingly, and with only minor grumbling.

CHAPTER THIRTY-SIX

The oldest devil was first on the scene when the vehicle lurched away along the rutted track. He'd eaten enough road kill during his life to know it was worth revisiting the scene of last night's feast, just in case the smelly, noisy vehicle had miraculously supplied new offerings of tucker.

Or in case some other element had changed—he hadn't forgotten the unreachable, unattainable but oh, so enticing carcass that his nose told him was still there, still hung high in the tree above where the vehicle had sat.

As he approached, new scents intruded, and he cast his head in the air, sensitive nostrils quivering. Then, ignoring the thrashed-up ground where the vehicle had been, where last night's feast had been, he turned and waddled off along the track toward the cabin, following his nose. Aware he would soon be joined by others of his kind. Determined to get there first.

He couldn't get up on the tailgate of Stafford's vehicle. But he tried. Many, many times. He reared up as high as he could reach, but his claws couldn't get purchase on the metal. He managed to clamber up into a wheel well, but couldn't figure out how to get from there up onto the tailgate, where he *knew* there was meat. Fresh meat.

The old devil's growls of frustration drew in others of his kind, and soon there were five there under the tailgate, noses lifted, their ears crimson with a blush of frustration, their voices an unholy complaint about the unfairness of it all.

One of the younger animals made a mighty leap and actually got both front paws and his snout up on the tailgate, but he couldn't hang on for long. His rear legs thrashed in thin air as he gradually slid away from the prize and landed upside down in the mud.

. But by this time, the oldest devil had lost interest. He was strolling in his rolling, uneven gait along a different scent path, this one leading from the vehicle to where light showed through the partly open door of the shack. The creature's sensitive nose informed him of old blood here, and blood less old.

New blood. Fresh blood. And with it, the scent of fear. The oldest devil mumbled to himself as he shouldered his way through the doorway, then halted, blinking in the light, testing the air with his nose, peering nearsightedly, his whiskers twitching as he evaluated the situation.

The prey was large. That was the first thing. And frightened . . . the stink of fear was unmistakable. And the blood was fresh; a trickle of it still moist on the prey's head. The creature stank of man-smell, but the shape was strange, all bent and contorted like that sheep he'd once found caught by its own wool in a jungle of barbed wire fencing carelessly discarded.

Dangerous? It never hurt to be at least a little cautious, but time was an issue here, too. Behind him, the oldest devil sensed the arrival of other devils, younger, less cautious maybe, certainly more impetuous.

And equally hungry.

Soon they were seven. Heavy-shouldered creatures with jaws powerful enough to crush the leg bone of a horse. Mouths that gaped hugely in yawns that weren't yawns at all. Scavengers of the finest order, occasionally predators if the opportunity arose.

Like now.

The oldest devil was almost entirely black, but several of the others had the more usual white blazes that ran like distorted lightning through the fur on chests and rumps and shoulders. None were pretty . . . merely efficient.

None were overly brave. When the creature writhed and screamed and thrashed about just at the sight of them, the devils rocked to and fro on their front feet and looked at it, none quite ready to be first, none wanting to be last to feed, either.

They were unconcerned about the noise of the creature's screams. The oldest devil again recalled the sheep in the wire coffin. It, too, had screamed. For a while. Nor was the thrashing of this creature more than a brief concern. There were no hooves to lash out, apparently no teeth that, like their own, could rend and tear flesh.

The screams intensified when the bravest of the devils dashed in, jaws open in the hellish gape for which the animals were infamous. The oldest devil lurched forward, second in the scrum but unconcerned. There was space here for all of them, and sufficient meat for them, too.

CHAPTER THIRTY-SEVEN

Charlie locked up Ian's .22 rifle in the rear of the vehicle with Viv's ancient shotgun, then hustled around and got into the driver's seat. Whereupon old Viv thrust the much-maligned map in front of Charlie and pointed with one tobacco-stained finger. "Tell your mob to come up this road here," he said. "It'll take them longer than us, might be, but we should run across them about *here*. Maybe. Might be the wrong road entirely. I can't tell from this stupid map, and we're going round by a different route that isn't on this map at all, see?"

Charlie thumbed on his radio and relayed the information as best he could, knowing he could be sending everyone on a genuine wild goose chase but having no choice in the matter. "Just keep it quiet," he ordered into the radio. "No noise, no sirens, no flashers. Make sure you stop and check out anybody you find if they're headed down out of the hills. And be careful." Then he turned the vehicle and headed south toward the Tasman Highway and the maze of crude forest tracks that led even further south, into the rugged country above Loila Tier.

"I hope you know where you're taking us, Viv," he said to his geriatric co-pilot, who was calmly rolling a cigarette and would have, Charlie knew only too well, been yanking open the tab on a tinnie if he'd had one. Old Viv was no respecter of authority even when he wasn't dealing from a position of power.

Practically from that moment on, the trip became a nightmare. Once across the Tasman Highway and into the maze of forestry roads, Charlie could only follow his headlights and Viv's shouted, often barely coherent directions through the night, the vehicle bouncing and jouncing like a live creature.

They plowed through swampy areas Charlie would never have dared to face under normal circumstances. His vehicle was in four-wheel-drive and needed it every inch of the way, just as Charlie needed his nerve. At one point they navigated an ancient logging bridge he thought would surely collapse and plunge them to perdition in the swift-moving creek below.

Charlie wanted to nose his way cautiously over the thing, but old Viv screamed, "Give her hell, Charlie," and he did, and they virtually flew across the chasm, to his great relief.

In the back, Ian Boyd moaned and screamed and occasionally argued with the old man about which direction to go at intersections Charlie could barely even distinguish as intersections. And every time Ian opened his mouth, that damned dog would start in yapping and yodeling and carrying on like a pork chop.

"Dammit, Viv . . . can't you shut the mongrel bloody dog up?" Charlie shouted at one point. Only once. Bluey, clearly delighted at having someone else to pester, took the complaint as an invitation to try and clamber onto Charlie's shoulders and kiss him on the ear. That nearly caused Charlie to drive fair into a mammoth peppermint tree beside what he thought was probably the track—it was the only space wide enough to drive through, anyway.

After that, though, he shut up and drove, letting the old man and the prisoner make the decisions and praying silently that somehow, magically, they would make it through to the *real* road that would take them to where they could turn back north again and reach Ian Boyd's shack.

If it exists. If we survive this nonsense. If I don't stop and get out and shoot the lot of them . . . especially that damned dog.

On and on and on it went, Charlie fighting the wheel as the vehicle slithered and slid and bounced and splashed and careened its way through the scrub, over logs and under gigantic, spreading stringy barks and blue gums, plowing through bogs and spewing mud and gravel and bark and leaves behind it. If there was any given moment when all four wheels were actually on the ground at the same time, Charlie couldn't identify it, any more than he could ever be sure of where they were or what direction was which, there in the jolting and the cacophony of shouted instructions and yodels from that damned dog.

Until, suddenly, he was faced with a seemingly impenetrable wall of eucalypt saplings, with bigger trees on both sides and nowhere to go and hardly time even to stop.

"Give it to 'er!" screamed Viv.

"Don't stop!" yelled Ian Boyd from the back.

And that damned dog yelped in his ear and tried to kiss him as Charlie floored the police vehicle, which flattened saplings for what seemed like half a mile before bouncing up and over a berm of dirt and through a shallow ditch to land in a shuddering, skidding stop right in the middle of a real, genuine road.

"You beauty!" an impressed Viv told Charlie. In the rear, Ian only groaned and hunched over his wounded testicles, his contribution to the expedition essentially finished, now.

Charlie sat for a moment, gasping for breath and trying to get his balance back. And his composure. Even so, he had to struggle to get out the words, "Which way now?"

CHAPTER THIRTY-EIGHT

Kendall couldn't help being embarrassed by it all. He felt like he was sixteen again and caught in his grandfather's old Chevy on one of the back roads along the Qualicum River on Vancouver Island. With a girl. Necking, it was called then, and he had indelible memories of a uniformed RCMP constable telling him: "Put your neck back in your pants and take her home. Now."

Kirsten merely thought it was funny, at least after they'd realized the vehicle bathing them in its headlights was a police car and the approaching figure with the flashlight was a policeman and not Ian Boyd . . . or worse.

Although she was quick as Kendall to scramble into her jeans and tug down her bush shirt, he distinctly heard her chuckle as she apparently realized there'd be no time to struggle into her bra, so she casually tossed it into the rear of the vehicle and flashed him a cheeky grin as she did so.

"Takes you back, doesn't it?" Kirsten quipped with an even wider smile. Then they were out in the road, attempting to explain to Charlie's youngest, newest constable the convoluted tale of their abduction, their escape, and the threat still posed by Ian Boyd.

"And Stafford," Kirsten said. "I won't be convinced *he's* not a threat until I see him hang. We have to get back there and make sure about him."

"They don't hang anyone in Australia," said the constable.

"And I have orders not to proceed further until Sergeant Banes arrives—especially now that we know you two are safe. If you say this Stafford person is safely tied up in this cabin, wherever it is, I expect he'll keep for awhile."

"The RCMP thought he'd been eaten by a cougar, and look what's happened," Kirsten replied. Sharply. Insistently. "He's already killed at least one other person that we know of and lord knows how many we don't."

"Yes, but according to you there's nobody else there for him to kill," replied the constable, already well trained by Charlie to maintain an appearance of calm no matter what the crisis. "So even if he gets loose, he can't get very far without a vehicle, for which you have the keys, and you say you didn't see this rifle he's supposed to have."

Further discussion lapsed, then, as a new set of headlights appeared along the road, and moments later they were treated to the sight of Charlie's vehicle, slathered with mud to the roof line, still festooned with bits of leaf and twig, as it slewed to a halt.

Charlie took his young constable aside, listened to his brief report, and merely raised an eyebrow at being told the situation the constable said Kirsten and Kendall were in when he'd arrived. Charlie dearly wanted to laugh out loud, but managed to hide the urge. He did throw them a glance that Kendall, looking as guilty and embarrassed as he felt, obviously interpreted quite correctly. Charlie could see the blush even in the questionable light.

She has got to be one tough woman, but then you already knew that, I suppose. I can see why me old mate Kendall is smitten, but I wonder if he's up to dealing with her, long term.

And Kirsten, too, had caught that aspect of the constable's report, Charlie noticed. When Kendall formally introduced

Kirsten to Charlie, she as much as told him so just by the look in her eye. And silently dared him to say a single word about it, too.

Not on your Nellie, darling girl. Not to you, any road. But I'll stir me old mate Kendall about it before he leaves Tassie . . . you mark my words. Lucky bugger.

"All right—here's how it's got to work," Charlie said once the bare bones of the situation had again been discussed. "You" (to the constable) "will take our little mate Ian here back to town, get him medical treatment, and then lock him up. And take these two" (Kirsten and Kendall) "along with you and drop them at Mrs. McKay's B&B. I can get their statement—"

"No!" The two of them spoke in unison, almost as if the response had been staged, rehearsed.

"What do you mean?" Charlie asked. "Don't tell me you actually want to go back there?"

"I don't want to, but I have to," was the reply from Kirsten. Uttered in a voice flat with determination, cold as a winter wind. "He got away in Canada and I won't sleep, now, until I see you take him away in handcuffs and lock the bastard up forever."

"Fine." Charlie could only sigh. No sense arguing with this woman, he thought. Easier to give in; they didn't have time to argue. So again, he turned to the constable, who was helping Ian Boyd make the transfer from vehicle to vehicle.

"Take old Viv along with you, then," Charlie said, "and see that he gets a ride home afterwards."

Viv didn't even bother to argue. He simply glared at Charlie, spat contemptuously on the ground sufficiently far from Charlie's boots that it couldn't *really* be interpreted as anything but a deliberate miss, then marched over, dog at his heels, and plunked himself down in the front passenger seat of the police vehicle.

Charlie's police vehicle.

Viv never so much as glanced at Charlie, but Bluey cast an evil yellow eye over the old man's shoulder as he hopped in after his master.

The young constable prudently looked the other way and busied himself on his radio, assembling the rest of Charlie's people now that it was certain where they were needed.

Kirsten and Kendall looked at Charlie, then at each other, and took refuge in their need to embrace, ignoring the fact they'd already done sufficient of *that* before Charlie's arrival.

All of which left Charlie between a rock and a hard place. Nothing he could say or do at this point was going to change anything. He couldn't physically throw old Viv out of the vehicle and leave him here in the middle of nowhere, and he couldn't arrest the old bugger either, although the thought did occur to him. Briefly.

That damned dog would eat me alive and the old man would let him. I'm surprised he hasn't already sent him over to piss on my bloody boots.

And he couldn't help looking down to check, more than a little certain it must have happened and he'd somehow missed the insult.

CHAPTER THIRTY-NINE

They lingered at that final turn-in, sitting in an uncomfortable silence as they waited for Charlie's troops to arrive.

Charlie stared out through the mud-smeared windscreen, pondering a plan of action and wondering if there was anything he'd forgotten in his planning. It had come to him suddenly, as they made the last bit of the journey, just how important this situation was—to his career, to his friends, to his future.

And I can't even control the situation here in my own bloody vehicle. Good one, Charlie.

In the rearview mirror he could see Kirsten, snuggled into the protective curve of Kendall's arm around her shoulder. Her eyes were closed . . . she might have been asleep but for the hand that reflexively stroked the rough fur of *that damned dog,* who had hopped over the seat and was now snuggled against her thigh with all the aplomb of a real dog. Well, a lap dog, anyway.

Occasionally, he heard her murmuring to the evil beast, telling him what a splendid creature he was, how clever he was, how utterly beautiful and noble and dignified. She'd insisted, immediately, on seeing the blood-soaked fur, on being given something to wipe away the blood and cleanse his wound—and only then, Charlie had noted with some amusement, deigned to do the same thing for the dog's master.

At least you've got your priorities straight. Sort of. I think the dog's injury was the worst of the two. Have to remember to stop by the vet's when this is all over with. Maybe he'll give me a cut-rate price to stitch up the both of them.

Beside Charlie, old Viv also stared, although out of the side window. And smoked. And—Charlie was certain—deliberately exhaled out of the corner of his mouth so as to send as much of the noxious smoke as he could in Charlie's direction. Viv had pointedly ignored him all through the journey thus far. Never looked at him, never spoke. He'd spent the time building a wall between them, laying his indignation and insult down brick by silent, reproving brick.

And Charlie didn't know how to deal with that, either.

Silly old bastard. I should have realized he'd want to be in at the end of it all. He was there at the start, as he's never let anyone forget. Okay, old man . . . I'm sorry.

But he couldn't say it. Not here and now, anyway, in front of witnesses. And not least because he knew any apology would be thrown back in his face.

And rightly so. Don't even bother to try and deny that.

He was highly relieved when the first of his people arrived and he could get out of the vehicle, return to real, proper police attitudes and circumstances, giving orders, taking reports about what had been done and by whom, and who was still to be expected in this lonely place tonight.

But all too soon, or maybe it wasn't soon enough, a move had to be made. Charlie's vehicle led the parade of those sufficiently bushworthy to follow him. He'd been forced to leave one officer out there at the road because his standard police cruiser wouldn't have made it through the final bit of track in a fit.

Rose's partially dismembered corpse hung like some grotesque pale fruit in the top edges of the headlight glow as they reached that spot, and Charlie noticed in his mirror that Kirsten and

Kendall both bowed their heads, unwilling to look again at a horror they'd already seen, would probably never forget.

The old man merely grunted something incomprehensible. He'd seen worse, as Charlie had, when Stafford's human discards were being removed from the old mine shaft up on Blue Tier.

When they reached Stafford's vehicle with its grotesque tailgate cargo, Charlie merely glanced at it in passing. It was too close to the shack for him to be worrying about it at this stage. What lay ahead was more important.

He parked with his headlights on high beam and illuminating the decrepit structure, huddled in the ferns with the door halfway open and a feeble glow of lantern-light visible within. From this angle, Charlie could see the Vaime sniper rifle propped against the side of the shack, a sight that prompted a silent sigh of relief.

At least now I can assume Stafford hasn't done a runner. He'd have taken the rifle, surely, if he'd got free.

"Right," he said, opening the door and stepping out, his eyes on the doorway of the shack. "I want you all to stay here. Got that?"

Kirsten and Kendall both nodded, the look on their faces suggesting they might now be regretting their insistence on coming along for the final scene. Viv glared at Charlie, but granted him a tiny nod.

And as Charlie stepped back to issue instructions to those in vehicles behind them, *that damned dog* erupted through Charlie's still-open door and charged toward the cabin, screaming out his battle challenge in a series of high-pitched yodels and yelps almost loud enough to wake the dead.

"God *damn* it!" Charlie cried, then—like everyone else who watched—was struck dumb in astonishment as seven Tassie devils scurried out of the open doorway, fading like shadows into the night as Bluey appeared in the doorway behind them, hopping up and down on his stubby legs and yodeling his triumph.

"Damn it, Viv. Control your dog!"

Charlie was only half aware of the old man's whistle as he rushed to the doorway, afraid of what he'd find, *knowing* what he'd find. He paused at the entry, head bowed, unwilling for a moment to look inside.

And when he did, it was to see essentially what Kirsten and Kendall had described to him . . . the camp cots, the folding table, the discarded lengths of chain, the lantern. And Dr. Ralph Stafford—what was left of him.

Oh dear God!

A devil can consume half its body weight in thirty minutes. How the hell do I know that? No matter. It's right. So . . . seven of the buggers . . . or was it eight? Ten—fifteen pounds apiece? And Stafford would have been about thirteen stone—a hundred and eighty pounds, say . . .

Charlie closed his eyes again to the horror of it, unable to do the math. Didn't *need* to do the math. Nobody *could* do the math, not accurately, except maybe some forensic specialist on a mission.

The professional policeman in Charlie took solace in the fact that the devils hadn't chewed away Stafford's fingers. Or at least not all of them. Enough of the man's hands, still bound by the cable ties, remained for a positive identification when that time came. The face was mostly undamaged, but that mattered less because it was obvious even in death that the doctor had undergone extensive reconstructive surgery to change his appearance.

But the human being in Charlie wasn't able to take in the horror with such cold professionalism. Not all at once, not even knowing, intellectually, that Stafford had likely gotten only what he deserved, given his record of murders and mutilations. Stafford, whose death mask screamed as loudly as the man himself must have screamed, whose body was still in that backward bow, wrists linked to ankles by the cable ties, just as Kendall had described it. Gone to his destiny without any chance to defend himself, without any more mercy than he'd shown the pretty young women he'd slaughtered and eaten.

Charlie had to turn away from the carnage before his humanity and his stomach betrayed him. He gulped and gasped to hold back the bile as he lurched outside, slamming the door of the shack behind him and gesturing a firm, definite, *STAY AWAY* to everyone waiting in the vehicles. As he fumbled his way around to the side of the building and confirmed that yes, he actually had seen the Vaime sniper rifle propped there. Charlie stood and stared at it until his stomach settled and his mind began to clear, until his mind actually began to work.

It needed to work. There was much to be done.

They'd been too late to save Stafford. Never had any show of getting there on time. The brief delay while he waited for backup wasn't relevant to anything—Stafford was devil-tucker already, at that point.

Just don't think about how it must have been for him.

Too late to save Rose, not that there'd ever been a chance of doing that. Poor Rose, driven by envy and her own shallow principles and lord only knew what else. She hadn't deserved to die like this, but there was nothing to be done about that except to treat her remains with due respect.

At least we've got all of her, Charlie thought. Then remembered the lower half of that amputated leg. The thigh was on the tailgate of Stafford's vehicle—where was the rest?

Charlie had a vivid, *noir* flash of forensics technicians having to prowl the area for a mile around, collecting devil droppings to be sifted through in the lab for splinters of bone. Then dismissed the mental picture, hoping as he did so that it would stay dismissed but knowing it would come back to haunt him, probably at a singularly inappropriate time.

This wasn't the time, anyway. Now he must concentrate on doing his job. Consider his options, do what he could for the dead and what he could do to consider the living. What had to be done.

"It's over," he told everyone as they gathered around his police vehicle. Charlie looked from face to face, keeping his own expression neutral, firm, but *willing* them to accept that he was in charge and things would be done as he said they would be done.

And they were. Kendall and Kirsten were sent back to St. Helens with one of Charlie's people. Another was designated to stay and man the turn-in from the main road, to guide the forensics people when they eventually arrived.

"I'm going to have to stay here until they do," Charlie said. "I'd really appreciate it, Viv, if you could stay with me . . . but I can have somebody take you home if that's what you'd prefer."

He kept his voice flat, direct, professional. But the pleading was there—in his eyes, in his very soul, as he met the old man's stern, still-indignant gaze.

CHAPTER FORTY

Kirsten threw Charlie a curious glance when she read through her statement in his office the next day. She raised an eyebrow, parted her lips as if to speak, then firmed those same lips and signed the statement with a firm, bold hand.

Kendall wasn't quite so obliging. He was a man of words—he read the statement slowly, carefully. Charlie found himself holding his breath as his friend read. He could feel Kirsten's eyes on him, tried to ignore that, too.

He'd hoped Kendall might just skim through the report (which had taken Charlie most of the morning to concoct) and miss the fact that there was no mention of how Kendall had handcuffed Stafford with cable ties, used them to shackle his ankles, then joined both sets of shackles together.

"Are you sure about this, Charlie?" asked Kendall. "I was sure those cable ties would hold . . . and if they didn't, why didn't he run, I wonder?"

Charlie shrugged. "You didn't do a very good job of it. Those damned cable ties can be tricky . . . look like they're holding and then slip. Good job you're not supposed to be an electrician. No need to mention that, though. Be a pity to destroy your handyman status."

He grinned, only it emerged as a wince because he shook his head as he did so, and a spasm of pain lanced in behind his red-rimmed eyes. It had been a long, long night.

"Anyway, there's no way of telling how he managed to get

free or what happened later. Might be he fell and hurt himself after he'd cut himself free. Maybe the devils gave him such a fright that he had a heart attack or something. They'd have given me one, I can tell you that. We'll never know, I guess."

In actual fact, Charlie wasn't sure if there was a recorded case of Tassie devils actually having eaten anyone. Ever. He knew bushmen, and old Viv and Ian Boyd would have also, who told tales of being stalked by the creatures, bushmen who swore blue that they'd be terrified of being caught in the wilderness with a broken leg or similar injury.

But he'd thought such tales to be the stuff of local legend. Until now, when he was forced into *this* charade in order to protect his friend. And his friend's lover, who probably didn't need protecting. And he had the worst hangover he could ever remember. His mouth tasted foul and his head throbbed, sensitive to any sudden movement. This was, he decided, *not* the best time for doing something like this. But there was no other. It had to be now.

He paused then, firmed his voice for the clincher.

"It doesn't matter."

Enough, Charlie. Say no more or he'll figure it out. Probably will anyway, but not now, not here, not in time for it to matter.

"No, it doesn't. What matters is that your Tassie devils are more efficient than our cougars at home," said Kirsten. Backing Charlie up, and they both knew it. Doing her best to get this part of it over quickly, for all their sakes.

She knows. Or at least suspects. Kendall's no more a handyman than he is an aerospace engineer. It'll be her that changes the tap washers and stuff like that when they finally get their act together.

He met Kirsten's gaze and had his opinion confirmed. She *knew!*

She also knew, just as Charlie did, that Kendall would be tormented beyond endurance if he had to live with the fact of having bound Stafford up to be eaten alive by the Tassie devils, able to watch it, forced to endure their consumption of his flesh with no possibility of escape or defense. Because of Kendall.

Kendall, who would have nightmares about all this anyway. Who would probably carry guilt to his own grave because of what had happened to Rose, the ex-wife who'd tried to have him shot. Kendall looked from his lady love to Charlie, shrugged, then scrawled his name at the bottom of the statement Charlie had so carefully, cunningly, he thought, laboriously constructed from the facts he knew, the facts he'd suspected and the facts he'd totally, deliberately ignored.

The previous night had been a damned long night indeed!

Charlie and old Viv had stood outside the shack, not talking, not looking at each other, or at much of anything, as Charlie's instructions were followed through. They definitely hadn't looked down the track to where Rose's body still hung, had tried not to notice as the departing police personnel—every one of them—slowed, if only ever so slightly, unable to avoid taking a final look.

Just as Viv had to look inside the shack, which he did after firmly commanding *that damned dog* to sit beside Charlie's vehicle and stay there. Charlie left him to it. No sense arguing, and at least Viv had exhibited the common decency to keep *that damned dog* from going back into the shack and probably pissing on everything in sight. It was easier for Charlie to walk a ways down the track, lean up against the solidness of a huge blackwood tree, and think it all out. If he did this wrong, his career could be on the line. Maybe even if he did it right. Well, it needed to be done right. It needed to be done . . . that was the point!

Charlie and his curmudgeonly old friend didn't have to speak. Charlie knew what he was going to do, what he *had* to do. All Viv had to do was stand outside, guard the door, and keep his mouth shut later.

Nor did it take very long. There wasn't that much involved, after all. Charlie put on latex gloves, took up a boning knife from the collective kitchen tools on the picnic table, and slashed through the cable tie that held Stafford's wrists to his feet, then the one holding his wrists together and the third one that held his feet together.

Snick. Snick. Snick. Simple as that.

Far simpler than the memory of how the savaged body of the victim sprang free of that ghastly bow-shape to flop limply on the floor, a dead man, now . . . not a tortured specter from some horror film. Far simpler than the memory of having to grip the remains of Stafford's right hand around the knife before Charlie dropped it in what he hoped was a logical spot for it to be found if anyone looked. Far simpler than thinking of the consequences if he somehow managed to stuff this up royally.

Then he'd left the shack, quietly closing the door behind him and testing to make certain it would stay closed. He moved to the rear of Stafford's vehicle, where he found that somebody, probably Viv, had carefully spread a tarp out to cover the half-carved thigh, the cheesecloth and the carving utensils that had been used to hold the cheesecloth down.

Now, Charlie could spare a moment to think what had to be done about Rose. And it only took a moment, because there was really nothing sensible he could do. What lay ahead, like what would happen inside the cabin Charlie would never enter again if he could help it, was to be determined by the crime scene specialists, the forensics people. Who might get there by morning. Or might not. There was no screaming panic involved, now. No hostages, no danger to anyone, no real need for the forensics people to wander around in the middle of the night when they could wait for daylight before even starting out from the city.

I never thought about that, damn it. Wonder what else I didn't think about? Wonder if I can risk going out to the haul road and sending that young constable in here to baby sit, so Viv and I can go home to bed.

He looked around then, to see that the old man had taken it upon himself to give them a fire to spend the night by. Well away from the actual crime scene, thank goodness, but where they could sit, be warm, and still keep an eye on things.

You beauty, Viv. Trust you to think of the important things.

Charlie made his way to the fire, and was halfway to seating himself on a convenient log when he realized that the old man had done more than just build a fire. He was sitting there, the dog with its ugly head in his lap, and in his hand was—impossibly but undeniably—a bottle of wine.

"Where the hell did that come from?" Charlie cried, getting up even faster than he'd sat down. Noticing as he troubled to look that the old man had a whopping great camp cooler sitting there beside him. Where had *that* come from?

From Stafford's truck. Charlie knew it without having to ask, almost didn't dare to ask anyway . . . not now, when it was definitely too late to change anything. But what if the cooler held . . . ? He suppressed a mental picture of Rose's tidy ankle even as old Viv answered the unasked question.

"No part of her in here. I looked. Lots of damned good plonk, though. Reckoned we might as well have it . . . your mob'd only steal it, I reckon. 'Sides—finders keepers. You want some?"

He extended the bottle and Charlie hesitated only an instant. He was definitely thirsty. Doubtless the old man had been thirsty too. Somewhere in Charlie's vehicle there would be bottled water, maybe even a few aged granola bars. But this— this was Piper's Brook. By almost any standard the finest wine produced in Tasmania . . . in Australia!

And it was evidence. Or had been. Or should be. And it

was . . . 2:15 in the morning and he'd just finished manipulating evidence far more important than this was, if for much better reasons. And old Viv was, at least, speaking to him again.

"Don't mind if I do," said Charlie.

They passed the bottle back and forth until it was empty, then replaced it with a fresh one. Charlie tried not to think of where Viv had picked up the corkscrew he wielded like a pro, tried not to think of too much at all. It was easy enough until the old man got serious.

"What'll happen with Ian Boyd?"

"It's not up to me, Viv. You know that. But I'd reckon manslaughter, at the least. I don't believe he meant to shoot that gundog judge, but it happened while he was committing another crime, with an unregistered, illegal firearm. It'll go hard for him."

"So you won't be needing me to press charges, I guess."

And having to admit to having that damned antique shotgun, never mind shooting it at somebody? Okay, in self-defense. Maybe. I'd give odds 'twas you fired first, old man. Probably just damned good luck there's no pellets in Ian as well as tooth marks.

"I can't see much sense to it, unless you're bound and determined to have your day in court," Charlie said.

Which is exactly what you want, you cunning old bastard. Nothing you'd like better than to be the center of attention, I'd reckon. My God!—what a bun fight it would be. Trouble is that once they got you going you wouldn't stop until you'd insulted somebody important, or got cited for contempt, or something. You're worse than that damned dog, once you're fired up.

"But it'll go in the record somewhere how he attacked me, how me wonderful dog saved me? Saved us both, didn't he? I'd want that known, I reckon."

"It will certainly be part of the arrest record," Charlie said. "I'll make certain of it."

Which seemed, at least for the moment, to satisfy an old man who didn't actually want to admit he'd needed a shotgun to deal with a man twenty years his junior, twice his size, and high on drugs. Bad enough to admit he'd had to call the police, but he could slide past that formality by skiting about his new cell phone and how it worked out there in the wilderness where he lived.

And Charlie suddenly realized there was more, yet, to the old man's attitude about this. Good, bad or indifferent . . . Ian Boyd was one of his own, a local, somebody he'd grown up with. It was, therefore, perfectly all right for Viv to have stomped Ian into the ground for shooting the dog, and he'd have done so without a qualm if he could have. Or shot him. But taking the man to court, to be judged by strangers, was . . . something else.

Charlie understood that. Sort of. As much as he understood anything about the unique culture of rural Tasmania, where the rules were different than elsewhere in Australia, different, even, than in the cities of Tasmania. He understood it enough, anyway, to know when to change the subject.

Once the statements were signed, Kendall and Kirsten hovered. There was no better way to describe the situation—they wanted to go but felt obliged not to rush away. And they couldn't quite hide it, nor the guilt that it carried.

It took some organizing, but eventually they found a pristine copy of The Book, which both Kendall and Kirsten inscribed to old Viv—and, at Kirsten's insistence, to Bluey as well. But neither had any enthusiasm for having to go bush to deliver it. They'd seen enough of the east coast bush for the moment, perhaps for a lifetime.

Charlie was mildly annoyed to find that although old Viv had *his* cell phone number, he didn't have the old man's, so he couldn't even phone to suggest that Viv make a trip to town to pick up his gift. And his shotgun, which Charlie had managed to have declared an inoperable antique to avoid having to confiscate the damned thing.

Everybody's got baggage, because of that goddamn Stafford. Except maybe old Viv. He's old and he manages to travel pretty light. Lucky bugger.

Kendall had come halfway around the world, in part to see his old friend, only to have the visit shaken by an unbelievable but nonetheless horrifying set of circumstances. He'd brought the woman he loved halfway around the world to show her the place he often thought of as his spiritual home, only to have . . .

Charlie understood.

How could Kendall even hope to spend a fortnight showing Kirsten the scenic wonders of Tasmania when—in her mind—a devil lurked behind every bush, a semi-butchered corpse swung from every stringy-bark?

How could his friend lurch from book signing to book signing anywhere in Australia with the media feeding frenzy poised not on his current book, but with fangs bared, pack voice screaming as they imagined the book Kendall hadn't even begun yet?

But would. Probably. Eventually.

"I've cancelled the signing in Hobart," Kendall said then, as if he'd been reading Charlie's mind. "We've got a ride back to Launceston and I've booked a flight out later today, so we'll have to get on the road pretty soon."

"I'd reckon so."

Hell. What else can I say? Nice to see you . . . here's your hat . . . what's your hurry?

Easier to turn his attention to Kirsten and practice the gallantry he hoped to exhibit later, with a different woman, when this business was done and he could manage the time. Soon.

"It has been wonderful to meet you after all Kendall's said. And I have to say that even *his* words don't do you justice." Charlie laid it on with a trowel, heaping compliment upon compliment, until finally he ran out of pretty words and had to slow down, then stop.

Kirsten kept it more simple. "You've been a good friend to Kendall and I thank you for it," she said, then turned and gazed admiringly into Kendall's eyes. It was the look of a smitten bubble-gummer, Charlie thought. But effective.

"Kendall is my hero," Kirsten sighed. And sagged, body language tragic, her giggle verging on hysteria, into her lover's arms.

At which Kendall tried not to blush and Charlie tried not to laugh.

CHAPTER FORTY-ONE

Linda fell apart with laughter when Charlie recounted to her the tale of his rescue by old Viv's dog. And laughed even louder when he admitted his apprehension about what he described as Kirsten's great scene.

"Here's this woman who's twice, at least, proven herself to be tougher than most men could even dream of being, and what does she do? She sighs, 'My hero' and collapses in Kendall's arms. The bugger was so surprised he nearly dropped her."

Charlie accompanied his exaggerated and not quite accurate tale with overdramatic gestures of his own, waving one arm, looking (he hoped) longingly upward to the ceiling. He had to look ridiculous, knew it, didn't care. Worth it just to see Linda laugh. He loved her laughter.

"It was like something out of the worst soap opera," he said ruefully. "She had to be having him on . . . must have been. Not that the poor bugger noticed—he was too happy just to have her where she was, and all of a piece, and I can't blame him for that. But . . ."

Linda's laughter slowed and she shook her head almost sadly, a contrast to the smile that still played on her lips.

"Sometimes, Charlie," she said, speaking slowly, enunciating each word, holding him with her eyes to be sure he got her message, "a girl's just gotta do what a girl's gotta do.

"Speaking of which . . ." Linda rose from her seat and walked over to Charlie with one hand extended and the other undoing her blouse buttons. Slowly, deliberately, extremely provocatively. She took Charlie's hand, squeezed it in a gesture of encouragement, then turned and moved away.

Obviously, Charlie thought, he was expected to follow.

So he did.

ABOUT THE AUTHOR

Gordon Aalborg is the (actual) author of "The Specialist"—a Five Star Publishing mystery, 2004.

He spent more than twenty years in Tasmania, and has traveled in the area where *Dining with Devils* is set. A keen gundog enthusiast, Gordon is a life member and foundation president of the Tasmanian Gundog Trial Association. He now lives on Vancouver Island, in Canada with his wife, fellow mystery author Denise (Deni) Dietz.

Visit his Web site: www.gordonaaalborg.com